STONE HEARTS

OLYMPIAN AWAKENINGS BOOK 1

CB SAMET

BOOK ONE
OLYMPIAN AWAKENINGS
TRILOGY

 STONE HEARTS

CB SAMET

ebook ISBN: 978-1-950942-31-2

paperback ISBN: 978-1-950942-53-4

CHAPTER
ONE

Madison adjusted her sunglasses as she crossed the threshold into the mansion. Her emotions mingled with part awe and part intimidation, but she would maintain her usual professional demeanor.

"This way, Miss Katsaros," the butler beckoned. Fitting that a home of this magnitude would have a silver-haired butler, though the penguin suit seemed excessive.

She followed him along a corridor where bold columns stretched high to a vaulted ceiling and down to accentuated white floors so polished she could practically see her reflection in the marble as her short heels clicked. Inset coves held gold statues of ancient warriors with gladiator swords, their expressions some mix of surprise or anguish. Oddly, these weren't the usual fearless battle gazes of Greek art.

Gold was also an unusual choice. While the gleaming color contrasted beautifully with the white walls, Madison knew from her work in art restoration that most Greek sculptures were made of marble or occasionally bronze. Why had someone painted them gold?

Farther down the hallway, they passed magnificent oil paintings of Greek mythology—Achilles falling in battle, an arrow through one heel, hands touching on the ground while crushing defeat hung his head low; Hercules conquering Cerberus with one of three heads dangling limply as the other two snarled with rage-filled red eyes; Perseus wielding the head of Medusa to petrify Phineas and his coconspirators. Myths and legends—or so the world believed.

Madison shivered at the last image. The demon, snake-headed woman had turned many men to stone before being decapitated, and even in death, she'd been deadly. Her story was even more tragic, considering how she'd been cursed simply for being beautiful.

The butler paused before the entrance to a sitting room. "If you would please wait here for Master Chloros."

Master? This is twenty-first-century America. Who calls anyone master?

Madison had grown up in England and only noted the word "master" still used occasionally when addressing a young boy not yet old enough to be called "mister."

Nodding, Madison stepped into the room. The space looked equally lavish with a stone fireplace, more paintings of Greek misery and triumph, and more strange gold statues capturing people in moments of shock and awe. The exquisite detail of the work made them lifelike, but what could have been works of beauty were rendered creepy by their expressions.

Movement near the window startled her. A man, perhaps thirty with brown hair dusted in blond highlights, turned toward her. His sapphire eyes were stunning, the depths of which spoke of hidden secrets. His chiseled face had a couple of days' stubble covering his jaw. With his khaki trousers, airy off-white button-down shirt, and thick-soled shoes, he needed only a machete to look fresh from the jungle.

"You're not Mr. Chloros," she said.

"No. I'm Rex Alderman." His voice sounded deep, rugged, and American. He walked over, extended a hand.

"Madison Katsaros." When they shook, a warm, tingling sensation spread through her.

He didn't smell like jungle. His scent was a manly musk with a hint of cinnamon. Rex Alderman. Something in the name caught her attention and set her mind churning. Releasing his hand, she took a step back and distanced herself from the allure of him. Personal involvement was a complication she didn't dare entertain ... with anyone.

"Do you work for Mr. Chloros?" Rex asked.

"No. I'm an art conservator. He invited me to discuss a restoration project." She began to regret accepting the invitation. She preferred to work in solitude, and already she'd met a butler and this man. Yet, Mr. Chloros had paid a generous upfront fee for her to come in person and learn about his project.

"Interesting. I'm an archaeologist," Rex said. "I too was invited to discuss a business opportunity."

"Archaeology." She couldn't contain the fascination in her voice or the double-take at his appearance. She wondered what his civilization of interest was when the name triggered a memory. "Wait. Rex Alderman."

He gave her a lopsided grin as though flattered she'd heard of him.

"*The* Rex Alderman who pulverized a two-millennium-old Scythian crown?"

His smile faded.

Stepping closer, she hissed, "You desecrated a priceless artifact. Took me weeks to restore that crown to something resembling the original." When she'd been assigned the job to repair the fresh dents and chips, she'd wondered how the man who'd discovered it could even call himself an archaeologist. She'd heard the entire grave site had been a disaster, as if trampled by a horde of drunken centaurs.

He cocked his head to one side, seemingly unfazed by her scolding, as his grin returned. "They say never meet your heroes." He raised his hands shoulder-high as if in surrender.

Taking a retreating step back, she bristled even as her core warmed to the sight of his cocky mouth. Her body's reaction irritated her further.

"You, sir, are not my hero."

"I could be."

She did a double-take. Was he flirting with her? Preposterous. He was the Tasmanian devil of his field, and they were here to discuss a job. She hoped it didn't include cleaning up his messes.

Before she could devise some retort to wipe the self-satisfied look off his face, he asked, "You fly across the Atlantic to come here?"

"No. I live in New York."

"But grew up in London? The accent," he added. "But your last name, Katsaros, is Greek."

She shook her head. "I grew up in a little town in England called Dunchurch where my mother's family is from." Madison walked around the room, feigning admiration of the art so she'd stop admiring him. There wasn't enough space in this room for his ego and the two of them. "My father was American, but his father immigrated from Greece."

Small talk risked the personal involvement she meticulously avoided, so she changed the topic of conversation back to work. "Do you suppose Mr. Chloros accidentally scheduled us at the same time, or that his project involves you finding an object and me restoring it?"

"We'll soon find out. Your, uh, glasses are particularly dark." Rex tapped next to his eye.

Ah, yes, the inevitable question—or implied question—about

why she wore dark glasses indoors. And so came the well-rehearsed lie. "I'm photosensitive."

"All the time or you just came from the ophthalmologist?"

"Always and forever."

The butler swung the doors open wider. "Mr. Alderman and Miss Katsaros, I present Master Chloros."

A large man entered, dressed in an iridescent blue suit. A swirl of black hair topped his head and appeared to contain enough gel to hold up a palm tree in a hurricane. "Thank you both for accepting my invitation." His voice had a medium-pitched Southern twang. His mansion may be in upstate New York, but he'd clearly been raised in the South.

When Madison had spent three months at the Mississippi Museum of Art on a restoration project, she'd found the dialect charming. Chloros's shadowy mysteriousness, however, was anything but charming. Her initial relief that his arrival meant the meeting would be underway and she could avoid further conversation with Trampling T-Rex Alderman was replaced by an unease from Chloros's demeanor.

The butler closed the door behind him as he left.

"You have quite the collection," Madison began, hoping to keep the conversation professional and brisk. "And I've only seen the hallway and this room." She'd already begun cataloging items in her mind, a remnant of her college days working in a museum basement and a by-product of her belief in order and tidiness.

"I've spent decades collectin'," the man drawled.

Rex turned, lifted a sword off one rack on the wall. "It's a fantastic place. This is a gladiator's sword." He twirled it. "Weighted perfectly."

Mr. Chloros stiffened slightly, making Madison wonder if he didn't like his trinkets touched—or if he knew of Rex's propensity to damage priceless artifacts. Turning toward her, Chloros smiled broadly with gleaming white teeth, though something calculating glimmered in his gold-flecked eyes. He glanced at Rex who played with the sword as Chloros moved toward Madison.

"Should we discuss why you need my services?" she asked.

Something about Mr. Chloros slinking toward her had her skin crawling. In a word: *dodgy*. She also didn't care for the young Indiana Jones lookalike slaying the air with a sharp object. Though she didn't consider herself claustrophobic, the room felt suddenly small and the closed door paradoxically too far out of reach.

Rex set the sword down and walked over to inspect a golden statue—a hoplite soldier wearing a muscle cuirass shirt.

Mr. Chloros eased even closer to Madison. "I am interested in your particular talents." He extended his hand toward her.

They had already dispensed with introductions and hadn't settled on an agreement of any specific work, so the handshake seemed oddly timed. Whatever. She could be polite until she could politely leave. This place, despite its lavish expense and pristine cleanliness, had a disconcerting feeling crawling up her spine.

She swallowed back her discomfort as she extended her hand. "What do you need restored?"

When she touched his hand, it felt like gripping ice straight from the Antarctic tundra. Cold—sharp and bone-deep—spread rapidly from her hand through her chest and abdomen and into her other extremities. She opened her mouth to scream, but her entire body became immobilized.

CHAPTER
TWO

Rex Alderman needed funding for his next archaeological expedition, so when he'd received an invitation to upstate New York to talk about financing, he had booked the soonest flight. Once inside the mansion and its trove of artifacts, he was certain he'd found his cash cow. He only needed to convince Mr. Chloros to be his benefactor. Rex could be charming, so he'd been mentally rehearsing his pitch since walking through the front door.

His mind had momentarily gone blank when Madison Katsaros had entered, a slim five ten and wearing a pencil skirt showing off shapely legs, conservative pumps, and a Louis Vuitton crossbody purse containing her phone. Spiraling strands of pale blond hair, almost white, dripped down from a soft updo. Deeply shaded sunglasses obscured her eyes, though he could see the edge of dark, shapely eyebrows. She was impeccably dressed, like a work of art herself. Her voice held a rich British accent, akin to the actress Eva Green. And Madison had heard of him. Sure the Sky Wrath's dig wasn't one of his best sites, but he'd been lucky to leave that place alive, much less with a few marketable trinkets like Kharon's crown.

Now, Rex gaped at the lovely young woman who'd just metamorphosed into a gleaming gold statue, an expression of shock and terror in the raised eyebrows and shape of her open mouth. He knew enough Greek mythology and had witnessed enough strange events, even ones he'd thought impossible, in his lifetime to understand what had happened as Chloros lifted his hand off Madison's still form.

The man turned toward Rex slowly, golden eyes now positively glinting with a demonic and terrifying glee. Rex grabbed the sword he'd been playing with moments ago in his now sweating hand.

He pointed it toward Chloros. "What the hell do you want?" He'd been in dangerous situations, and he'd seen unbelievable magic, but this was both combined.

"Redemption. I destroy the two of you, and I will once again be in the good graces of the master."

Rex's heart rate kicked faster as his senses narrowed to focus on the threat. The man was dressed like Elvis, spoke like a Southern Baptist minister, and wielded the power of Midas's touch.

And had Rex backed into a corner—wall on one side, chaise lounge on the other.

"What master? I don't even know you, man." Rex would sure as hell skewer him if that hand got too close. He glanced over Chloros's shoulder. Yup, Madison was still a hundred and thirty pounds of solid gold.

Chloros smirked. "He watches even now." His gaze flicked back to Madison. "I had to handle her first. She's particularly deadly."

Madison? Rex had only met her for five minutes and had assessed her as introverted, gorgeous—despite the dark sunglasses—and utterly harmless with her prim and proper demeanor.

Now, she was dead. Dead or suspended? If she was as lethal as Chloros claimed, making a risky next move might pay off.

Rex gripped the sword in his hand tighter as he shuddered and summoned his saddest memory. With his left hand, he wiped at his eyes. He faked right, then lunged left, leaping over the chaise lounge. As he landed, he swiped a finger across Madison's smooth, gold forehead.

Behind him, Chloros dove toward Rex, who pivoted, narrowly missing the demon's outstretched hand. A pulse of fear spiked through Rex as he slashed the sword. His attacker jerked his hand back before Rex could cut it.

After fumbling the door open with sweating palms, he backed out of the study. On his way, he grabbed at another statue—this one of an armed gladiator—and yanked.

Rex had envisioned bringing the statue down as a barrier to slow Chloros's pursuit, but the damn thing was actual gold—*Duh, Rex*, he scolded himself—which meant it weighed a freaking ton and didn't budge.

Arms wrapped around Rex from behind, pinning his biceps against his chest while he jolted in alarm. Shit, of course, the butler was in cahoots with this psychopath. Rex struggled against the man restraining him. Anger warred with terror, both causing his heart to beat wildly, as Chloros closed in.

"I will have my redemption," the man declared.

Jerking his head back, Rex slammed his skull into the butler's nose with a satisfying crack. The man's grip slackened enough for Rex to pull away, turn, and launch a right hook into his face, made all the firmer by the sword handle in his grip.

The retaliation cost him precious time. Time enough for Mr. Chloros's metallic touch to extend toward him. Rex brought his sword around but already knew he couldn't chop the man's arm off before those creepy fingers grazed him. Then what? Would he become another hallway decoration for this monster? Dead and fixed in time or imprisoned for eternity in an immobile hell?

Golden Elvis was a mere inch away from touching Rex when his hand halted, spasmed, and flew to his abdomen where a long spatha gladiator blade protruded.

Heart threatening to pound out of his chest, Rex stumbled back out of reach, putting more distance between himself and the Elvis-Midas hybrid. Then he saw who had impaled the man. The warrior who'd been frozen gold when Rex tried to topple him was now flesh and blood. Rex had never been more grateful for his powers than this moment. If his remnant of tears on his hand had reanimated the gladiator, did that mean—?

"Hey, tosser!" Madison's furious voice came from the study.

Chloros turned his head in surprise. He snarled as his entire body went rigid with his back to Rex. His skin paled while the color seemed to leach from his bright blue suit. All of him turned a sickly gray filled with cracks and imperfections.

When Rex peered around the stone Mr. Chloros—a move he would later reflect on as quite careless—Madison was adjusting her sunglasses back in place, cheeks flushed crimson.

Ah, well, not so harmless after all.

"Master! No!" The butler flung himself at stony Elvis. "You monsters!" Red-faced, he reached into his jacket pocket.

Rex spun toward him and tightened his grip on his sword. Before the butler could withdraw what Rex suspected would be a gun, the gladiator brought his bloody blade around, cleaving the head off of the butler's body.

"Oh, my, God. I'm going to be sick." Madison stumbled out of the study and skirted around the stone figure, avoiding the blood pooling around the stone statue from the butler. Her heels clicked on the white tile as she scurried down the hall.

Rex trailed after her. "Wait. What the hell just happened?"

She didn't stop until she neared the front door. Brushing pale hair out of her paler face, she bent over to catch her breath. "Well." With one hand pressed to her stomach, she fanned herself with the other as she took several steadying breaths. "Seems Midas lured us both here with a promise of work when his real intention was to turn us to gold, apparently to earn favor with his master boss—whoever the hell that is. You reversed his magic by touching me, and you also freed our decapitating helios."

The Greek warrior approached, sword lowered, and watching with a curious, nonthreatening expression. Rex could figure out his story later. For now, he focused his attention on Madison.

"You omitted the part where you turned golden Elvis to stone." With the threats seemingly managed, his heart rate slowed to normal, but he kept a grip on the sword in the event further surprises awaited them.

"Elvis?" She glanced back at the stone statue, turned a shade of green and looked away. "Oh, yeah, I get the reference. So, yeah, I don't have the ability to turn things to gold—if I did, I wouldn't be here looking for work."

"You petrified him."

"I'm cursed." She tugged at her blouse a few times rapidly as if to cool her body. "Any living thing that looks into my eyes turns to stone."

Rex took a moment to digest Madison's words. "So ... not photosensitive?" he asked.

"No. Are you finished with your questions, officer? Can I leave now?" she said on a huff. The tension around her lips and jaw suggested she was holding herself together, but barely.

"Sure, but I think we should stick together until we sort this out. Apparently, Midas has a boss who wants us both dead—or out of commission." They were more likely to uncover who was after them and why if they worked together.

"Fine. What about him?" she asked.

They turned to look at the bronze-skinned gladiator who'd been studying their conversation with quiet interest and who didn't seem the least concerned he'd just beheaded someone. For now, the warrior seemed to be on their side and Rex intended to keep it that way. His gaze slid down to the sword the man held and the slow trail of red blood on pristine white tile it had made down the hallway. Perhaps if Rex had been a warrior imprisoned as a statue for a few thousand years, he wouldn't be fazed by spilling blood either.

"We certainly can't leave him here," Rex said. "He doesn't so much blend in with upstate New York, and we can't have him slaying people."

"I am Alexios." The ancient Greek spoke the words slowly and carefully.

"Oh, English. Didn't see that coming." Rex couldn't place Alexios's accent; then again, he'd never heard an ancient Greek speak English.

"I listen. I learn. First time speaking English." He grinned as though pleased with himself. The smile was disarmingly out of place on such a muscled fighter holding a bloodied sword.

"You're doing amazing," Madison said. "But can we go now?" She hugged herself while looking around as though expecting another attack.

She could be right.

"OK," Rex agreed. "I took a rideshare here. Alexios, I'm guessing, doesn't know what a car is since being solid gold for, oh, roughly two thousand years. Have you got wheels?" Rex asked Madison.

"I have wheels." She took out a pair of keys, dangled them in the air.

"I know cars," the Greek warrior interjected. "I watch movies when I was at Chloros's home—until he moved me out of the entertainment room. I drive?"

"No," Madison and Rex said in unison.

The three of them dashed down the hall to the front door. Rex glimpsed the many statues as a tingling sensation slipped down his spine. He suspected many of these were still alive, frozen and watching as Alexios had been. The battle-hardened warrior had fortunately come to their aid. What of the rest of these? Friends or foes? And how would they acclimate to a world they'd watched evolve around them for thousands of years? How many would have abandoned sanity from that sort of slow torture? He made a mental note to come back here and try to free who he could when he could safely return.

Rex glanced at Alexios as he hurried ahead of him to ensure he rode shotgun. Outside, a crisp April breeze greeted them, and Rex instantly felt calmer in the expanse of fresh air.

"Before you get in my car," she told Alexios, "wipe that thing off." She gestured to the sword.

When Rex slid beside Madison, she was already cranking the engine. No. It had already been on, which meant she had the forethought to start it remotely.

Smart, quick-thinking, and kept herself together under pressure—all attractive qualities. Too bad she could turn men to stone. She could just leave those glasses right where they were, and Rex would be sure to keep his distance.

When everyone was inside the white Camry with doors closed, she zipped down the long driveway bordered by an immaculate lawn. She spun onto the main road and didn't drop to the speed limit until they were back near civilization.

Head straight, she focused on the road as she gripped the wheel with white knuckles. She looked like she was still fighting for composure. Who wouldn't after seeing a man beheaded?

"Are we going to talk about what just happened?" Rex asked. "I feel like we should talk about it."

"I'm still hyperventilating over the fact I just killed a man."

Rex decided he'd omit his speculation that Elvis might not be technically dead, but suspended the way Alexios had been. Rex's life was all about movement and freedom. Rex couldn't imagine a worse curse than what Midas was about to face. The butler, however, was very much dead, and Alexios wasn't so much distraught as he was ... smiling in the back seat of the car like a boy on his way to his favorite burger joint.

Jeez. The guy would probably want a meal soon.

"We talk," Alexios said. "On the way to Milopas."

"Milopas?" Rex asked.

"It is a Greek island near Naxos," Madison explained.

"Yeah, I know where it is," he snapped. "I want to know why Alexios wants to go to the same island I've been dreaming about."

Madison turned her head sharply to look at him, mouth parted in surprise, before turning her attention back to the road.

"Ah, so we're apparently all summoned to go there." Rex crossed his arms and leaned back in his seat, thinking of this strange mental tug he'd been experiencing for several weeks imploring him to go to Milopas. "Well, seeing as how our last invitation almost turned me into currency, I'm fine keeping my life just the way it is." He wanted to know who Chloros's master was but not at the cost of traveling halfway around the world.

"I think it's something important," Madison said, voice conspiratorially low. "I've been putting off the pull to go there, because I can't make sense of it and I don't do adventure. I restore art. Alone. I travel for clients only, and even that's a risk. After today, though, what if we're supposed to go? What if going provides us with answers?"

"What if going only gives us more questions? What if it has more demons, like golden Elvis back there?" Rex asked.

Madison shook her head. "What if something at Milopas has the answers to who and what we are—don't smirk at me, Rex. I know I have Medusa's powers. But why? And what if there's a cure? You have powers too. You restore life to the inanimate. Do you know why?"

He shook his head. "I heal. I didn't actually know if my tears would work to free you until they did."

"Do you know why you have powers others don't?" she pressed.

"We go," Alexios said. "We get questions and answers, and more monsters." His brown eyes lit with excitement.

Rex gestured to Alexios as he listed exactly why they shouldn't go, but Madison just raised her dark eyebrows above her glasses expectantly, as if silently asking if Rex would back down from a challenge.

Rex could have bailed and felt certain there would be times in the future he wished he had. But he'd become an archaeologist out of genuine curiosity about the world. He couldn't temper that tendency just because someone was throwing around the word *monsters.* He also had some fairly badass companions to travel with—surprisingly feisty Medusa Madison and a Greek gladiator unafraid of danger and not squeamish around dismembered bodies.

"Fine. We'll go," Rex said. "Some of the best advice I've taken has come from ancient Greek guys—Aristotle, Plato, Socrates. Why not take Alexios's advice?"

The warrior grinned like a schoolboy. "I met Epicurus. 260 BCE in Colophon. He founded Epicureanism. He is now a famous Greek ... *guy.*" He said the last word like he was trying out the sound of it.

"Pleasure above all else. I can appreciate that," Rex said with a playful wriggle of his eyebrows.

"Not quite," Alexios said. "Pleasure is the highest good. Mental pleasure more so than physical. And the ultimate pleasure is freedom from anxiety and mental pain."

"I'm liking this Epicurus's outlook," Madison said. "I don't think I would recognize life without anxiety and mental pain."

"You must learn emotional calmness," Alexios said.

"You certainly have. You'll have to teach me."

An unfamiliar irritation crawled along Rex's spine. He didn't like the idea of Madison learning hedonism from Alexios, even though the Greek warrior wasn't making a pass at her. Surely, Rex couldn't be experiencing jealousy when he'd only just met Madison. He should be more concerned about her Medusa powers or that the three of them were all being subliminally summoned to a Greek island.

"Wait. Epicurus?" Rex turned to gape at Alexios. "That puts you alive around the time of Alexander the Great."

Alexios smiled broadly. "We conquered all the way to India."

Rex turned back to face the road, astounded into silence. The gladiator really was twenty-three hundred years old and didn't look a day over thirty.

Madison turned right at a stoplight. "Aside from the fact that we all just saved each other's lives, I don't know either of you. Still, today's events are prompting me to consider this trip to Milopas." Her voice sounded slightly breathless, showing she was still hyped on adrenaline. "I'll need to go home for my passport. You?" she asked Rex.

"Always have it on me because I travel so much," he replied.

She glanced back at Alexios. "How do we get him across international borders?"

꿸 꿸 꿸 꿸 꿸 꿸 꿸

MADISON DROVE south with two strangers in her car while she mentally planned how she would rearrange her life to travel to a Greek island. Today's events meant she needed to stop delaying the need to explore the pull toward Milopas. Thinking about this trip was preferable to thinking about what happened at the mansion.

She'd been turned into a freaking gold statue!

Then, a man with apparently magical tears brought her back from that momentary frigid hell, following which, in self-defense —and part retribution—she'd stoned another human being ... or mostly human.

Replaying events threatened to unravel the tiny threads of control she clung to. Cracking the windows, she let cool, spring air inside to ease her nerves. She tried to recall if she'd seen any cameras or touched anything that would have left fingerprints. Maybe there wouldn't be any proof she'd been there when authorities found the corpses ... well one corpse, one statue.

Athena, I'm hoping for answers in Milopas.

For so long, Madison had carried this curse as she tried to pass through life unnoticed by normal humans. What if more like her were out there? What if they were evil like Mr. Chloros?

She had to break the heavy silence in the vehicle, or her mind would keep spiraling. "I've always wondered if more people existed in the world with powers. Although healing is so much better than petrification."

In the back seat, Alexios flipped the middle console up and down like he'd never ridden in a car before—which, she supposed, he hadn't. He shifted his weight to put his nose near the partially open window like a golden retriever. Moments like this and when he smiled so boyishly made it hard to believe he was a deadly soldier.

Rex trailed a finger along the edge of the open window. "Not a manly trait when you have to cry in order to heal. Also, not a great gift when you're excavating in Iran—once ancient Persia—and inadvertently bring a Scythian soldier to life. But definitely handy when you fall down in a crypt and break your leg. Or you have to turn a block of gold back into a beautiful woman."

Madison swallowed. Rex had distributed the compliment so effortlessly, she wasn't sure he'd realized it. Was he flirting? His tone didn't suggest as much.

Flirting would get Rex nowhere. One careless move during a relationship and her date could become an outdoor decoration— the equivalent of a giant garden gnome. She'd tried to take the risk a few times, but dates always wanted the glasses off for intimacy ... not happening. Those who hadn't cared if she'd worn them, hadn't been worth dating.

"Or beautiful man," Alexios said, with a jovial innocence that made Madison chuckle and forget her self-pity.

"Or that." Rex laughed, a good-natured sound that had her wishing she could flirt with him.

"You healed your own leg?" she asked.

Rex shrugged. "Because I was already crying like a baby over the pain, wasn't too hard to sprinkle a few tears over the wound."

Madison smiled, hardly believing this rugged man who kept his wits about him while dodging the golden touch of death would ever cry. "Like a baby, huh?"

"Should you ever divulge that outside this trio of trust, I will adamantly deny it."

She chuckled. Wow, he was good at diffusing tension.

"I am good keeper of secrets," Alexios said.

"Good," Rex said. "Because the world you just joined doesn't believe in magic, Greek curses, or many-millennia-old Greek warriors reanimated from elemental captivity. Those are big secrets we all have to keep."

"I keep."

"You reanimated a Scythian soldier?" Madison asked him.

"Apparently my tears can bring back the dead, sort of. I'll tell you, he was not happy about it. Hell hath no fury like a resurrected warlord."

"What happened to him?"

Rex picked at the handle of the sword propped against the car door with its blade pointed down. "Ah ..." He cleared his throat as the humor in his eyes faded. "I had to kill him all over again. Not fair to him, but he made it clear it was him or me."

"How do you kill something that's already dead?" When she asked, she eyed him warily as she wondered how accustomed this stranger in her car was to violence and death.

"Well, he'd been sort of ... preserved. I think he was buried in a salt pit. Anyway, being somewhat mummified—which I think is why I could inadvertently revive him—I, uh, had to decapitate him."

"Seems like the theme of the day," Madison commented, swallowing back the repulsive images of a mummy and the butler's beheadings.

Alexios clapped Rex on the shoulder. "You are also a warrior."

"Nah, man. Just a survivor."

"Madison is a survivor," Alexios added. "She turned Mr. Golden Elvis to stone."

Rex grinned. "She sure is," he agreed. "Was he your first?" he asked her.

"Stoning? No." She pursed her lips. "He wasn't my first." Her voice was tight. The topic wasn't up for discussion. Mr. Chloros hadn't been her first, and she had a sickening feeling in the pit of her stomach that he wouldn't be her last.

FOUR

They picked up drive-through burgers on the way to Madison's apartment. She lived in the Upper West Side. Sweet spot. *Near The Met*, Rex noted. She parked the car in the lot, and they walked toward the building.

"You live in a high-rise," Rex remarked as they took the elevator up.

Madison rolled her shoulders. "Can't turn anyone to stone when you live on the twelfth floor. No one's looking into your windows way up here. It was either this or a basement. Actually, I did live in a basement apartment until I could afford this."

Rex thought about how difficult her life must have been. Still, she'd worked toward a successful career despite the challenges she'd faced. She couldn't look at people unfiltered, but she could look and restore the art they created.

Alexios kept trying to push the buttons on the lift once he noticed they glowed, forcing Rex to continually slap his hand away so they wouldn't stop on every floor. Fortunately, they'd left his sword in Madison's car, but the warrior still stood out like he was fresh from a Renaissance fair with his skirt and breastplate.

Rex followed her out of the elevator and into her apartment. Rex glanced around at the open-concept living area, which was airy and light thanks to tall windows that offered a sweeping view of the skyline. Soft gray walls served as a neutral backdrop for pops of deep emerald and gold. A sleek, modular sofa was draped with a cashmere throw, and a low, matte-black coffee table held a stack of art history books, one open to a page on Hellenistic sculpture. One wall was dedicated to framed sketches of Greek constellations. A small bronze bust of Persephone rested on a floating shelf.

As Madison set her keys down on the counter, he walked to the window.

"Try not to destroy anything, Rex." Her British accent held a mix of tease and warning.

"Come again?" he asked, detecting the teasing tone in her voice. "Wait. Are we back to discussing the crown? That wasn't my fault."

She walked to the kitchen and fixed herself a glass of water. "You know you have a nickname in the world of art restoration?"

"Oh, yeah?" He crossed his arms and grinned.

"Trampling T-Rex Alderman because of the damage you do." She drank her water.

"I've had a few unavoidable complications." He shrugged as he walked to the window. "You chose well. Great view. You're right, can't make eye contact with anyone up here."

When he turned back around, she stood still with one hand gripping the glass on the counter, but he couldn't read her expression through the sunglasses.

"Sorry," he offered lamely. "I'm sure it's a sensitive subject." He stuck his hands in his pockets, feeling like a schmuck.

A sound bubbled up from her throat. She folded her arms on the counter and put her forehead on them. Her shoulders shook.

Rex couldn't tell if she was laughing or crying. A good example of why he didn't get involved with people. People were complicated and emotional. Thousand-year-old buried treasures were not. A knot of guilt formed in his stomach for having upset her.

He looked to Alexios for help, but the man was unwrapping and intently sniffing his cheeseburger, unconcerned by Madison's behavior. He glanced around as if something else might offer assistance. Her galley kitchen was tidy and had brushed brass fixtures, open wooden shelves, and a Greek key backsplash in blue and white tile. Olive oil in a ceramic amphora sat beside a marble mortar and pestle.

Now what? Did he offer her comfort, or would she prefer he left her alone? He didn't want to be accused of being cold-hearted, though it wouldn't be the first time.

"Madison?" Rex asked.

After a moment, she lifted her head and sniffed, but her cheeks were dry. "It is *such* a sensitive subject. I've been keeping this secret, carrying this." She gestured to her sunglasses as she gave an ironic smile. "Suddenly, people know! People I helped and who helped me know. I'm terrified of the great unknown future, but for just a while I can enjoy not hiding the ugly truth about who I am."

"There's nothing ugly about who you are," Rex said. She was gorgeous, and that beauty extended to the inside of her too. She hadn't hesitated to help two men she didn't know and drive them away from the danger of the mansion and back to her apartment.

One eyebrow arched. "No? I'd like to believe that, Rex, but you've known me for roughly two hours. I don't have a happy past. You know how I first discovered my curse?"

"Tell me." He sensed she needed to tell the story just as he sensed it wouldn't be pleasant. As someone who studied the past, he wanted to know hers.

"I competed in beauty pageants when I was a little girl. Naive, competitive, and self-centered—that about sums it up. Not hard to imagine why the gods cursed me." She turned, pulled a cup from a cabinet, and poured a second glass of water. She slid it over to Alexios, who listened as he devoured his sandwich. "Nothing humbles you like having to exile yourself from society. Having to protect people from the monster inside you."

Rex regarded her. "You chose to protect people. Not everyone would have."

"On my sixteenth birthday. Want to know how my curse began? I spent the morning blaming my mother for the last pageant we lost." She paced the small kitchen. "I claimed she picked the wrong outfit, the wrong ensemble. I was such a brat." Shaking her head as if scolding her younger self, she ran a trembling hand through her hair. "I blew out my candles, wishing I would no longer be surrounded by incompetence. Instantly, I had a headache and blurry vision. I lay down and took a nap. When I woke up and opened my eyes, the first thing I saw was Zephyr."

"Zephyr?" he asked.

"My dog. The only thing I hadn't mistreated in my young life." Her head dropped as her shoulders slumped, obviously reliving the painful memory.

A lump formed in Rex's throat. "You turned him to stone."

"I did." She rubbed her neck. "I've kept him with me ever since. I keep him close to remind myself how the stone in my heart is just as cold as killing my dog."

Rex followed her gaze, looked over his shoulder, and spotted the stone statue of a mutt that looked part boxer, part Lab.

Madison straightened and wiped under her glasses. "Sorry to dump all of that on you. Can't tell your shrink in therapy that you petrified your dog without being committed and thrown in a padded cell. Anyway, I'm going to pack." She walked toward the back hallway where Rex suspected she needed some time alone and not just to pack.

"She is in pain," Alexios said between bites of food.

"Yeah, man. Must have been hard to live with that guilt. To live with the fear of who or what she might turn to stone next." Rex walked to the dog, bent to inspect him.

"She is better with us … *man*." Alexios drank the water Madison had fixed for him.

"Yeah. Healing takes time, though. Physical and emotional." Rex ran a hand over the cool stone. He tried to pick the dog up, not surprised it was heavy. The gold statues at the upstate mansion had been as heavy as gold, and the petrified dog weighed probably three times his weight as a living creature.

"Hey, Zephyr. What are the odds you're still in there, bud?" If Rex could reanimate a two-thousand-year-old gold warrior, could he bring a dog out of stone suspension?

He glanced toward Madison's bedroom. This might be something worth asking for her consent before attempting. Then again, he didn't want to get her hopes up if it didn't work.

Summoning tears—easy to do when he imagined the devastation of a sixteen-year-old accidentally turning her furry friend into stone—he tilted his head forward and blinked. He let the tears fall. A faint whimper preceded the feel of soft fur and a wet lick from a tongue.

Rex chuckled as he rubbed Zephyr behind the ears. He had soft black fur and white paws. He looked to be part Lab by the body, and part boxer by the more square face and shorter legs. The dog barked, spun in a circle, and dashed off toward Madison's room.

Female squealing ensued. "Zephyr. Oh my God, Zephyr! Rex! Oh, my sweet boy. Oh, I'm so sorry, boy." Some combination of laughing and crying followed.

Rex walked back to look out the window and hide more tears

from Alexios. Sliding his hands into his pockets, he tried to remember the last time he'd ever made someone this happy. Never. He kept a tight lid on his ability—avoided ties in general because the last thing he wanted was to become someone's lab rat when they studied him or bottled his tears to turn a profit.

"Now. You have a wife," Alexios said proudly.

Rex choked. "Ah, no, man. That's not how it works in modern times." Rex was so not interested in matrimony.

"You are both powerful. Both lonely."

"Lonely, eh? How do you figure that?"

"You both plan *big* trip—all the way to Milopas—yet call no one. Yes, I know what a phone is."

"Huh. You sure are observant. So, aside from being revived after a few thousand years, during which time you learned English and perhaps a keen sense of observation, what are your powers?"

"Warrior." He jabbed a thumb toward his chest.

"Can't argue with that. Between the getup and having witnessed you behead a man, I'm guessing you were a fine warrior of your time."

"One of the best."

Rex chuckled and raised his glass in a mock toast. "Modesty is overrated."

Lying on her bed beside Zephyr with her fingers sunk into his fur, Madison looked around her tidy bedroom. The space was more personal and serene than the other rooms with sage-green walls, sheer linen curtains, and a queen bed with a weathered oak frame. A vintage vanity held her daily essentials alongside delicate gold jewelry and small relics she'd picked up at auctions or flea markets.

On her nightstand, a glass dome covered a tiny restored figurine of Athena—Madison's first solo project. The mirror on one wall was the only dramatic piece. Ornate, gold-framed, and cracked in one corner—a subtle reminder of a curse she couldn't quite escape.

Was she really doing this? Was she taking a trip to Greece with people she'd only just met?

She had traveled around Europe. As a lover of art, she wanted to see works of art in person—the *Mona Lisa*, the statue of *David*, *The Last Supper*. Traveling to Milopas would be so much more. Good or bad, something waited for them there.

She ruffled Zephyr's hind fur, and he hopped to the floor, his wagging tail making her think he'd forgiven her. Dogs were amazing like that. She hadn't had a pet since that terrible day sixteen years ago.

Standing, she composed herself. She walked back to her living room and up to Rex, Zephyr at her heel.

Wrapping her arms around him, she said, "Thank you. Thank you so much."

He patted her back. "Oh, um. You're welcome."

When was the last time she hugged a man? Human contact was a luxury she could seldom afford. In her arms, he felt strong and warm and all man. The impulsive hug felt suddenly awkward with her body's quickly heating response.

Clearing her throat, she stepped back, hoping the warmth in her cheeks hadn't produced a noticeable blush. "Thank you," she repeated.

He shifted his weight and stuck his hands in his pockets. "Least I can do after you saved my life is shed a few tears."

She smiled. "OK. Travel plans." She walked to the fridge and pulled out lunch meat. She didn't have any dog food, but poor Zephyr had to be hungry.

Rex took his phone out of his back pocket, thumbs moving

over the screen. "Direct flight, New York to Athens. Then rent a boat to Milopas."

"International travel. Let's talk logistics." She laid the deli slices on a cutting board and chopped them into bite-sized pieces before setting the board and food on the floor for the dog to devour. "We don't know how long we'll be gone, but I can keep it down to one suitcase."

"I travel light," Rex said.

After looking him up and down, she gestured to him. "As in, this is it?"

"Yup."

"Change of clothes?" She fixed a bowl of water and set that beside the food as the dog ate.

"I can pick something up at the shopping center down the road."

"Toothbrush?"

"In my pocket."

"Hmm. Dodgy. What about these two?" She gestured to the dog and Alexios.

Zephyr had moved from the empty cutting board to the bowl where he lapped up water.

"You're taking Zephyr?" Rex asked.

"He goes where I go. There's plane cargo transport for animals." *Long, miserable flight in confinement, though*, she thought. And he'd been confined in stone for the last sixteen years.

They both looked at Alexios.

"No identity," Rex said glumly.

"No passport," Madison added.

"What if he's cargo, too?" Rex asked the question slowly, giving Madison a tentative expression. "What if they both are?"

Her heart did a slow, lolling thump at the thought of turning her newly animated best friend back into stone. And surely poor Alexios would be terrified at the thought.

"How do you travel?" Rex asked her before she had a chance to address his last earth-shattering question. "What I mean is, how do you get past airport security without making eye contact?"

"I have a system," she said.

Rex used attentive silence to convey that he wanted details.

Madison picked up the cutting board and washed it with soap and water. She said with a sigh, "I've a pair of contact lenses. They're designed for light sensitivity, like wearing sunglasses, but when I wear them and cast my gaze askance without making direct eye contact, I can avoid turning the TSA agent into stone."

He rubbed his chin. "First, kudos for the use of *askance* in a sentence. Second, I am trying to envision how you tested this contact lens hypothesis. Did you just try it, and it worked?"

"No. I wouldn't risk accidentally stoning someone. I performed a rigorous trial-and-error process with multiple different contact lenses. I think the ones I settled on worked the best because they're thick and uncomfortable. I can honestly only stand to wear them for a short time. But long enough to get through security."

Alexios, sporting a wide grin, sat on the floor and began to pet the dog who wagged his tail with eager ferocity.

"What did the trial and error involve?" Rex asked.

Madison pursed her lips. Pushy, this man. He was putting her on the spot, but he seemed genuinely curious. She hadn't been able to talk to anyone about her situation. Now she could, even if reluctantly.

"I'm not proud of what I had to do," she said. "But a person can't spend his or her entire life alone in isolation. I mean, they can, but I wanted to travel."

"You had to have turned something living into stone to test the contacts. Make sure you didn't accidentally turn a person to stone."

"Snakes." She shifted her weight uncomfortably. "It's not fair to them, but I would get snakes from different pet stores for my experiment. I tried insects, but they don't make eye contact with you."

Rex nodded, expression contemplative. "Since I am thinking about all the many dark holes and jungles I've traversed and probably lost the most sleep over fear of snakes, I'm not judging you on that one."

"Thanks?"

He shrugged. "Better snakes than people."

How did he do that—lighten her mood just by being inquisitive and congenial?

"What worries me more than security are these two," Madison said, gesturing to Alexios and Zephyr. "I can't imagine the psychological trauma of being a golden statue for over two thousand years, and now you're asking about turning him into a stone statue. He is completely dependent on us to revive him. God knows what will go through Zephyr's mind when he's immobilized once again."

Rex turned to the man. "Alexios, what says the almighty Greek warrior?"

Zephyr licked the Greek's hand and face as he grinned and ruffled the dog's fur. "If I need documents to pass through countries, and I have no documents, I cannot go to Milopas. It seems my only option is to travel as cargo. I will hold Zephyr and take care of him while we are stone."

Both men turned to stare at her. Zephyr turned toward her and sat, looking up at her as though sensing her distress.

"Ugh. Bugger me sideways," she grumbled. "OK," she added more resolutely. "But we'll wait until the absolute last minute before the shipping company takes you. They'll still have days in transport as a statue."

"They shouldn't be too heavy for air cargo, but they will be too heavy to move out of your apartment."

She recalled using a dolly to move Zephyr alone. "You're right." Madison tapped a finger on her chin. In the world of art restoration, she'd shipped items overseas. She suspected an archaeologist had as well. Making the entire trip by boat would be entirely too long for Alexios and Zephyr. "We'll have to take them to the shipping company and somehow turn them to stone there without an audience."

"May I request a bag over our heads? Or a black cloth?" Alexios asked.

"What is the significance?" Rex asked.

"When I am in darkness as a statue, it is as if I am sleeping. Blocks of hundred years at a time have passed when I was in storage and slept through the darkness."

"Wow. Like pressing the fast-forward button." Rex sounded as though he wanted all those details of when Alexios was awake versus asleep.

Of course he did, Madison thought. The ever-inquisitive archaeologist. She imagined Alexios the statue emerging from storage to see a drastic change in human culture based on innovations or advancements, cluing him in to the passage of time.

"We can do that," Madison said. "That's a relief, actually. I hope turning you to stone will have a similar effect. Goodness, this makes me nervous. If you're damaged in transport, break something—"

"Madison," Rex began, tone dismissive.

"I'm serious," she snapped, not willing to have her concerns brushed aside by a man who traveled with little more than the clothes on his back and a toothbrush in his pocket. "I've moved before, and crap gets broken. All. The. Time. I don't care how much you pack it in bubble wrap." The gory imagery of body parts of stone snapping off had her breathing faster as her heart kicked up a notch. Maybe this was a terrible plan.

"I can fix it," Rex said, calmly. "If any damage happens, I'll fix it." He stepped closer and rubbed his hands up and down her arms.

"Yes. That's true. You can do that." His touch had the intended calming effect, and her breathing and heartbeat slowed to normal. "I'm warming up to this plan." *And him*, she thought disconcertingly. "Cut me some slack, though. This goes against everything I've been doing my entire life in avoiding turning people and animals into stone."

"I get that." His tone was soothing. "Take your time and wrap your head around it." He gently squeezed her arms as his hands lingered there.

Alexios stood and cocked his head to one side. "How can she wrap her head around anything?"

"It's a phrase meaning wrapping her mind conceptually around something. Her thoughts. Thinking about something until it's acceptable." Rex dropped his hands and stepped back.

The combination of haste in his actions and reluctance in his eyes puzzled her.

Alexios stepped forward and rubbed Madison's arms up and down in mechanical motions. "Wrap as much as you need. The plan is acceptable."

Rex grinned in obvious amusement at the sight of Madison's bafflement as Alexios tried to mimic Rex's comforting gesture.

"Thank you," she said. She raised her hand and patted Alexios's cheek, a friendly gesture that vanquished the awkwardness of the moment.

At the door, Zephyr whined.

"Oh. Oh, right. I'll take him out. Ugh. I don't even have a leash."

"I've got this." Rex pulled a ropelike bracelet off his wrist and unwound it. "Paracord." He looped it through Zephyr's collar. "Bag?"

"Um. Yes." She retrieved a plastic grocery bag from under the kitchen counter and handed it to him.

"I must also use your room of resting," Alexios said.

"Ah, certainly. There's only one. This way." As she led Alexios toward the bathroom, she watched Rex casually leave the apartment to take Zephyr for a walk, as if he'd been doing such a task every day. As if he hadn't just spared her the anxiety of a public interaction while her dog took care of business.

CHAPTER
FIVE

ex walked Zephyr along the sidewalk, passing pedestrians. With tail wagging, the dog sniffed the ground with the enthusiasm of a detective on the hunt.

"Take your time, my furry friend," he told Zephyr. Poor thing hadn't smelled the world in sixteen years.

Madison lived among a classic slice of city life—vibrant, noisy, and full of texture. The street buzzed with movement. Cyclists wove through traffic, delivery vans double-parked, and pedestrians hustled past, phones in hand and earbuds in. The scent of roasted coffee beans and garlic from the Mediterranean deli across the street mingled with the occasional pungent note of car exhaust. The chaos was somehow comforting, a steady rhythm of normal after a bizarre day. Rex wondered if Madison found a sort of anonymity amid the noise and motion ... the perfect place to hide in plain sight.

The tree-lined block had early 1900s buildings rising shoulder to shoulder, their iron fire escapes zigzagging down facades like ladders to another era. Her building sat halfway down the block, tucked between a trendy espresso bar with minimalist signage and a secondhand bookshop.

Today had taken a vastly different turn compared to how it had begun. Rex was now planning a trip to the Mediterranean where, hopefully, answers awaited … and something more. Discovering why he had the power to heal meant learning its true purpose. He was sure the magical gift wasn't solely to heal himself during his archaeological adventures.

In addition, he'd met a remarkable woman and a two-thousand-year-old Greek warrior. He could see a friendship in the making with the two of them. Rex had many casual acquaintances, but few friendships.

Madison, though … Madison was understandably guarded, and Rex wanted to ease himself under that hard exterior and discover the woman beneath. That desire puzzled him, because he didn't form attachments with women. Usually, the less he knew, the better. Madison may turn people to stone, but he'd been accused of having a heart of stone. The lack of attachments had always been a survival technique. With his power, relationships were tricky because he needed to prevent the unwanted discovery of his magic. Trust wasn't something he gave easily. Madison had earned it in a surprisingly short time—easy to do when they'd saved each other's lives while simultaneously revealing their secrets to each other in the process.

The ability to turn a living creature to stone was wickedly impressive. Tragic too, considering the burden she'd carried alone for so long. She'd persevered. Maybe she'd been a brat when she was younger, but she'd taken adversity and forged her way, creating a career for herself.

Alone.

He recalled how she'd shed tears over her newfound friends knowing her secret. Rex had chosen to be alone, enjoying the peace of solitude unless he wanted company. Madison had never had a choice without risking someone's life. No friends. Any lovers?

None of his business.

Zephyr found a suitable spot, and Rex cleaned up after him before finding a trash can for the bag. He let the dog sniff around a few minutes longer, weaving through pedestrians. Inside and outside, people carried on with their lives to and from work or shopping or to the gym, unaware of the threads of magic woven into the lives of some humans.

Answers at Milopas. He hoped so, but if the three of them were drawn there, who or what else might be?

Rex walked off the elevator and down the hall toward Madison's apartment door. Before he could reach it and knock, the door across the hall from Madison's apartment opened and a pixie-cut blond in short shorts and a cutoff shirt stepped out, phone in one hand and enormous purse in the other. He gauged her to be mid to early twenties as she flashed a brilliant smile of ruby lips at him.

"Well, hello there. Are you new to the building?"

"Just visiting."

Zephyr wagged his tail as if waiting for an introduction. When the woman didn't show any interest in the dog, Rex took the slack out of the leash to make sure the animal didn't bother her.

"You're visiting Madison?" She leaned back on her doorframe, arching her back and drawing Rex's gaze down to a plump set of pert breasts. The curve in her lips suggested she noticed his lingering gaze.

"Yeah. We just met." He brought his eyes back up to meet hers. They loomed large, chocolate, and inviting. "Are you two friends?" he asked.

She gave Madison's door a derisive glance. "I don't think she friends anybody. Like, I don't see anybody ever visiting her. And she's so ... totally aloof. Hashtag British snotty. Hashtag no social life."

Keeps to herself, Rex thought. He could relate to that. But the woman who saved him and cried over her dog wasn't snotty.

Beside him, Zephyr sat patiently, calmly resigned to not receiving attention from this particular human.

The neighbor toyed with the gold chain around her neck, but Rex didn't fall for the ploy this time to draw his gaze lower. Instead, he glanced back at Madison's door.

"So, like, are you two dating or what?" the neighbor asked.

He tried to clear his head from the distraction of her bosom, floral-scented perfume, and her grating use of the word *like*. "No. We're colleagues, sort of. We just connected through a work thing ..."

"I'm Mimi." Her face brightened as she pocketed her phone and extended a beautifully manicured hand. "What work?" The skin over her delicate hand was soft when he gently shook it.

"Rex Alderman. Archaeology."

Her lip drew down. "Like ancient civilizations?"

"Like treasure hunter," he said. Absolutely ancient civilizations. They were fascinating, but that line of conversation didn't interest most women. He recalled Madison's initial reaction had been one of intrigue.

Mimi's bright green eyes sparked. "Treasure hunter."

One side of his mouth curved reflexively at her interest. "Yeah. I dig up secrets, chase myths, and try to avoid curses when I touch things I shouldn't. You could say I specialize in finding trouble ... and buried treasure. Sometimes they're the same thing."

His standard line to invoke intrigue felt flat even as Mimi seemed more enchanted by him. A conversation with this woman about archaeology wouldn't be as intellectually stimulating as it would with Madison. He wondered why that mattered. He hadn't selected dates based on mutual interests and education levels before.

Mimi gave a little giggle as she released his hand. "When you're done with your work thing, you should totally drop by. I'm headed out for a latte with some friends, but I'll be back in an hour."

Long legs moved gracefully as she walked down the hall, hips swinging. She was attractive and entirely too shallow for his taste. Looking down at the hand that had briefly held hers, an icy shiver ran through him, thinking of the last handshake he'd seen where Chloros had turned Madison into gold.

He'd been lured to that mansion with the promise of work and funding for his next excavation. The promise of financial backing was a weak point of his to exploit, which made him think of his other weaknesses, like beautiful women. Mimi had once been right up his alley—someone who would invite him to her room after a sixty-second acquaintance and was purely interested in the physical and sexual. Someone who would never venture into the depths of who and what he really was. But now the invitation felt hollow. Something larger was at play and such a diversion no longer appealed. He needed answers about who or what was after him and couldn't risk walking into any other traps until he had them.

When he knocked, Madison opened her door with a "thank you" for him and a pat for Zephyr. The words were brisk as she only looked at the dog, making Rex consider how quickly she'd opened the door. Had she been eavesdropping on his conversation with Mimi?

Without looking at him, Madison went to her laptop at a small kitchen table and began clicking like a fiend.

Was she jealous? That would be absurd. Then, he recalled his words: "*I dig up secrets, chase myths, and try to avoid curses when I touch things I shouldn't.*" The line was a harmlessly flirtatious way to earn the interest of the opposite sex—one he'd employed on several occasions. Harmless, as long as the woman hearing the words didn't consider herself cursed, which Madison did.

Rex unleashed the dog, who dutifully went to his owner. "Met your neighbor." Might as well clear the air as soon as possible.

Madison rubbed a hand through his fur. "You met Mimi." A slight acidity tinged Madison's voice. "I think she works in social media, but I don't know the specifics." She didn't look up from her computer.

He rubbed his neck, unsure how to patch up the harm he'd inadvertently done. He suspected Madison wouldn't like being called out for listening to their conversation. "She seems friendly."

"To the Y chromosome, yes. I'm sure she would welcome you into her revolving door of men." Her tone was matter-of-fact as she continued to focus on her typing. "She's got good taste, though. Never seen an ugly or unfit one leave her place, and they all seem to leave with a smile on their faces."

"Not interested." The words came out of his mouth before he could think, but he realized they were true. He pondered why and figured it must be because of his earlier rationalization of wanting to stay focused on the task.

"Where's Alexios?" Rex asked.

"Hopefully taking a shower. I told him the basics while you were walking Zephyr. Alexios said he'd seen it on the telly before. Based on the excited noises, I think he's both entertained by the shower and successful at using it. I'm trying not to envision the puddles of water he's probably making everywhere." She may have tried to sound dismayed, but a note of adoration slipped into her complaint.

Rex understood her tone as Alexios was somehow both fierce and adorable at the same time.

She typed more. "I found a cargo service. We can drop them

off in two days, and they'll fly them to Athens the day after that. We'll have to pick them up at the warehouse there and boat them to the island ourselves."

He walked over, placed his hands on her shoulders and said, "Book it. We'll do our flights next." Because he wasn't sure how to smooth over his earlier words, he'd just have to show her he wasn't afraid to touch her. In doing so, maybe she would see that he didn't think she was cursed.

She looked up at him, lips curving. "Someone is now all in for this adventure."

"Adventure keeps me sharp."

"Is that why you chose archaeology?"

"I didn't study for a decade to play it safe. Myths aren't written for passive reading in libraries—they're meant to be discovered in carved stone and sealed tombs."

He pulled up a chair beside her and sat. "I initially hesitated because I like to weigh the pros and cons. But once I decide, I don't waffle."

She glanced down, seeming to take note of the small space between them. In order to see the plane flight schedules, he needed to be close. He certainly wouldn't treat her like a leper just because she had Medusa's abilities.

"And the danger of those buried myths?"

"If there's not a curse, a trap, or a monster, artifacts are rarely worth sealing," he murmured with a grin.

Madison's cheeks flushed as she turned her attention back to her screen. Intriguing. She felt the chemistry too, then. A few days of harmless flirting mixed with their travel plans would help the time pass.

CHAPTER
SIX

The next morning, Madison woke and cooked eggs and sausage while Rex took Zephyr outside to relieve himself. Last night, she'd given Rex and Alexios each a pair of loose pajama shorts for them to wear. Rex had slept on the sofa and Alexios on the floor beside the sofa.

The entire arrangement seemed bizarre—cramming two grown men into her apartment—but then so were two men in tight shorts, stretched over their quadriceps like the Hulk, at her kitchen table eating her food. Despite the oddity, she was relaxed with their presence and had slept soundly, which seemed like quite an accomplishment after being turned to gold and fearing for her life. Nothing like two muscle-packed sentries outside her door to bring a sense of safety and comfort.

"I completed all the electronic paperwork online." She scraped scrambled eggs from the pan onto three separate plates beside the warm sausage. "We'll take them to the shipping company tomorrow and turn them into ... statues." Her voice cracked at the last words. She set the plates down in front of them before turning to fix Alexios a glass of orange juice. "This feels fast. Are we moving too fast?"

"First," Rex began around a mouthful of food, "thank you for the food. You didn't have to cook for us, but it's appreciated. Second, I don't know about you, but I don't want to wait around for whoever this 'master' is to come after us. I like being proactive. The sooner we get answers in Milopas, the sooner we know what the hell is going on."

Right, the man doesn't waffle once his mind is made up.

Alexios swallowed a bite of sausage. "I would like to see the city you live in. But," he added with a sigh, "I would like to see all the world. It can wait. This feels important." He took a sip of the orange juice and wrinkled his nose. "It is very sweet."

"Yeah. Made from concentrate." She took his glass and added tap water. "We'll tone it down a bit." She slid the glass back in front of him. She imagined there weren't many sugary foods in existence during his time. Today's doses would absolutely shock his senses. For this reason, she'd omitted the soda when they'd ordered drive-through yesterday.

"What did you eat in ... Where were you born?" she asked.

"Aegea in Macedonia during the reign of Philip II. Maza—uh, barley bread—was a staple. Fish and goat for protein. Lamb if we were lucky. Garlic and onion, lentils, figs, and goat cheese."

She cracked a few more eggs to cook for Zephyr and made a mental note that she would need to buy dog food in Athens. "That sounds really good, actually."

"I thought I'd take Alexios shopping today," Rex said. "Grab a few clothes and toiletries. Maybe a little sightseeing if it's not too much sensory overload for him."

She nodded as she scrambled more eggs for Zephyr. "I'll pack." She could use a few moments of space to herself before the international trip. "Oh, but we should exchange phone numbers."

"Good thinking." He swallowed his sausage bite and drank his coffee.

"Do you think it's safe to split up?"

Rex shrugged. "Stop worrying."

Irritation rippled through her with surprising gusto. She whirled and pointed the spatula at him. "OK," she snapped. "If I asked if it was safe when the most dangerous thing out there was cloudy with a chance of rain, you can dismissively tell me to stop worrying. About this, I'm not overreacting. We don't know what else, like *Midas*, is lurking out there, so I think my question is a damn legitimate one." She paused, gripping the spatula firmly and giving Rex—what she hoped was conveyed despite the glasses—a look daring him to tell her to calm down.

Blinking, he carefully set his mug down, picked up his napkin, and wiped his mouth. Her gaze slid to Alexios, who was looking back and forth between the two of them with wide-eyed interest as though watching a Wimbledon final.

Rex leaned back in his chair. "I concede the point. We don't know the danger on the streets. Worrying is a logical reaction to the unknown."

She took a moment to replay his words and detected honesty without patronization. Lowering the spatula, she turned off the stove burner with a flick of her wrist. "Thank you. I didn't appreciate your subtle insinuation that I was overreacting."

He nodded. "We'll keep to public places. No upstate mansions for us. Anything else?"

"We can set up our phones to track each other," she suggested, scraping the cooked eggs onto a plate to let them cool for the dog.

"Good idea. And you'll stay safely in your apartment?"

She nodded. "Except when Zephyr needs to go out."

"Then we'll walk him before we leave and not be gone more than four hours to walk him again when we get back."

Moved by his consideration, she gave him a soft smile. "That's ... that's perfect. Thanks."

"HE MIGHT COME BACK ANY MINUTE," Rex commented, unable to keep the irritation out of his voice as he looked nervously around the warehouse.

The cargo bay at JFK was a concrete and steel cavern. Fluorescent lights buzzed overhead, throwing stark shadows across rows of towering wooden crates and shrink-wrapped pallets stacked on metal skids. Forklifts beeped as they crisscrossed the space, the acrid tang of fuel and machine oil mixing. A rolling bay door yawned open to the tarmac, where aircraft engines growled in the distance.

In the shadows between a line of crates, Madison and Rex had carved out a pocket of secrecy—just enough cover to do the impossible: turn Alexios to stone before crating him for his flight across the Atlantic.

"I know," Madison fired back. She wore black leggings and a short t-shirt that rode up slightly, giving Rex glimpses of a bare abdomen he shouldn't be fantasizing about licking. He'd spent several days now in close proximity to her, and her allure seemed to grow during that time.

He crossed his arms. "We've been over this. They'll be fine." As soon as the words escaped his mouth, he regretted them. She had a right to her worry. This was no small psychological undertaking. If they were going to work together and navigate these murky waters of myth and magic, he couldn't be dismissive of her feelings. He placed a hand on her shoulder in an offer of support.

"I know," she repeated, this time with less conviction.

Alexios had dressed in his warrior outfit with his sword at his side as the imagery made for a better statue. He held Zephyr in his arms, waiting patiently.

Madison's throat bobbed in a swallow as she lowered her sunglasses and peeked over the top. Rex crossed his arms and kept his gaze straight ahead at Alexios and the dog. The warrior gave her a reassuring smile, even as the color bleached out of his skin and everything hardened to gray stone right before Rex's eyes.

Fascinating. How many times on his various archaeology adventures could that little trick have helped him? But if Rex had to choose between tears and stone, he would choose tears. He didn't envy Madison's gift. It had obviously isolated her for years and caused her pain. Rex, on the other hand, had chosen to isolate himself from his peers. He liked his freedom and being responsible only for himself. After they found answers in Milopas, he could return to his way of life. He guessed she could too, though perhaps it wasn't a fulfilled one.

Madison slipped her glasses back up and sniffed, looking a little gray herself. He wanted to comfort her in some way, which obviously clashed with his self-image as a loner, but he could dissect that contradiction later. At last, he decided on an arm around her, which must've been the right move because she leaned into him and laid her head on his shoulder.

They stayed comfortably linked like that for a moment until the warehouse attendant approached and Madison straightened.

As she walked over to greet the man in overalls and show him her electronic paperwork on her phone, Rex walked up to the statues. He settled Madison's smartwatch on Alexios's wrist—a way to track him if he didn't arrive in Athens as expected. Next, he pulled the two knit hats Madison had provided and slipped them on—one over Alexios's head and the other over Zephyr's.

"Sleep tight, boys. We'll see you on a beautiful island. Dream of friendly women and large dog biscuits." He tugged the hats down to cover their eyes.

⌘⌘⌘⌘⌘⌘

MADISON FIDGETED with the book in her hand. She'd bought a Frieda McFadden thriller novel at the airport but felt too wired to focus on reading it. She was literally traveling to the great unknown and with a man she barely knew.

She and Rex had passed through security without incident. When the plane was in the air, Rex reclined his seat the fraction of an inch it would allow. He had the aisle, and she had the window.

"Can you look in a mirror without your glasses and not turn yourself to stone?" he asked.

"Yes. And if you think about it, that's how Perseus defeated Medusa, using her reflection to locate her and behead her. I can look at anyone through a reflection and not turn them to stone."

"Ah. Right."

Wanting both a distraction and to know Rex better, she said, "Tell me about your greatest archaeological adventure."

He grinned, eyes crinkling at the edges, as if to suggest she was in for a treat. "The Black Sea Coast, Crimea. First, the backstory. Two thousand years ago, Kharon the Sky's Wrath was one of the most feared warlords to ride across the vast Scythian steppes. A brutal conqueror, he led his bloodthirsty cavalry over the Black Sea region, raiding Greek colonies, annihilating rival tribes, and demanding tribute in gold, slaves, and weapons." His tone was enthusiastic and engaging, the archaeologist in his element.

"Kharon believed the Sky Father—Papaios—favored him and that his destiny was to unite the Scythian tribes under his rule, no matter how many had to die for it. He earned his name after slaughtering an entire enemy village under a stormy sky, claiming the lightning was a sign of divine approval. His warriors burned entire settlements to the ground, their inhabitants left to the vultures."

Madison shuddered. "I restored a Peter Paul Rubens painting on Kharon—*Epic Battle Chaos.* A grand, disturbing battle scene full of motion, muscular warriors, and supernatural elements, like *The Fall of Phaeton.*" She recalled the high energy of the painting conveyed through horses rearing, bodies tumbling, and dramatic lighting illuminating Kharon as the divine executioner beneath swirling storm clouds that filled the sky. "But ... continue your story."

"He sought immortality, believing that as long as he ruled, the Scythians would never fall. To achieve this, he turned to dark rituals, sacrificing captured enemies and even his own warriors to the gods in exchange for eternal life.

"His arrogance angered the priests of Papaios, who warned him that no man could defy the gods. Enraged, Kharon stormed their sacred temple, executing the high priest and seizing the Crown of the Sky Father, an artifact said to grant divine wisdom to Scythian kings." Rex's blue eyes sparkled as he talked animatedly, clearly a skilled storyteller.

"But the gods had seen enough. The sky darkened, and a supernatural storm raged for three days, forcing Kharon and his warriors to take shelter in their most secure burial kurgan. The priests' ultimate curse took hold—the ground swallowed him and his treasures whole, sealing him in an underground tomb of salt and stone, where his soul would suffer in endless darkness."

"I suspect," she began, "based on your ambitious nature, you were after the Crown of the Sky Father and all that divine wisdom from the gods."

The corner of Rex's mouth twitched. "Just the crown. Wisdom is earned, not taken—or divined—from an artifact. Besides, I didn't necessarily believe in the power of it, just the reward for finding it and the gold that would have been buried with him. The Scythians were master goldsmiths. Legend claimed that buried with him was a golden pectoral intricately designed with mythological animals and warriors in combat, gold plaques and belt buckles, and gold-covered weapons—ornate akinakes, arrowheads, and sword hilts inlaid with precious gems."

"Plus, buried war gear would be there." She imagined the booty—and the millions it would be worth. "A modest aspiration for a modest treasure hunter," she quipped and wondered why he was looking for work at Chloros's mansion if he'd found Kharon's windfall. And she knew he'd found it, because she'd had to repair the damage to the crown—nicks and dents that had clearly been a recent desecration of it. She needed to hear the full story.

"Hey, I'm a modest kind of guy."

She chuckled and shook her head.

"So, you found the burial site?" she prompted, practically on the edge of her seat with anticipation.

"After a year of research, I assembled a team, and we dug out an ancient underground chamber lined with thick layers of salt. Weeks of back-breaking work. At the center of the tomb rested a Scythian warrior, his body strangely intact despite two thousand years having passed. I think it was the salt, though after having met you and golden Elvis, maybe it was the curse from the priest after all."

He rubbed his chin before continuing, "In any case, the salt and dust had my eyes watering, and I dripped sloppy tears right onto Kharon. Next thing I know, he's bolting upright, cursing—so I suspect—at me in a language I didn't know, and swinging a bronze sword at my head as if I'm the one who killed him the first time."

"What did you do?" Her breath wisped out in anticipation, and she placed a hand on his forearm.

"Pulled a sword off one of his soldiers and we hacked at each other a while. He was twice my size and battle-forged. Only thing in my favor was being faster and his joints were a bit tinman-ish after two thousand years of salt preservation."

"Where was your crew?"

"Running for their lives, convinced I'd cursed them all. They didn't know my tears had brought him to life. They thought our disturbing the graveyard had unleashed the supernatural to kill the modern invaders."

"So you killed Kharon all over again?" she asked.

"Yeah. Decapitation, but not before he got a few of his own good licks in."

"And you found the crown and sold it?"

He nodded. "Solid gold except for embedded emeralds and rubies. Got less than it was worth due to the fresh damage."

She nodded. "I remember it was shaped like a wreath of lightning bolts and eagle feathers symbolizing both the Greek Zeus and the Scythian Sky Father, Papaios. How did you damage it?"

He grimaced. "Might have had to use the thing as a shield at one point."

She thought about the fresh nicks and dents. That scenario fit. Ha! She'd made the repairs to the crown all the while thinking some rogue archaeologist had been careless, but he'd been fighting for his life.

"And the mystical properties?" She'd certainly never put the thing on her head.

"Sold it. No idea." Rex shrugged, though a twinge of regret was in his voice.

"Bollocks!" She smacked him lightly on the arm before leaning away and crossing her arms. "You had a priceless, possibly magical, artifact in your possession and you just sold it without testing it first?"

He chuckled at her outburst. "I'd spent a fortune in research and manpower just to discover the location and uncover the site. I needed the money more than I needed the wisdom."

"What about the rest of the treasure?" she demanded.

"Once my hired help saw the crown, they put fear of curses aside and looted the rest. I was outnumbered but managed to get away with the crown and Kharon's sword."

She leaned her head back against the seat, absorbing it all. "That is quite the story. Where's the sword?"

"I rent a climate-controlled storage unit in Atlanta with all the sentimental artifacts I can't part with."

"Storage? Treasures in storage?"

He shrugged a shoulder. "If I ever have a home, I'll put them on display."

CHAPTER
SEVEN

After a ten-hour, nonstop flight, they arrived in Athens where Madison was grateful to stretch her legs on the way to a taxi. Though she'd only slept a few hours in an impossibly uncomfortable position, jet lag and a sore neck couldn't dampen the nervous anticipation of going to the island.

The taxi rattled through the city streets, weaving between mopeds and compact cars. Athens unfurled outside the windows in a blur of contrasts—ancient stone wedged between modern concrete, graffiti-splashed walls giving way to whitewashed balconies hung with laundry. As the cab descended toward Piraeus, the traffic thickened, and glimpses of the sea flashed between warehouses and shipyards where ferries and fishing boats bobbed side by side. The closer they drew, the more the city gave way to salt-stained docks with cranes arching overhead.

At the docks, they rented a boat to sail to Milopas. The *Delfináki—Little Dolphin*—was a charming, modest vessel. Madison thought it perfect for a more leisurely journey across the Aegean. It also fit their budget.

Painted a sun-washed white with accents of pale turquoise, the eighteen-foot wooden motorboat had the look of a bygone era, well-maintained but also well-traveled. Its hull was rounded and slightly weathered, with hand-painted lettering on the stern bearing its name in both Greek and English.

Powered by a single, quiet outboard motor, the *Little Dolphin* cruised at a comfortable pace, allowing Madison to enjoy the gentle roll of the sea and the breathtaking coastal views while Rex had the wheel. A striped canvas canopy stretched over the middle third of the boat, offering shade to a cushioned bench seat and a simple wooden steering console.

While Rex maneuvered the vessel, Madison stared out at the vast blue sea, enjoying the salty breeze and cool April temperature.

The boat cut through the vibrant, tranquil water. The buzz of the engine and whisk of wind were the only noises. Past tourist boats and fishing boats, they sped to a foreign destination. Did the place hold answers or only more questions?

The local who rented the boat to them had explained that no island named Milopas existed in this sea, so Rex had feigned a mispronunciation and pointed to a different island on his phone app when he paid a week's worth of rent on the *Delfináki*, not knowing if they'd need it for three days or three weeks.

Rex and Madison could see the island on the map of their phone apps—a small mass of land that apparently didn't exist, at least not to anyone else.

As they neared Milopas, the shallower water turned emerald green. She'd seen paintings of the Aegean Sea, but living it was more vivid and breathtaking. Rex slowed the boat, circling the landmass. The thunderbolt shape was cleaved into the sea as if Zeus himself had borne it into existence.

Jagged cliffs rose from the water, their sheer faces scarred with streaks of golden veins that shimmered, suggestive of remnants of the lightning god's celestial touch. The island's body consisted of craggy peaks and lush valleys, where the land descended into crescent-shaped beaches kissed by turquoise waters.

At the one and only dock, they parked the boat and disembarked.

Rex tied it securely to the post. "You OK?"

"A bit revved up. A bit chuffed. I'm sure the jet lag will hit me later, and I'll be knackered." With her hands on her hips, she inspected the immediate area. The sun beamed merrily and she was comfortable in her navy shorts, boat shoes, and pink cotton shirt surrounded by the smell of sea and sand.

"Up or around?" she asked. The path diverged both ways.

"How about up? Get an idea of the layout."

She grinned. "You want the higher ground in case we're attacked." She could tell he was on alert. "Now who's worried?"

"Doesn't hurt to be cautious." Rex wore khaki slacks and a light blue button-down shirt with the sleeves rolled. He slung his backpack over his shoulder. It contained toiletries and clothes for him and Alexios. "Although, something about the place feels safe. Too quiet. But safe."

"I agree." She followed him up the stone staircase, deciding she would grab her suitcase later after they'd found a room or bungalow to rent.

The first clearing, about two stories up, had a vast platform. To the left stood weight machines; to the right spread an obstacle course. The middle looked to be an open-air sparring ground with a weapons rack.

"It's a training facility," Rex said.

"For who?" Madison asked, not liking the newness and emptiness of it all.

He cast her a sideways glance and continued upward without answering.

At the summit, an enclave of six sturdy cabins was arranged in a half circle, their exteriors a blend of smooth marble and timber. A larger building opposite them completed the circle. They entered the building, noting a picnic-style table near a kitchen. At the other end was a sitting area with sofas.

Rex walked to the kitchen faucet and turned it on. "Running water. Maybe piped up from a reservoir beneath the island."

Madison flipped on a switch. "Electricity."

"I think I spotted rooftop solar panels on each cabin and this building."

Rex opened the refrigerator, a large, double-door steel contraption. Cool air spilled out.

"Stocked with food?" Madison gaped. "Someone went to a lot of trouble to put this place together. Do you think they're somewhere else on the island?"

"Ours is the only boat at the dock. I think we're alone. Maybe he, she, or they went out for supplies."

"This place is immaculate." She looked at the kitchen island with a six-burner stove above side-by-side ovens. "Like it's not even been used." The floors were clean, the table spotless, and the couches unruffled.

She left the building and walked to one of the cabins—also pristine with running water and electricity. It had a bed, dresser, and bathroom, complete with toilet, shower, and mirror. One by one, she explored, undecided if finding other people would be more or less anxiety-provoking.

Rex joined her. "They're identical."

"I'd like to find the owner. Ask if we can rent a room for the night." She backed out of the cabin and moved into the center of the compound. "Look at this writing." The stone floor had letters carved into it.

"Looks Greek to me," he quipped.

"Very funny." She bent and touched the letters. "Wonder what it says?"

The letters rose, floating in the air before her. She sucked in a breath and stood, backing into Rex, who gripped her arm as though prepared to move her out of harm's way should something happen.

On a shimmering ripple, the letters morphed to English.

Forged by divine hands
Let this be a place of refuge
A proving ground.
Warriors six, sharpen your skills
Embrace the gift of the gods
Prepare for your destiny.

Gooseflesh sprang along Madison's arms. "Six warriors?"

The words drifted back to the floor where they settled.

"Appears that way."

"What destiny?"

"I don't know." He ran his hands up and down her arms as if trying to dispel the chill that had run through her or maybe needing a little reassurance himself, grounded in the feel of something tangible.

She found the gesture touching, as it had been the first time. "I suppose we're here until we do know."

Rex nodded. "Magic letters and all. I wonder what else is enchanted?"

"Shall we continue to explore?" She wanted to know who else was here. Who had stocked food supplies, towels, and toilet paper?

He took her hand in his and led her back to the stairs. "Good idea."

REX AND MADISON explored for hours until they tired and returned to the compound for water. As best he could tell, they were the only two people on the island. The path branched in different directions. One led to a waterfall, another to a beach. Rex was so skinny-dipping in that amazing shoreline while he was here.

"How about we shower and reconvene for dinner?" Madison suggested.

"Knackered?" he asked on a grin.

"Immensely."

"Meet you back in the kitchen in an hour?"

She nodded.

After a quick shower, Rex rummaged through the pantry and refrigerator, finding salmon and salad contents. While the oven heated, he spread seasoning over the fish. He chopped salad components—lettuce, tomato, onion, hearts of palm, green pepper, and cucumber. He was whipping up an oil and vinegar dressing when Madison arrived, clean with damp hair over her shoulders and wearing a summer dress with sandals.

She smiled, and he wished, not for the first time, he could see her eyes when she smiled. They were forever obscured by those dark sunglasses. The oven light flashed, indicating it had reached his desired temperature. He slid the salmon onto a pan inside it.

"You've been busy," she said.

"I was thinking how nice fish would be on an island and, sure enough, I found it in the fridge. I've also noticed you like salads and found all the ingredients for that too. Maybe you can scrounge us up a bottle of wine and some glasses."

"I can work on that." She glanced around the room. "There appears to be a wine bar."

Rex cocked his head and stared at the mahogany wood with a

dozen bottles, neatly stored and shelves holding white glasses. He didn't recall that furniture being there on their first pass-through.

As he whipped up the salad dressing, he said, "This place needs a firepit out in the middle with a couple of chairs. It would make a nice relaxing post-dinner spot."

"That sounds lovely." Madison fetched a bottle, two glasses, and a corkscrew. She set them down on the kitchen island. "The sitting area in here would make a cozy after-dinner spot also."

He drizzled dressing over the salads and carried them to the picnic table.

She opened the bottle of wine, sniffed the rich scent, and joined him. After pouring a glass for each of them, she sat and took a bite of her salad. "This is so delicious."

The smell of butter and garlic from the salmon filled the room.

"Easy to make it good when the ingredients are so fresh," he said.

A light breeze floated through the building. Everything about this place was open—windows with no panes and entryways with no doors. He peeked out of the mess hall entryway and saw a firepit with two deck chairs.

Chuckling, he shook his head. He ate the salad, flavors bursting on his taste buds.

"What?" The word fizzled on her lips as she followed his gaze and her mouth hung in astonishment. "Did you just wish that into existence?"

"I noticed a pattern. I mumbled about needing a phone charger—well, an adapter for the type of outlet here—before I took my shower. When I emerged, I had one bedside. I thought about wanting fish for dinner. I found fish, but I'd said that aloud too. I looked around for a dessert and didn't find one, but I didn't say audibly that I wanted a dessert. So I think, yeah, you can wish things into existence here by asking for them."

"I don't know whether to be thrilled or terrified by the amount of magic thrown around this place."

Ah, the worrying, Rex thought. Perhaps at times he was a bit too nonchalant, and they balanced each other out.

A HALF HOUR LATER, Rex leaned back in his chair, watching the flames in the outdoor firepit. "Beautiful island. Amazing amenities. A man could get used to this lifestyle."

Madison scoffed. "Not you. You're the restless sort. Always looking for the action."

"Takes one to know one." His tone teased.

"I suppose you're right." She chuckled, a sound he enjoyed. The fire's flames reflected in her dark sunglasses. Beneath them were her gorgeous, full lips—ones he'd stared at for entirely too long while she'd slept beside him on the plane.

"I'm not much for idleness unless it's moments of reflection and tranquility like this. You, on the other hand, look like you're waiting for the other shoe to drop."

"You know it will," she countered.

He raised his hand, let it fall. "Everything comes at a price. We're on an island crafted by gods and pulsing with magic. They want something from us."

She recited the engraving:

"Forged by divine hands
 Let this be a place of refuge
 A proving ground.
 Warriors six, sharpen your skills
 Embrace the gift of the gods
 Prepare for your destiny."

"The question is, when will our destiny be revealed?"

"Tomorrow, maybe," she speculated. "After we pick up Alexios and Zephyr."

"Alexios makes three. There are six cabins." He swirled the wine in his glass.

"Six warriors. Assuming we are two of the six warriors—which I do not consider myself—three more will join us to meet their destiny."

"My suspicions exactly. Everything here is by design."

Madison drew up her knees and wrapped her arms around them. Her lips straightened into a tense line as she stared into the fire.

"Hey. We'll stick together, OK?" he assured her. "I imagine our new colleagues will have magic too. You don't have to share what your gift is until you're ready."

"Gift?" She jerked her head back.

"Yeah. Like I said, everything here is by design. I suspect part of why you're here is the ability to turn living things to stone."

"I'm not a warrior. And despite your intentions, you're not making me feel better about the situation." Her tone was matter-of-fact and not admonishing. "If gods—or whatever powerful beings they are—brought me here for a destiny that involves training with lethal weapons and turning enemies to stone, my ability still doesn't seem like a gift."

He drank the rest of the wine in his glass as he considered her concern. "That's fair. Maybe we should go back to enjoying the fire."

"Yeah, maybe so." She rested her chin on her knees and stared at the flame.

"Want another glass of wine?" he offered.

"I'd love that."

Hopping up, he headed for the kitchen, glancing back at Madison by the fire. They would find the answers they sought about why they had the powers they did, but Madison was right;

they might not like those answers. She was right to worry, and he couldn't rationalize to himself why he wanted to ease her concern.

The crackling fire and the half-moon shining down felt tranquil.

They also felt like the calm before the storm.

CHAPTER
EIGHT

t sunrise, Madison woke and stretched. She'd slept soundly in an amazingly comfortable queen bed that wasn't her own. A quiet, steady ocean breeze filtered through the window, though the cabins were too far from the shore to hear the waves. No hum of bustling streets below her high-rise polluted the sounds of nature—rustling leaves and chirping birds. While she'd always valued the city as a place to blend in and disappear among the crowd, this island was bliss. She'd gone to bed restlessly worried and woken refreshed.

As was her morning habit, she checked her phone. Surprisingly, they had internet under the network "Milopas" and cellular service. She checked work email and answered a few of them, declining and apologizing for being unavailable for consulting work on any projects for the immediate future. She cringed, knowing her bank account could take the hit in the short term ... and hoping this diversion was short term.

She dressed in capri trousers and a floral shirt for the day before slipping on her sunglasses. Today, they would pick up

Alexios and Zephyr. An anxious anticipation buzzed through her, and she went in search of Rex.

He wasn't in his bungalow, nor the kitchen. The boat, perhaps? As she descended the rock stairs, halfway to bottom, she heard a scuffling noise.

Following the sound of shuffling feet and grunting noises, Madison took the path down the stairs toward the training grounds, stopping with a terrified jolt at the sight before her.

In the center, Rex clashed swords against a fierce creature who had the body of a red lion with sleek fur and a spiked tail. Smooth, bat-like wings were tucked behind it on its back as it attacked Rex. The Neanderthal-shaped humanoid face had an overbite and thick brow ridge. The animal lashed at him with wicked claws, gnashed three rows of sharp yellow teeth, and thrashed its spiked tail.

Madison's heart thudded wildly as she dashed toward Rex. Lurching one step forward with his name poised on her lips, she clamped her jaw shut, not daring call out and risk distracting him. Drawing to a halt at the edge, she puzzled at the scene. Now that she had a closer look, she tried to make sense of what she was seeing.

As the creature ducked and slashed its tail, it opened its mouth to scream or roar but no sound emitted. It shimmered like a glitch on a screen. When it next snapped its teeth, Rex ducked before thrusting up with his sword.

The impaling lethal blow bore no blood on the creature's chest. After a pause, it simply vanished into thin air.

"What the hell?" She raised a hand to her chest, willing her thundering heart to slow.

Rex straightened and turned toward her, a wide smile spreading his lips like a boy who'd just scored his first home run. He wore only a pair of shorts, and his shirtless torso glistened with sweat as he held the sword loosely at his side.

A woman's projected voice around him said, "Congratulations, warrior. You earned your first badge. Level three unlocked."

"Cool, huh?" Rex said.

"It's a holographic training ground?" Madison gaped.

"Exactly. Like virtual reality, except no clunky headset where you lose your peripheral vision."

The terror she'd experienced seconds ago drained out of her. "No sound either."

"Well. When I activated the system, I didn't know if it came with sound effects—roars and battle cries and how loudly that would carry. I asked the system to go on mute. Didn't want to wake you."

"Wake me? You mean send me into a panic? When I saw you fighting just now, I thought we were under attack."

"Sorry. Just sparring. Want to try?" He gestured to the rack of swords, axes, spears, arrows, and shields. "When you step into the inner circle of pavers, the game invites you to play. Your opponent appears, and off you go. It's fun. And satisfying the way winning at a video game is."

Eyeing the weapons, she decided the entire setup was too daunting. "Uh. No." She had an eerie feeling she would find herself in that circle with a sword in hand sooner than she'd like. With art as her passion, she'd never taken an interest in video games.

That wasn't entirely true. She'd met a man online through a virtual escape room game once. They had flirted harmlessly until the day he'd asked to meet in person. She couldn't bring herself to follow through and risk another relationship of half-truths when he seemed like a nice guy who deserved better. Leaving the game marked the end of her adventures in online gaming.

She shook off the memory. "I would like to go to the mainland to retrieve Alexios and Zephyr. Maybe do a little shopping."

Rex set the sword down by the other weapons. "Shopping? I

thought we established that this island gives you whatever you ask for."

"And I thought we established how those gifts will come with a price," she countered, bristling in part from the scare moments ago and because the future seemed more uncertain than ever.

"Agreed." His expression softened as he added, "But I don't think asking for less will change the price."

"Hmm." She didn't have a counter for that.

"If you want to shop, we can shop. Let me get cleaned up, and we'll go."

ⵣⵣⵣⵣⵣⵣⵣ

REX SHOWERED and considered the holographic manticore he'd battled. How many levels did the game have, and how many types of creatures? And if they sparred with Greek monsters, who would show up for the real fight?

When he emerged from the shower and toweled off in the bedroom, he found clothes exactly matching the attire he'd worn here. Khaki pants and a cotton button-down shirt. They were clean and a little too pressed for his taste, but the material felt soft on his skin.

"Uh. Thanks," he said to the empty room in case the clothing fairy was eavesdropping.

After dressing, he filled a backpack with water bottles and a change of clothes for Alexios. He snatched an apple from the kitchen and ate it as he descended the stairs. At the bottom, he found Madison sitting, staring at the sea, her blond hair glistening pale gold under the sunlight. She wore capri pants, a floral print spaghetti strap shirt, and boat shoes. Her pale, smooth skin had his fingers tingling to know what skimming them along that surface would feel like. And what her reaction would be.

So far, she hadn't minded the few times he'd touched her or

taken her hand. He wanted more. With those glasses, he wouldn't be able to see the emotion in her eyes, but he was learning to read her mouth—the lovely O it formed when she was surprised, the dip at the corners in displeasure, the straight line of concentration or worry, and the beaming white of teeth when she was happy.

When he took another bite of apple, the sound had her turning toward him. She looked up at him.

"Ready?" he asked. "The sea beckons, lass." His pirate impression could use improvement, but had the desired effect of making her smile. He extended a hand. When she took it, he pulled her to her feet and up against him.

"Oh!" She put a hand against his chest as her surprised mouth made that delightful O shape.

He wanted to kiss that mouth. Kiss her. Maybe he could earn one. But he could wait—enjoy the interactions during the wait—and pick a better time when she wasn't anxious to get to her friends.

"Want to drive the boat?" he asked.

"Yes. I'd like to learn." Her breathless words didn't go unnoticed.

Good. The closeness affected her as much as him. That would make the future kiss he was scheming even more delicious. For now, he wanted proximity to her and conversation with her while they enjoyed a boat ride on a beautiful day.

"Climb aboard," he said, dropping his arm from around her.

She did, walking to the helm. He untied the boat, tossing the rope on the deck as he finished the apple and chucked the core onto the island where birds and ants could finish it off.

"You've already had the safety talk from the rental company, so we'll dive into driving. Check your gauges—fuel, RPMs, battery, oil pressure, temperature." He pointed to each as he spoke. "Ensure the engine is in neutral. Some boats, you prime the engine first. Turn the key to start."

She turned it, cranking the engine.

"Good. Shift into reverse and use minimal throttle to ease away from the dock."

He lifted her left hand and set it on the wheel, keeping his hand gently on top. He did the same with his other hand, guiding hers to the throttle. "Minimal throttle to move away from the dock with smooth, slow movements." He applied gentle pressure over her hand to ease the throttle forward. The boat glided away from the dock, and he turned the wheel with her hand. Soft hands. Slender, tapering fingers. "There's no power steering like a car, so get a feel for how much strength you might need to turn it. The boat leans into turns slightly, so make wide, gradual turns at higher speeds."

"What's the red cord?" she asked.

"Safety. If you're boating alone, you can attach one end to your shirt or belt. If you fall overboard, the cord pulls, cuts the engine."

"Ah. Like on a gym treadmill."

He chuckled. "Yeah, like that."

He dropped his hands and stepped back to give her full control. "Cruising speed is usually between fifteen and twenty-five knots. Let's do fifteen for your first time. Gradually increase power to avoid bow rise."

"Bow rise?"

"The front lifting too much."

He watched her hands move—steady and gracefully—as he kept his distance. As a woman who restored art and had an attention to detail, he suspected that steady grace had come from years of practice. Every touch of her made him want to touch her more.

Madison wasn't a quick tumble under the sheets before his next adventure in Dubai. He was enjoying getting to know her and could take his time. One, because she was the type of woman —with everything she'd been through—who needed time. Two, because he had the time to take. Considering how they had their own self-sustaining compound, he suspected this assignment—whatever it was—would require time.

He had always felt himself up for new adventures. Getting to know Madison Katsaros was an adventure all its own.

CHAPTER

NINE

After they docked, Madison bounded onto the deck. They had two hours before they could pick up Alexios and Zephyr. The buzz of anticipation mingled with the excitement from her first experience driving a boat. Not to mention the little thrill that ran through her body every time Rex touched her. When those deep blue eyes were focused on her, all her worries seemed to vanish and they were just two people sailing the sea. When those large, calloused hands touched her, she felt cared for, like she meant something to another person. She couldn't remember the last time she'd felt anything like it.

"Let's do a little touring while we wait," Rex said, taking the lead.

She gave him a grateful look because he clearly intended to distract her from her anxious waiting by filling the time with site seeing. His gesture was as thoughtful as when he'd taken the time to teach her to drive a boat.

From the dock, they walked to Monastiraki Square, a bustling hub where ancient and modern collided. Street vendors sold souvenirs, jewelry, and antiques, with the Acropolis visible in the distance. The air was filled with the smells of freshly baked koulouri, sizzling souvlaki, roasting chestnuts from street vendors, salty sea air from the nearby port, and blooming jasmine in hidden courtyards.

They walked past the Plaka Neighborhood, full of narrow, winding streets lined with neoclassical houses, bougainvillea, and quaint cafés. Musicians played soft melodies on traditional instruments. Beyond the Plaka Neighborhood, they strolled to Anafiotika with its whitewashed, island-style houses, quiet and picturesque, and cats lounging in the sun.

The Acropolis and Parthenon were an amazing sight, packed with tourists taking pictures of the massive Doric columns and intricate friezes. Madison and Rex climbed up the rough stone steps as the scent of warm earth and ancient marble lingered.

At the top, she took in the breathtaking cityscape. "It's magnificent," she told Rex.

"You can see the Erechtheion and the Caryatids." He pointed toward a temple with a unique asymmetrical design due to the uneven terrain. "It's the site of the legendary contest between Athena and Poseidon for the city's patronage." He turned her toward another spot. "The Temple of Athena Nike."

Perched gracefully on the southwest edge of the Acropolis, the small yet striking temple stood on a bastion overlooking the city, appearing almost delicate compared to the massive Parthenon columns. The white Pentelic marble of the temple gleamed in the sunlight, and its columns were elegant and refined, perfect for the goddess of wisdom and the arts. Though smaller than the Parthenon, its position on the edge of the Acropolis made it appear almost floating above the city. Beyond the temple, the view stretched toward the Saronic Gulf, where the blue waters shimmered in the distance.

They stood like that for a moment with his hands on her shoulders, facing Athena's temple and admiring the beauty.

Madison was tempted to call the view and the company romantic, but she didn't think that was Rex's intention. He was being friendly, as he had on the boat. And yet, her body warmed at the contact and ached to lean into him.

"And over there is the Odeon of Herodes Atticus. Still used for performances today." He pointed to a well-preserved ancient stone theater.

When she turned toward him, he dropped his hands but didn't move away from her. "Let's make our way to the warehouse. We'll be a few minutes early, but we can walk slow."

"Thank you for this. It's all so lovely, and took my mind off the wait. Even though we don't know what the future holds, I feel fortunate to have met you and have a friend in this."

He gave a slight but genuine smile as he took her hand. "Feeling's mutual."

They descended the stone steps and moved on to Ermou Street, a lively shopping strip where they passed perfumeries, bakeries, and high-end boutiques. The scent of fresh bread and coffee filled the air.

As she dragged Rex along a few detours, he patiently endured her shopping. She bought dog food and chew toys, despite Rex mentioning, again, how she could probably just ask the island for these things. She didn't like the idea of owing anyone anything—even, or maybe especially, magical beings. At a clothing store, she bought shorts and t-shirts for Alexios to add to his meager collection of modern clothes. She had to stop at shoes, though, because she didn't know his size. She also had to stop because they were reaching the limits of what they could carry and still walk around. Rex's backpack was bursting at the seams, the dog food bag was slung over one shoulder, and she carried a sack of goods.

Her final purchase was pasteli, thinking the sweet treat would make a nice introductory gift for the others when they arrived.

Three more guests, to be exact, assuming the bungalows and "warrior six" represented the total number of expected guests.

Next, they took a taxi to the airport. At the cargo terminal, they exchanged their receipt for an enormous crate inside a cavernous warehouse. Their footsteps echoed slightly with every step on its smooth concrete floor. Overhead, massive steel beams supported a high roof fitted with rows of fluorescent lights and skylights, casting harsh white light and patches of sunlight across the space. The air smelled faintly of oil, metal, and the dust of cardboard and wood.

Cargo was stacked in neat zones, segregated by destination or content. Pallets of goods—ranging from industrial equipment to luxury vehicles—were shrink-wrapped or crated in reinforced wooden boxes. Painted lines on the floor marked lanes for forklifts and safety zones for workers.

Metal shelving units along the walls held shipping supplies—straps, shrink wrap, labeling machines, heavy-duty gloves, and barcoded tracking tags. Digital screens displayed incoming and outgoing shipments, with time stamps and gate assignments.

A section of the warehouse was dedicated to loading and unloading, with retractable loading dock plates and rolling metal doors that opened directly to the airport tarmac. Overhead cranes and hoists hung from ceiling tracks, ready to lift oversized or unusually heavy cargo. A constant hum of activity filled the warehouse—forklifts beeping, a radio playing Greek pop quietly from a corner, and the occasional barked instruction in Greek or English. The buzz of nearby planes taking off and landing seeped in through the steel walls.

Excitement had Madison practically bouncing on her toes. In all her art restoration days, she'd never had this reaction waiting to open a crate. Rex set down their supplies and took her hand as if wanting to help her remain calm.

"Where's your truck?" the attendant asked.

"On its way," Rex lied.

The man frowned. "Well, I need the forklift in hangar three. Call me when your truck is here."

"Will do, thanks," Rex said.

When the man left, Madison looked around to ensure they weren't within earshot of anyone before turning to Rex. "Can you open it?"

As he scanned the warehouse, she followed his gaze. Scattered across workstations or resting against crates and walls were tools commonly used in cargo management, including box cutters, ratchets, barcode scanners, label printers, gloves, hand trucks, and crowbars.

"Bingo." Rex picked up a crowbar.

Madison picked up her own, and they set to work, rushing and hoping to open the crate before anyone could see what they were doing. When her hands shook, she doubled her efforts. She didn't want her friends immobilized for a minute longer than absolutely necessary, but she also didn't want to get caught and have to try to explain what they were doing.

When the last nail was up, they each took a side of the lid and lifted it off. A pressure in her chest eased. Inside, her friend and her dog were stone still and whole, as she'd left them.

Rex was quick to summon tears and swipe a moist finger over Alexios and Zephyr. The reanimation was swift with a sudden burst of color followed by movement. Rex snatched the hat off Zephyr who leaped out of Alexios's grasp and to the ground before Madison's feet.

With a giddy squeal, she knelt and hugged him to her. "Who's a good dog? Is that you? Yes, it is."

Alexios climbed out of the crate and took off his head covering. "Athens?" he asked hopefully, looking a little dazed.

Rex clapped him on the back. "You have arrived at your destination. We'll take a taxi back to the docks where we have a boat waiting to sail to Milopas. But first, there's a restroom over there where you can change clothes."

She looked up at the Greek warrior and stood. "You're well?"

"I am well. You succeeded, Madison." As he had at her apartment, he smiled broadly and ran his hands up and down her arms in a mechanical motion, trying to mimic the way Rex had soothed her.

She patted his hand, so he'd know he could stop the sweet but awkward gesture. Then, because the relief was too much to contain, she leaned in and placed a chaste kiss on his cheek. "I'm glad you're OK."

While Rex and Alexios took out clothes, Madison found the dog treats among their purchases and gave one to Zephyr. She attached a leash to his collar.

When Alexios rejoined them, he wore modern clothes, though he still wore his ancient sandals.

"I'll keep your sword in my pack," Rex said. "This is not the era for wearing weapons in public."

THE TAXI RIDE was quiet with Alexios staring out the window, mouth open in childlike awe. They had the cab driver drop them off a block from the docks so they could grab a meal before departing. Madison held Zephyr's leash and her coveted pastries as the men unloaded her purchases from the cab. She was happy they didn't have to carry her shopping haul very far now and she had two men to help.

As the taxi drove away, Rex clapped Alexios on the back. "I imagine this city looks different compared to the last time you visited."

"Yes," Alexios said with a smile. "I was here twice. The Lamian

War in 322 BCE and Cassander's war in 317 BCE. I was a veteran soldier by that point."

"You helped Cassander take Athens? He abolished the city's democracy." Madison didn't keep the distaste out of her voice. She turned to Rex. "Cassander installed a puppet ruler, Demetrius of Phaleron. The city was under strict Macedonian rule, and Greek resistance leaders were exiled or executed."

Alexios gave her a forgiving half smile. "We are what we are conditioned to be. I was a soldier. A soldier who follows orders is one who is able to retire and settle down with a family. A soldier who doesn't is buried with the enemy. I was too young at conscription to even know my own principles. Staying alive was my prerogative. I have seen empires and countries rise and fall and have yet to see one without fault—democracy or otherwise."

She realized then that despite his youthful grin and boyish curiosity about the world, this man was rich with knowledge.

"Right. You're right. I'm sorry for the judgment in my tone. It's a short walk to the marina."

"Gyros?" Rex asked, gesturing to a street vendor.

"I would like to eat."

On the way to the docks, they ate their sandwiches. Madison enjoyed the savory meat wrapped in pita bread. With her friends —all of them—by her side, she relaxed.

Alexios looked around at the streets, watching cars and pedestrians with interest. "From the different homes I resided in over the years to the movies I watched on people's televisions, I knew the world changed as I slept. But to walk those streets now ... it is a gift. The gods have given me a gift."

"Wait until you see Milopas," Rex said, amusement in his eyes.

Madison stared at Alexios, marveling at his disposition. Here was a man cursed to immobility and to watch the world change around him—never knowing if his eternal curse would be a thousand lifetimes of paralysis. He could be damning the forces that confined him, damning the Fates for waking him to a world he knew little about. Instead, he exuded gratitude for being alive and free while openly embracing friendship with new people in his circle. She could take a lesson out of the pages of the book of his life.

WHEN THEY ARRIVED at the *Little Dolphin*, she coaxed Zephyr onto the boat as Alexios boarded, deposited the goods he carried for her as Rex did the same. Her furry friend sniffed the ground and seats, circling the small space. He could swim—had done so growing up, but because this was his first boat ride, she hoped he wouldn't jump off the moving craft.

While she cranked the engine, Rex untied the boat from the dock and shoved off with one leg while hopping aboard. Throttling up, she eased the boat away from the dock, around other boats and buoys, and out to sea.

As she drove, Rex talked about the amenities at Milopas with Alexios. Half an hour later, they moved on to discuss fishing. Surrounded by friends, with the sun at her right and a breeze in her hair, a deep calm ease caressed her soul. She'd been missing this sort of peace all her life and wondered how to make it part of her future.

"If you need to swap and take a break, let me know," Rex told her.

"I'm good. Maybe next time out, I'll teach Alexios."

"See one, do one, teach one." Rex nodded.

Zephyr hopped onto the bow and began barking. Though he was in unfamiliar territory, he'd never been a dog who barked without cause. Alarm bells rang in her head. Rex and Alexios came beside Madison, gazes scanning the water.

"There!" She pointed port side at movement in the water

while keeping the boat on course to Milopas, whose white cliffs and green peaks rose in the distance.

"What is it?" Alexios asked, squinting at whatever parted the sea.

Rex raised a hand to shield his eyes from the sun.

Madison swallowed. "Looks like a fin. A big, fast-moving fin." Dread coiled in her stomach like a tangled slinky.

If that fin was any indication of the size of what swam beneath the water, the shark was massive—assuming it was a shark. Whatever it was, speed was its middle name and the *Little Dolphin* wasn't fast enough to outswim it.

"That thing is heading straight toward us," Rex said.

TEN

Gulping back her panic, Madison pushed the throttle up. Maybe they could reach the safety of shallower water around Milopas where the creature wouldn't risk getting beached.

Alexios turned and rummaged through Rex's backpack, withdrawing his xiphos. The double-edged iron gleamed in the sunlight. Rex lifted one seat, pulling out an orange flare box.

Close now, the living thing rose out of the water and unleashed a deafening roar.

"Hold on!" She cut the boat hard right, hoping no one would fly off.

As the boat turned, she glimpsed the horrific beast. It spanned at least forty feet long with the head of a boar, complete with wickedly curved tusks and a blunt snout. The eyes, black as oil, were offset to the sides slightly, like many marine predators. Gills flailed low on the jawline. The gray body appeared sharklike with glistening water sluicing off the thick hide.

It slammed down, back into the water, barely missing their

boat but sending their sea vessel nearly tipping from the wave it generated.

Zephyr flew into the air, legs pinwheeling and eyes wide with fear, before landing in the water. He splashed into the tumultuous sea and sank beneath the sloshing surface.

"Zephyr!" Madison cut the throttle back to idle, gaze searching the water for her furry friend. Sweat broke out along her forehead and neck. Her hands became suddenly slick on the wheel.

Meanwhile, the creature circled back around in a wide berth, giving itself time to gain speed underwater for its next attack. They were a stationary and easy target.

"He's here," Rex cried. "C'mon, Zephyr. Good boy."

When Madison ran to the stern to help Zephyr into the boat, Rex took the wheel, flare box still in one hand. She doubted that creature would leave them alive long enough to signal for help. With soothing words she didn't feel, she coaxed the wet, paddling dog to the steps and reached for him.

As soon as she locked her arms around him, she cried, "I have him!" She held tight, panic still clogging the back of her throat.

Rex revved the engine, but the boarshark veered toward them, slamming his broad head into the side of the boat as he lifted upward and speared the belly of the *Little Dolphin* with his tusks. At that same instant, Alexios leaped off the boat, sword in hand. He soared through the air in a mighty leap and plunged the blade down into the animal's head.

Wood beneath her splintered as Madison went airborne. Time seemed to momentarily slow as she watched her friends scatter through the air. Rex flew sideways, twisting then tucking his body as if experienced with bracing for impact. With a violent shake of the creature's head, Alexios was tossed aside like a rag doll, the sword wrenched from his hands and left sticking out of the boar's skull.

Madison screamed before crashing down into the water. The impact knocked the wind out of her and jostled her hold on Zephyr loose. Her clothes, instantly drenched, weighed her down.

Panicked and heart racing, she flailed and fought her way to the surface, gasping for air.

She was blind. Everything burst painfully white.

Treading water, her pupils adjusted. Not blind, but her dark glasses had been lost to the sea. Fear clawed at her chest. *No, no, no.*

She squeezed her eyes shut, not wanting to inadvertently stone her friends or her dog, fearing they would sink to the bottom of the sea, lost forever. Straining to listen, she couldn't hear events around her between the noisy sloshing of water over her ears and thunderous beat of her heart.

She had to risk a look. Peeking, she quickly absorbed the scene. Alexios clung to what remained of the *Little Dolphin*. His long, wet hair was plastered to his head and face and he wore a grim expression.

Rex treaded water the farthest away, swimming toward them. Behind him, the creature circled, then closed in. The menacing fin slicing through the water as surely as its tusks would slice through Rex. He was completely defenseless.

No!

The bright orange flare gun box floated several feet away from her. Furiously paddling her arms and legs, she swam to it, snatching it open. Fumbling, she loaded a flare, hands wet and shaking. Water filled the box, making it sink below the surface and taking all the other flares with it. Would the gun still fire dripping wet? Surely.

Taking aim, it occurred to her that she'd never fired a weapon. Certainly she could hit the broad side of a barn, which was exactly the size of the animal's head.

As he lifted his snout out of the water, she fired. Red and silver streaked through the air before the flare struck behind his eye. The hit was little more than an annoyance, but had the desired effect. He turned his attention from Rex and swam toward her, submerging below the surface.

Ignoring Rex shouting her name, she dove underwater. The animal, sword still protruding from the top of his skull, barreled toward her.

Look at me, you ugly sonofabitch. Look at me!

Against the sting of salt water, she kept her eyes open, then felt the tug of magic as their gazes locked. Power pulsed in waves to the beating of her heart and pushed into his black pupils in unseen ripples like sonar in the water. His eyes opened wide— shock and terror etched on his distorted face as the gray skin blanched and cracked.

Holding her breath while submerged, she continued to stare even as her lungs burned with the demand for air. Heavy, like the stone he'd become, he quietly sank into the depths of the sea.

Madison's vision blurred and head spun. She fought her way to the surface once again, this time also fighting to maintain consciousness. Kicking, she surfaced and sucked in air, but kept her eyes closed.

"Madison!" Rex called.

"I'm here. I'm OK." She treaded water as she caught her breath. "Boarshark is turned to stone. Alexios, are you OK?"

"I am floating on what is left of the boat. I am here with Zephyr."

At his name, the dog barked. Relief washed through her. Alive! They were all alive.

She swam toward the sound of the barking. "I can't risk opening my eyes. I lost my glasses."

"I'm with you." Rex's voice was suddenly close as his arm hooked around her waist.

"Extend your hand," Alexios told her.

When she did, he grasped it and pulled her onto the floating wreckage, assisted by Rex's hands around her waist hoisting her higher.

Zephyr licked her face.

"Thank you, both of you."

She felt around the wood splinters and swaying of the wreckage until she found a relatively smooth surface that seemed to balance the weight. When the boat rocked again, she suspected Rex was joining them.

"I am rusty," Alexios said. "I aimed for the Cetus's eye. A wound there would have slowed him more from the pain. Instead, I hit thick skull."

Madison, world still black from keeping her eyes shut, began to shake. The reality of almost dying followed by the fear of not seeing her surroundings was too much.

"Hey. Hey," Rex said. "Everybody's fine." He wrapped an arm around her.

"I can't see. I can't stand not seeing if something else is out there." Her voice was rocky. She felt like such a liability under the circumstances.

Warm hands cupped her face. "Hey. That's twice you've saved my life now. You were incredible. Now, trust us to watch out for you. The horizon is clear. Hear that? Zephyr isn't barking. Nothing to fear."

She tried to shrink back from Rex's proximity for his own safety, but he didn't let her pull away. "I can't stand the fear of accidentally opening my eyes and risk stoning one of you."

"I'm not worried about it." Rex was so close that the exhaled breath of his words ghosted her lips.

"Rex ..."

He pressed his lips gently to hers. The wet, salty kiss was brief but packed with an emotional punch that left her breathless. The angst over her current predicament eased.

His thumb ran over her bottom lip. "Alexios and I will kick this driftwood to shore. Hold Zephyr. There you go. We'll be right here the whole time."

Trusting, calmer now, she nodded. "I fancy I'll need replacement sunglasses. With any luck, there will be a pair on the dock, waiting for me. Everything I bought today is now at the bottom of the sea. I had gifts for the new arrivals."

Zephyr, seeming to sense her distress, nuzzled closer against her. She ran a hand through his matted fur, not caring that he smelled like the wet dog he was.

"We can get more," Rex said gently.

She appreciated that he didn't point out how she was basically surrendering and asking the island for glasses and supplies. After this most recent experience, she wasn't ready to sail again anytime soon.

The men slid into the water. She readjusted her position to balance the floating wood.

"What did you call that thing?" Madison asked.

"Cetus," Alexios replied. "A vicious sea serpent with the head of a boar."

"Yeah. Boarshark," she said. "That's what I thought."

"Legend says Poseidon sent a Cetus to plague Troy as punishment for King Laomedon's refusal to pay him for building the city walls. Heracles killed the creature with a bow and arrows."

She snorted, feeling some of her angst ease. "Arrows? Against that thing? Rubbish."

꒷꒷꒷꒷꒷꒷꒷

REX WAS WATERLOGGED and exhausted by the swim, reminiscent of toddler training days with a foam kickboard, except youth swim training never included deadly sea creatures. Paddling took an hour for what the boat—if it'd had a functional engine—could have done in fifteen minutes, but they safely reached the dock without further attacks.

After making sure his aching legs were steady, Rex helped Madison climb onto the dock where a new pair of sunglasses awaited her. He placed them in her hand. "The island answered."

As Rex tied the bow remnant onto the post, Alexios helped the dog onto the dock and Madison slipped her glasses on.

"Not getting our deposit back," Rex quipped, looking at the splintered hunk of what had been the bow. He thought of his nickname according to Madison in the archaeology world— Trampling T-Rex Alderman. But damn. The damaging events were never directly his fault.

Madison wobbled slightly.

"Hey." He cupped her chin.

"We'll need another boat. A much bigger boat," Alexios added.

When Rex turned back toward Madison, she wrapped her arms around his neck. Liking the contact, he slid his arms around her to reciprocate. Her damp blond hair hung down in thick strands while wet clothes clung to her body.

"You all right?" he asked.

"A little shaken, but OK."

He tucked a strand of hair behind one of her ears. "When you went under, I thought I'd lost you. I should've known you'd handle him. That was brave." He pulled her into his arms and kissed the top of her head. She fit perfectly against him, and, wow, he'd liked the feel of her lips against his earlier, even though the kiss had been brief.

"Good to walk back up?" he asked.

"I am now. Thanks."

When he released her, they headed along the dock toward the stairs leading up. Looking at the path ahead of them, his body inwardly groaned. His legs had threatened to cramp more than once during the hour-long swim. Now those long steps looked like a whole new level of taxation when he was already exhausted.

"A new boat?" Alexios paused ten steps up, gaze aimed toward the dock.

Rex turned to look out over the water. A huge yacht sailed toward them.

"That's no boat. That's a space station," Madison said.

"What is a space station?" Alexios asked.

"It's a movie reference," Rex said. He pointed at Madison. "You just became even more attractive, if that's possible." He moved his finger to point at Alexios. "And you just got enlisted to watch the entire *Star Wars* saga with me."

The boat made a straight line for the dock, which meant whoever was aboard knew about the island and could see it. Its hull gleamed in the Mediterranean sun, a pearlescent white with navy blue accents that caught the light like polished marble. The bow rose elegantly, slicing through the waves with practiced ease, while silver railings and tinted windows gave it an air of privacy and quiet opulence. Solar panels lined the roof above the flybridge, hinting at an eco-conscious design, while the name *Calypso* curved in silver script along the side near the stern.

"You don't think ...?" Madison said.

"Alexios's words brought it into existence?" Rex shook his head. "I don't know."

Rex decided he would explain the island to their Greek friend while they waited for the yacht to arrive. He'd already described the cabins, kitchen, and training facility, so he explained the magic. "It seems to listen and grant wishes."

"Wishes?" Alexios's eyes widened.

"We asked for a firepit and outdoor seating and—*voilà*—they appeared."

"This place is a gift from the gods. You think the boat sailing toward us is because I said we need a bigger boat?"

"Not sure. Seems awfully coincidental," Rex said.

"But someone has to be driving it, right?" Madison sat down at the edge of the dock.

Rex scanned the sea for any disturbances or giant dorsal fins, but saw only tranquil sea.

"I would ask the island for a woman," Alexios said.

Rex chuckled.

Madison snapped her head around to look at Alexios, who grinned. Rex wasn't sure if it was because he was making a joke or because he found her incredulous glare humorous.

"Be careful," she warned. "We don't know the powers we're toying with."

Rex clapped Alexios on the back but spoke to her. "Lighten up. Poor guy's been in captivity since before Christianity was born. If I were him, the first things I'd want are a twelve-ounce steak and sex."

"Sex, yes," Alexios agreed. "But I was thinking more about companionship."

Madison's mouth quirked. "How very twenty-first century of you. And you should know that in this century—even if the gods give you a woman—she has free will and right of refusal."

The corners of Alexios's mouth fell. "I would never force her to do anything she didn't want to do."

"No, you wouldn't. I'm sorry." Madison's shoulders slumped. "I didn't mean to suggest you would. The history I've learned about your era is all about the spoils of war, concubines, and arranged marriages."

"That may be someone's history, but it is not mine. We are not all equally represented by scholars writing of a time they never lived in," Alexios said.

"Of course. And in only a few short days of our acquaintance, I've seen you're a man of integrity. I'm sorry for suggesting otherwise." She turned back to the water and stared at the approaching boat.

After quietly watching the exchange, Rex sat beside her, hooking an arm over her shoulder.

"I didn't mean to offend him ... again," she murmured.

"You smoothed it over. It's not in his nature to hold on to hard feelings. He'll accept the apology and move on."

Zephyr sat beside her.

She bunched her hand in his moist fur. "I'll need dog food. Zephyr's bag is now fish food."

Rex said nothing. He understood she was asking the island, as much as she hated to. If trips to the mainland were going to be scarce, owing to enormous and deadly sea creatures, they would be relying on the island for many things.

When the yacht arrived, Rex helped tie it to the dock, taking the rope tossed from a flaming redhead who had her right arm in a sling. Madison and Alexios stood to greet her. Zephyr wagged his tail in excitement.

After Rex secured the rope, the woman opened the door and stepped onto the dock. In the sun, her spiked hair was the color of vibrant red flame. She wore rugged jeans with the bottoms rolled and a tank top that showed strong, shapely shoulders.

Alexios stepped forward, dropping to one knee. "You are magnificent. Are you a goddess?"

The woman looked down at him and snorted. "Uh, no. Would a goddess have one jacked-up arm in a sling?"

Red-cheeked, Madison stepped forward. "I'm Madison. This is Alexios. And this is Rex."

"Welcome to Milopas," Rex said, amused by Alexios's behavior and Madison's embarrassment on his behalf.

"I'm Zoey. American, British, and—?" She pointed to each of them.

"Alexios is Greek," Madison said.

"As in ancient Greek, Alexander the Great Era," Rex added, then gauged Zoey's response.

"Time travel?" Zoey asked. "Can you stand back up, please? Not a goddess."

Hmm. Not put off by the supernatural, Rex noted. He wondered what her exposure to magic was, but there would be time for that discovery later. With the mood lighter after the Cetus attack, he could wait to share that information with them also.

Alexios stood. "I did not travel through time, except perhaps linearly as all do. I was trapped as a statue by the power of Midas for two thousand years."

"Ah. And still mostly sane. I guess we'll let that goddess thing slide then." She grinned, revealing a dimple, and Alexios looked like he might bow before her again.

Rex took Alexios's arm and tugged him back a step. "Let's give our new guest some breathing room."

"Rex freed me," Alexios said. "He has the power to heal. What happened to your arm? Were you wounded in battle?"

Zoey's mouth drew into a line. "Something like that."

"She was injured saving my life." Everyone turned to see another woman approaching. She had a sultry voice, midnight black hair, and olive skin. A purple dress with a plunging V-neck flowed around a shapely figure. "I'm Layla Sinclair."

"The actress," Rex said. That explained the multimillion-dollar yacht.

"Yes. How long have you all been here?"

"Just a day," Madison said. "Long enough to get the lay of the island."

"And have our boat destroyed by a Cetus," Alexios added.

So much for waiting on that story, Rex thought.

When Layla stepped onto the dock, Zephyr approached, tail wagging.

"Who's this adorable guy?" she asked, bending to pet him.

"You're all wet. You like swimming? I bet you do." The wet dog smell didn't deter her from rubbing behind his ears.

Madison smiled, looking like she was instantly friends with a movie star who would show kindness toward her dog.

"What's a Cetus?" Zoey asked.

Rex said, "Forty-foot-long monstrosity. Head of a boar, body of a shark." Because these women didn't seem shocked by an ancient Greek or the idea of Rex's healing powers, perhaps he shouldn't be surprised that a Cetus hadn't fazed them.

"It destroyed your boat?" Layla straightened.

"Small boat," Madison said. "Nothing like yours. You weren't attacked at sea?"

Zoey shook her head. "Smooth sailing all the way here from Sicily."

"Maybe there's only one of those," Rex said.

"Did you kill it?" Layla looked back out over the water.

"Madison turned it to stone," Alexios said, pride in his voice.

Well, shit. Rex could practically see Madison's stomach sink. He'd had a conversation with her about opening up to the others when she was ready. Now, that ship had sailed. He slid beside her and took her hand.

"Really?" Zoey's face lit up. "You can do that?"

"I have to wear these dark glasses; otherwise, I turn living things to stone."

"Badass. Give it here." Zoey extended her fist to Madison, who bumped it hesitantly.

Having been reclusive, owing to her secret, Rex was sure Madison hadn't formed female friendships in her life. Was this the start of one?

"So, healing power, Medusa power, and warrior," Layla said. "Can you tell us why we've been summoned here?"

"No," Rex said, putting on a smile. "But we can give you the ten-million-dollar tour."

CHAPTER
ELEVEN

Rex led the group to the top plateau, feeling a renewed energy with the arrival of two more people blindly summoned to the island. He thought saving the intimidation of the training center for last would be best. When they arrived up top, Layla and Zoey did a slow three-sixty to take in the compound and view.

"Wow," Layla said, hands on her hips. "Makes that climb seem worth it."

"This place is amazing. Is anyone else here?" Zoey asked.

Madison shook her head. "It was empty when we arrived yesterday."

"Beautiful and a little surreal," Layla added.

Rex beckoned them to the inscribed words near the firepit. "Then there's this."

The letters rose on display for the newcomers.

Forged by divine hands
  Let this be a place of refuge
  A proving ground.

Warriors six, sharpen your skills
Embrace the gift of the gods
Prepare for your destiny.

Layla reached out, and her hands went through the floating letters.

"We don't know what it means exactly," Madison added in a hesitant voice.

"Um ... that's ominous. Moving on," Zoey said.

The women explored the cabin and kitchen while Rex watched, wondering what powers they possessed. Neither of them had offered to share their secrets. No matter. They probably felt like Rex and Madison had the upper hand, having arrived on the island first. The women would share when they were ready. When they trusted.

He'd seen several of Layla Sinclair's movies, mostly the action and adventure ones. She was beautiful—the type who wore it with dignity. But her yacht and expensive clothes were a kind of high-maintenance class he usually avoided.

The redhead looked like she would be tough in a fight but didn't contain her wondrous fascination at this place. She stuck close to Layla in almost a protective fashion, and he wondered if that had been before or after she'd saved the woman's life.

As they descended the stairs to tour the training facility, Zoey irritably adjusted her sling and grimaced. She hadn't mentioned how long ago she'd hurt her arm, but it obviously still pained her.

"Are you right-handed?" Rex asked.

"Yeah. I've been learning to do everything with my nondominant hand. Months in and I'm still clumsy."

"I can try to heal that for you," he offered. He wanted to help, but he also hoped that healing her would build a bridge of trust. If the six of them had to sharpen their warrior skills, they probably had a fight ahead of them. He sure hoped it was a fight against something and not themselves.

She glanced at him skeptically. "How does that work, exactly?"

"No strings attached," he said. "A few drops will usually do the trick and heal wounds."

"A few drops of what?" She wrinkled her nose.

"Tears."

She snorted. "You're offering to cry onto my mangled arm?"

He shrugged as he led them off the stairs and toward the level sparring area. "Up to you."

"Is he for real?" Zoey asked Madison, her tone one of shock and unease.

Madison explained, "He turned Alexios from gold back to life, right before my eyes. I believed him when he told me he healed his own broken leg. I believe him when he says he thinks his tears could heal you."

"He can help you," Alexios added.

Zoey glanced at Layla who said, "A few tears won't hurt for sure. You should let him try. I'm curious myself."

Zoey relented. She took off the sling before easing off the sleeve that extended from her wrist to her upper arm. The jagged scars streaking along her forearm were pink and thick. Someone had tried to put it back together, but the tissue seemed to have been destroyed beyond repair. She held her arm up for him with her left hand.

"What happened?" Rex asked, helping support the arm as he worked to summon tears.

"Long story," she said in a tone to suggest she had no intention of sharing.

He tipped his chin down and blinked, letting the tears fall on her exposed skin. She sucked in a breath.

"Are you OK?" Layla rushed forward.

The scars receded, replaced by normal skin. Internally, the repairs would be similar.

"I'm good. I'm good. It's working." Zoey gaped at her arm, then groped it with her left hand as if to make sure her eyes weren't deceiving her. "It's healed. It's really healed!" She lunged toward Layla and wrapped her arms around her. "Oh, Layla!"

Rex swallowed back the emotion in his throat as he tucked his hands in his pockets. He'd never known the joy of healing others until these last few days.

"Alexios, grab a sword," Rex said, needing to focus on something less uncomfortably moving.

If the man was sweet on Zoey, Rex could play wingman and provide Alexios an opportunity to display his talents for her while also showing the new arrivals the holographic training center.

Armed with a xiphos, Alexios stepped into the center of the circular stone tiles.

"Thank you," Zoey said to Rex.

"You're welcome." He gave a brief nod before looking away.

"Warrior, identify yourself," a woman's voice said.

Rex nodded at him and ushered everyone back from the battle zone to give Alexios space.

"Alexios Nikandrou Pellaios."

"New warrior log created. Are you ready to battle?"

"Yes."

A nine-foot-tall creature appeared with the head of a lizard, torso of a man, and a tail where legs should be. He held a sword in one hand and a shield in the other.

Zephyr sniffed the air with his head cocked to one side, looking as though he wasn't sure what to make of the imaginary beast. Madison knelt to give him a reassuring scratch behind the ears.

Alexios and the creature carefully circled each other.

"It's an illusion?" Layla asked.

"The fight feels real enough," Rex said as he nodded.

Swords clashed, but Alexios moved with swift agility and a confidence honed by years of battle. In under a minute, he maneuvered inside the creature's defenses and ended him with a sword thrust through the heart.

The creature dissolved.

"Level five unlocked. Do you wish for another foe?"

Huh. Five. Rex supposed the programming accounted for skill and speed and advanced levels accordingly.

"Yes." Excitement lit the warrior's eyes.

A Cerberus appeared, three snarling heads with glowing yellow irises. The body was that of a dog, but the size of a bison. Alexios danced around it, dodging claws and gnashing teeth.

Zoey looked sufficiently impressed, so mission accomplished there. Layla appeared wide-eyed and horrified. Madison glanced nervously at Rex.

He walked over to her. "Did you see him skip right on by levels two through four?"

"I noticed. Jealous?" After giving Zephyr one more pat, she straightened and bumped her elbow into Rex's arm.

"Hell, no. Well ... Maybe a little, but I'm glad he's on our side."

"Have you been in there?" Layla asked Madison.

"No, but I'm sure I'm supposed to. Somehow, I think the program won't let me just turn all the holograms to stone."

Rex picked up the worry and unease in Madison's voice about the prospect of learning to fight.

"So we sleep, eat, and train here. Then what?" Zoey asked, eyes still locked on Alexios.

"That's what we're waiting to find out," Madison said.

"This is absurd," Layla said, crossing her arms. "Zoey and I didn't travel halfway around the world for gladiator fights against mythical characters. I'm not putting my acting career on hold to be maimed or die."

Madison looked nervously between Layla and Zoey. "Will you stay long enough to find out why something drew us here?"

Layla's dress billowed around her as she stared hard at Madison. "Zoey, what do you think?" Layla asked.

Rex didn't like the tension in the air. Layla had every right to her unease and every right to leave, which obviously included taking Zoey with her. Whatever was asked of them, it required six. Against the urge to implore them to stay a little longer, he kept his mouth shut. If maiming or facing death was part of their future, as Layla postulated, she would only resent anyone who coerced her to stay.

"We've come this far." Zoey pulled her gaze from Alexios. "What's a few days on a paradise island while we learn a bit more?"

Layla's defiant shoulders dropped slightly. "Fine. Let's take some luggage to the cabins."

"I'll make sandwiches while you both get settled," Madison offered.

⌐⌐⌐⌐⌐⌐⌐

WHILE REX and Alexios helped Layla and Zoey move their luggage to the cabins of their choice, Madison found dog food and set up Zephyr in the kitchen with a food bowl and a water bowl. When he finished following the newcomers around, he'd be hungry and thirsty.

"Thank you," she said to the empty space around her, feeling foolish. "While you're in the spirit of giving, I would like a bed for Zephyr in my cabin ... please."

She set to work laying out on the counter various meats, cheeses, and condiments for sandwiches for everyone.

Three women. Two men. One remained.

The best part about their new companions was how nice they

were. Even Layla Sinclair, who had every right to her skepticism. Like her and Rex, Zoey and Layla seemed to have accepted the bizarreness of being summoned to an island few knew existed. Layla worried about what it all meant, which Madison could empathize with. Everything about this island was both awe-inspiring and ominous.

Then there was the attack at sea. She hadn't had time to discuss it with Rex. Or the kiss, which seemed to her a defining moment as much as sinking the Cetus was. The man she'd initially appraised as cocky, reckless, and entirely too good-looking was full of depth and understanding. Perhaps in his studies of civilization, he'd come to appreciate singular human emotion as well. He looked at her, spoke to her, and kissed her like she mattered to him—and after such a short acquaintance. Even with the new arrivals, he provided quiet support of her in a look or when he chose to stand closer to her.

She thought of how he'd looked on the dock when she'd put on her new sunglasses after the boat ride with her eyes tightly shut. His hair had been damp and skin golden under the sunlight. His wet clothes clung to his muscular torso and biceps. And he'd smiled at her like there was nowhere he'd rather be than facing danger by her side.

"Need help?" Zoey popped into the kitchen, pulling Madison from her daydreaming. "I'm famished."

"Jump in," Madison offered. "We've got ham, turkey, Swiss, provolone, cheddar, and a few types of bread."

Layla joined them, and Madison wondered about any supernatural skills they might possess. No doubt, revelations would be forthcoming. Then what? Training? Fighting? Why was this place and their calling here shrouded in mystery?

The three of them had a normal conversation about where everyone was from, and Layla followed that up by asking about Madison's job and what it entailed.

"Basically, I take damaged or aging works of art—paintings, sculptures, sometimes frescoes—and carefully clean, repair, and stabilize them so they look as close as possible to how the artist intended."

"You bring the past back to life—one brushstroke at a time," Layla said.

Madison smiled. "Yes. It's kind of like detective work meets surgery—except no lives or limbs are at stake. I analyze old pigments, match centuries-old techniques, and sometimes uncover hidden layers or lost details." She smeared on a thin layer of mayonnaise covering the entire surface of the bread in an even layer. "It's delicate, slow, and a little obsessive ... but incredibly rewarding. I like the idea that I'm preserving beauty and history for future generations."

"What was your favorite?" Layla asked. She found glasses in the cupboard and set out five.

"The Artemision Bronze."

"Never heard of it," Zoey said, slathering on a blob of mayonnaise and smashing it even with a piece of lettuce.

"It's a bronze Greek statue of either Poseidon or Zeus—historians aren't sure because it's missing its weapon, a trident or a thunderbolt. It was discovered in a shipwreck off Cape Artemision around the fifth century BCE." She meticulously arranged overlapping cheese and deli slices to make her own sandwich. "Although its home is in Athens, I worked on it in England during the traveling exhibition in which it was featured. We had to stabilize the metal."

"Very cool," Layla said, setting out a pitcher of lemonade.

"Who do you think he was?" Zoey asked, haphazardly dropping meat and cheese slices before closing the sandwich.

"Poseidon," Madison said, without hesitation as she sealed and aligned the top piece of bread over her sandwich.

"Why is that?" Zoey asked.

"Just a feeling."

Rex and Alexios walked into the dining room. Zephyr trailed behind them, tail wagging. He went immediately to the food bowl and began eating.

"Hey, food. Need help?" Rex asked, sliding up behind her and placing a hand on her shoulder.

She smiled at him. "Assemble your selections, and we'll eat by the fire."

REX ATE his sandwich as he listened to the women talk. Madison engaged enthusiastically in conversation. She wasn't aloof, as her neighbor, Mimi, had claimed; she just needed the right group of women with whom to participate in discussions. Tension eased from Madison's demeanor as she spoke casually with Layla and Zoey. He suspected having camaraderie was rare for her, and he was glad she could start creating new bonds.

Zephyr lay on the floor beside her chair. Poor guy was probably tuckered out from the harrowing boat ride and excitement of new people. Rex certainly was.

They sat around a fire that burned hot and continuously without fuel. With the ambience, Rex could almost relax and enjoy the company of new acquaintances and forget the dark and dangerous undercurrent of why they were all here.

"I think my favorite scene was when you stood—battle-worn and covered in alien guts with a rocket launcher over your shoulder and said with defiance, 'mine's bigger,'" Madison said, voice light with humor.

Layla grinned. "That movie was so hard to film. We had all sorts of problems throughout the shooting. And my costar? Yeah, he was an unbearable tool."

"You never told me that," Zoey said, cocking her head to one side.

Layla shrugged as she took a sip of her red wine. "I was glad when it was over."

"What do you mean, a *tool*?" Alexios asked.

"He added tongue when the romance scenes required no tongue. This was a PG-13 action flick. The little touches and flirts? Ugh. Always trying to get his sweaty man-hands on me," Layla said.

Zoey frowned. "I'd have kicked his ass for you. You know, in a way that looked accidental or inadvertent."

Layla grinned at Madison. "What are friends for?"

Madison motioned between the other two women. "How did you meet?"

Zoey took a drink of her lemonade. "I was her stunt double."

"Really?" Madison's tone held fascination.

Zoey grinned. "I landed a gig as a pyrotech on one of her films. The director noticed we had similar builds and had me try out for stunt woman."

"She's a natural," Layla said.

"At least until I injured my arm. I thought my career was over." She flexed her fingers while shooting Rex a grateful glance. "I guess it's still over, because we are thousands of miles from Hollywood and waiting to hear what type of assignment six people with superhuman powers are supposed to take on."

"I showed you mine. You show me yours," Madison said, a teasing tone in her voice as she took a sip of her lemonade.

"Why not? Seems like a safe space here." With her right hand, Zoey flicked her wrist, and a ball of orange and red flame sprang to life from thin air and into her palm where it rested.

Alexios gasped. "I knew you were a goddess."

She chuckled. "Flattered, but no. I'm so not a goddess. I can control fire and can't be burned by it, but I can be injured in every other way … like a normal human."

"Yeah, well. So far, I think your gift is the hottest. Pun intended," Madison said. "No offense," she told Rex.

"None taken." *Fire probably was a better gift,* he thought. He could have done some damage over the years with a skill like that. He considered his rebellious teenage years. Hmm. Better for everyone that the gods hadn't given him the gift of flame.

"Layla, what about you?" Madison asked.

The actress adjusted in her seat and sat up straighter. Her mouth opened to speak, but no words came out as her eyes fixed on something distant. Her face paled as if she'd seen a ghost.

Rex turned to follow her gaze as a form approached from out of the shadows.

CHAPTER

TWELVE

R ex tensed as a man approached their fire. Zephyr bounded up and over to the new guest, tail wagging. Rex supposed that was as good an approval as any, although he suspected the dog had never met a stranger.

The man bent and patted the animal. He looked about thirty, with deep brown hair curling at his ears, and wearing blue jeans and a t-shirt. He had a backpack slung over one shoulder and a relaxed posture.

"Am I late to the party?" His voice was smoothly Southern and unrushed.

"And the sixth arrives," Alexios said.

Rex stood and walked over as the man approached. "Rex Alderman. Welcome to Milopas." He gestured toward Madison. "Madison and I have been here a day, and Layla and Zoey arrived a few hours ago. That would be Layla's yacht you may have seen docked down below."

"Tyler Callahan." He shook Rex's hand. Though he made no facial expression at the mention of a yacht to suggest he'd seen it, his warm smile had faltered when he'd heard the name Layla.

While grasping Rex's hand for the introduction, he looked around him to spot the actress. "You're quite the surprise."

Layla stood, clenching her glass of lemonade in one hand. Her cheeks had gone from pale to crimson. "What the hell are you doing here?" Her voice held shock laced with outrage.

Tyler released Rex's hand and addressed Layla's question in a calm tone. "I imagine the same as you. Something or someone seems to think I needed to be here. It wouldn't shut up about it."

Rex looked back and forth between the two. The animosity sparking between them threatened to singe him. Layla's flushed cheeks accentuated her blue eyes as they flared with anger. Tyler's expression was neutral, but the white-knuckled grip on the backpack over his shoulder betrayed a brewing temper.

"Well, forgive me." Tyler managed to smile as he drawled the words to address the rest of the group. "I have neglected my manners." He walked over and extended a hand to Madison. "Tyler. It was Madison, right?"

"That's right."

"Pleasure to make your acquaintance. British?" He shook hands with her as she nodded before he turned to Alexios. "And you are?"

"Alexios. I am a Greek warrior."

"Kudos." Tyler grinned.

Rex clarified, "As in ancient Greece, reanimated after two thousand years."

"You look good for your age, but you'll have to pardon my skepticism. How is that possible, exactly?"

"I will tell you the tale sometime," Alexios said.

Tyler turned to Zoey, who stood and crossed her arms with spite. "Zoey," she snapped her name out. "Layla's best friend, and you must be Kitty Hawk."

Tyler's eyebrows rose.

"She never told me your name," Zoey explained. "Just told me you did a number on her during her summer at Kitty Hawk Beach."

He cocked his head to one side. "Is that right?"

Layla stood, still with a death grip around the glass in her hand. "This is preposterous. I'm not staying on this island with you. I'll stay on my boat until I figure out why I'm here and determine my next move." The seething tone suggested her next move would involve being anywhere Tyler wasn't.

Above them, lightning split the dark sky at Layla's words. She didn't flinch, even though everyone else did. Where moments ago Rex had watched a clear night sky, storm clouds billowed above.

Crap. Did she control lightning? Rex wondered. That was a terrifying thought, and one that reminded Rex to stay on her good side.

Before Layla could storm away, as Rex suspected she intended to do, the flames in the firepit rose unnaturally high. An apparition appeared, shimmering into view. The smoke parted around her.

Everyone fell silent.

The figure of a woman wore a gown of flames with the deepest gold hair trailing down her back. Her flawless skin glowed sun-kissed brown, and her eyes were a rich blue flecked with silver.

"Gather, warriors, bold and true,
For fate has spun its thread anew.
A tale of old now wakes again,
Of gods, of war, of fallen kin.
Long ago, in shadowed strife,
Kronos sought to end human life.
Six gods rose with righteous might,
And cast him out in a ferocious fight.
A prison forged in realms unseen,

Bound by fate and magic keen."

As she spoke, she projected a mural for all to see, animated as if they were watching what happened in movie form. Six gods—Rex knew from Greek tales to be Hestia, Demeter, Hera, Hades, Poseidon, and Zeus—tangled in a mighty battle with an enormous glowing humanoid, all angry wrath and power. Kronos.

Rex could feel the cold cruelty emanating from the Greek titan. He was a towering figure, as tall as a house, cloaked in shadow, and wearing a robe that rippled like cracked stone when he moved. The sharp angles of his face held an ancient nobility weathered by bitterness and betrayal. Wielding a black scythe, he battled his own offspring to prevent being overthrown.

The six gods fought him back to the edge of a portal, beyond which raged an unfamiliar world of volcanoes with lava carpeting the ground and ash pouring from the sky. Heat spilled over, hot against Rex's skin as if he stood too close to a furnace as the smell of brimstone filled the air. He leaned back slightly as the team of gods forced Kronos into the gaping, frayed-edged hole before plummeting through with him and sealing the gateway to this world.

"Yet time's cruel hand now rends the veil,
  A wicked force rides on the gale.
  Kronos stirs, his hunger vast,
  To drown the earth in death at last.
  The barrier grows weak, his power swells,
  He calls from deep forbidden wells.
  But you, brave souls, are chosen now,
  To halt the storm and make a vow.
  Six must stand where six once fought,
  With wisdom, strength, and courage wrought.
  The path ahead is veiled in night,

Yet fate reveals the tools to fight.
Seek the relics, lost and old,
Of gods' tools in battles of old.
Each shall test your heart and soul,
For only the pure may claim them whole.
And when in hand, the six align,
The breach shall seal, the stars shall shine.
So rise, O warriors, take your stand,
The fate of all rests in your hand."

When the goddess vanished, the six of them stared nervously at each other. Rex considered the timing—the message had been delivered as soon as the sixth warrior arrived. He felt the bubbling rise of disbelief and panic both in himself and in the expressions of those around him.

"The six of us against a titan?" Layla asked, tone a mix of incredulity and outrage.

"That thing is trying to claw its way back into our world?" Madison's voice shook along with her entire body. She began to pace. "We can't let it do that."

Zoey choked on what sounded like the start of a bitter laugh. She rubbed her temples. "It took six *gods* to put him behind that barrier. We're supposed to keep him there?"

Tyler said, "What else do we do? We can't let him breach our side."

"Countries have armies for a reason," Layla said.

"For defending against titans?" he fired back. "Let's play that out—if the world sees a titan bringing Armageddon, they'll launch nukes, but by that time he'll already be through the portal and finish the job. Nothing left of us humans. Earth turns into whatever hell he came from."

Stopping her pacing, Madison added, "That's if he shows his

form. He could break through and destroy the surface with *natural* disasters—in usual Greek legendary fashion."

Zoey muttered, "So much for my theory that the end would come in the form of a zombie apocalypse."

"I guess I'm not getting on my boat, leaving after all," Layla said, barely above a whisper as her face transitioned from flushed to pale.

"Are we all staying, then?" Rex asked. His gut churned. He'd never banded with a team before, and certainly not for something as monumentally suicidal as opposing a titan.

"No small ask, but they seem to have picked us for a reason," Madison said.

Tyler adjusted his backpack as his tone turned bitter. "They don't play fair. Save the world or allow it to be destroyed. Your choice, but no guarantee we all live through this. I'm in, though. Just laying out the facts."

"Why can't the gods seal it shut again?" Zoey asked.

"Maybe they're trapped on that side and it can only be closed on this side," Layla suggested.

Alexios added, "Maybe they are busy fighting him on their side."

"We only have to reseal it, right?" Zoey said. "It doesn't sound as though we have to go through it like the gods did. We don't have to actually fight a titan."

"Also, doesn't sound like they're making it easy for us," Madison said. "We need relics—tools—to get the job done, but each will test our heart and soul." She shuddered.

Layla nodded. "And sounds like we need them in hand to seal the portal."

"Except we don't yet know what relics or where to find them," Rex added. He ran a frustrated hand through his hair. What if these relics were off the island ... where more Cetus roamed the waters?

"Athena will tell us," Alexios said. "She will return when it is time with further instructions."

"How do you know that?" Zoey asked.

"This is how Greek quests work," he said simply.

Rex supposed that was true. Gods delivered instructions piecemeal during a hero's journey—maybe that was what this was. Except—news flash—he was no hero. He was a glorified tomb raider. A fortune hunter. He wanted to cry or panic or punch something.

"Until then, we just stay on Milopas?" Madison asked in disbelief. "We have jobs we put on hold."

"We don't just stay here." Rex leaned forward, looking around at the worried group and finding his composure. "We train here." Based on their encounters with a Cetus and golden Elvis, Kronos —aka Chloros's master—intended to make their mission fraught with hazardous creatures. "Athena called us warriors twice in her recital. We'll need battle skills for whatever Kronos throws at us to try to stop us from keeping the portal sealed."

THIRTEEN

The next morning, Madison joined Layla and Zoey at the kitchen table for breakfast. The mood had been somber since Athena delivered her directive the night before.

Layla had ignored Tyler but stayed in a cabin instead of her boat. Madison felt safer with them clustered on this plateau and would have worried about Layla if she'd separated from the group. Easy pickings for the next creature that attacked them. Maybe not too easy, considering Layla's powers.

Madison cleared her throat. "So, uh, lightning, eh?" She poked at the granola and Greek yogurt in her bowl.

Layla grunted. "You noticed that?"

"Hard to miss the dark clouds rolling in unnaturally fast when Tyler's appearance upset you. Then, the lightning flashed right along with your temper."

Layla sighed.

"You're like Zeus?" Madison asked.

Layla shook her head. "Nothing that impressive. I can control the weather. Usually, I have better control. In fact, I've spent a long time learning how to keep my mood from creating rain and storms. Last night, my power slipped. I just ... I was so angry." She rubbed her temples.

Madison glanced at Zoey, then back at Layla. She didn't want to cross the boundaries of acquaintances sooner than Layla was ready for, but thought the woman might benefit from discussing her past. Madison had certainly felt better after talking to Rex about her former hardships.

"What happened between you and Tyler?" Madison asked.

"Doesn't matter. It was a long time ago."

"It matters to you," she said gently. She didn't add her worry that any disruption—like unresolved feelings or animosity—among the six could affect their chances of success.

Layla shook her head. "What matters is keeping big bad Kronos in his world. I won't lose control like that again. I promise no one will accidentally be struck by lightning because something—or someone—pissed me off. To pull off that promise, I'll need to train."

Zoey's face went slightly pale, making Madison wonder if she'd seen Layla inadvertently damage something—or someone—with her powers.

One by one, the men joined them, making their own breakfast bowls. The room remained quiet, heavy with the weight of concern about the magnitude of the task before them. Zephyr ate the food Madison had put down for him, then circled at their feet, waiting for affectionate pats or perhaps crumbs to fall.

After breakfast, Rex stood up and took his dishes to the sink. His efficient and graceful motions caught her eye every time. She thought of his kiss and proximity on the dock yesterday and wondered—now that six were on the island—if they would have any privacy for moments like that again. For now, there were more pressing issues at hand.

"I've been thinking about how we should organize every-thing," Rex said, addressing everyone. "We are obviously here to train. That we'll do. I think Alexios should take the lead there and come up with a training schedule that mixes the simulator, weight training, and cardiovascular for each of us."

"I can do this," Alexios said, looking pleased to have an assignment worthy of his skill.

"Next is meals. There are six of us, so we could rotate who makes dinner by the days of the week, with one day when we're either all chipping in or you're on your own."

"I like that," Tyler said. "And I'll add that on our rescue teams when we had temporary offices set up, kitchen cleanup duty was done by a different person or persons than those who had done the meal prep."

Rex nodded. "Then we'll rotate that, too. Laundry and basic tidying seem to be managed by invisible minions, so there's nothing to divide there. Am I leaving anything out?"

"Maybe a little breathing room for us to process Athena's directive," Zoey said with irritation, glancing at Layla. "We only just found out we're the only thing standing between humanity and doomsday."

"Right," Rex said, jaw ticking, like he was struggling between understanding and his own frustration at the situation. He'd obviously put thought into coming up with a plan of approach.

Madison put a hand on Zoey's shoulder. "I think his way of dealing with the assignment is to get busy. It's OK if you need more processing time."

"One day a week off from training," Layla interjected. "I'm all for working our asses off to train for whatever ungodly thing is in store for us, but I believe in physical and mental rest."

"Done," Rex said.

A born leader, Madison thought, looking at Rex. And one who tackled the task while making each person on the team feel useful and valued. He seemed to have some untapped skills he was now putting to use.

"And the relics?" Zoey asked.

"When we're assigned to fetch them, we'll fetch them."

REX LAY IN A RECLINER, staring at the constellations. The night sky was a sheet of velvet black dotted with twinkling stars. Without light pollution, the constellations gleamed clearly—unfiltered, untamed—like a tapestry the gods themselves once embroidered. Leo dominated the southern sky this time of year, its bright heart, Regulus, pulsing steadily. Rex thought of the Nemean lion, the monstrous beast Heracles once defeated with his bare hands. The myth lived again in the sky, the stars forming the powerful shoulders and curved back of the lion whose hide no weapon could pierce.

To the west, Gemini still lingered this time of year—Castor and Pollux, the twin brothers. One mortal, one divine. Overhead, Virgo was rising—often associated with Demeter or Persephone, a symbol of rebirth and shifting seasons. Rex mused on how Persephone moved between worlds, much like the path he and the others now tread: halfway between the mortal world and something older and more dangerous. Also in the west, Aries began to sink. And to the northeast, just beginning to rise, Hercules was barely visible—its boxy body foreshadowing the laborious trials ahead.

As Rex watched the constellations shift above the sea, he felt the press of history and myth closing in. The sky, after all, held more than stories. It held the past, present, and future. And tonight, it felt as though the gods were watching.

What had he gotten himself into? Follow the pretty lady to a mysterious island. He'd thought it would be an adventure, and he was always up for one of those. Now, though, he wasn't excited to be enlisted in a war against global destruction. He'd teamed up with five others, wondering how committed each of them would ultimately be as danger escalated.

No way he would allow a titan into his world, but teamwork seemed to be a crucial part of Athena's plan. This was a major deviation from Rex's usual solo work. Sure, he hired workers for some of his larger excavations, but that had been paid, delegated work—not the heart and soul pledging nonsense the goddess spouted.

When the fight began, six strangers had to work as a unified team or they wouldn't see success. They wouldn't survive. No one would.

"Am I intruding?" Madison breezed up beside him, looking majestic under the moonlight. The stars reflected in her glasses, and loose blond hair framed the lovely shape of her oval face.

"Never. How are you holding up?" he asked, gesturing to the empty seat beside him.

She was a sight, and he'd been wanting to be with just her. With six people on the island and rigorous training schedules, he would have to be deliberate if he were to succeed in securing one-on-one time with her. He thought about ways to see her—on a walk, during meal prep, or under the stars.

"Holding up?" Her mouth quirked as she reclined in the seat. "We're supposed to prevent an apocalypse with ancient toys we don't have and no instruction manual. Easy-peasy."

He grinned. "I meant more like leaving behind your life to take this quest. Joining five strangers ... "

She stared at the sky above for a long moment. "I belong here, Rex. And I've never felt that way in my whole life. I dread what we're up against, but at this moment, on this island, it's nice to belong."

He reached over and took her hand. "You belong, Madison. Look at those stars. As beautiful and shining as you. And you're part of the same history written up there."

"I wanted to thank you for how you handled the boat incident."

"You handled our attacker, not me."

"I'm referring to events afterward. I was blind and lost after, having to keep my eyes shut. It was terrifying. You calmly talked through everything, brought me back from the edge of panic. So, thank you."

He toyed with her fingers in his hand. "No problem."

"And then you kissed me."

He stilled, trying to discern any trace of irritation in her voice. "On impulse. I should have asked. You couldn't see that I was asking with my eyes. My timing was—"

"Perfect. I'm glad you did. The timing was right." She shifted in her seat as a small smile played on her lips. "And if you wanted to kiss me goodnight later, the timing would be right for that too."

Feeling a swell of excitement, he squeezed her hand and turned his gaze back to those wondrous stars smiling down on them. "I'd like that. I'll do that."

CHAPTER

FOURTEEN

Rex jogged beside Tyler. Ahead of them, Zoey and Alexios ran. Behind them, Madison and Layla. By the third day on the island together, they had a weekly schedule detailed and hanging in the common room near the kitchen.

"I should give you the skinny on everyone's skills," Rex told Tyler. "Alexios, you know. Greek warrior. I can heal, Madison can turn enemies to stone, and Zoey controls fire. And Layla ... I suspect the lightning on the night of your arrival was her doing, which would make her another formidable addition."

When Tyler offered no insight into Layla's powers, Rex suspected he hadn't known. Tyler also didn't offer up what his abilities were.

"Madison was right about putting our careers on hold. What kind of work do you do?" Rex asked.

"Search and rescue."

"Military?" Rex asked.

Tyler didn't look military with his dark hair past regulation at his ears. He held himself less rigid than servicemen Rex had met in the past.

"No. After college, I joined a specialized search-and-rescue unit in the Coast Guard rescue swimmer program and spent time in the fire department urban search and rescue—USAR—which is mostly structural collapse rescues. Some military pals let me learn pararescue with them. Picked up paramedic training, swift water and flood rescue, high-angle rope rescue, and dive search and recovery."

"That's quite a résumé." Rex considered how such training would make Tyler quick-thinking under stress and not afraid of danger. Valuable assets. "You've done a lot of search and rescue expeditions with all that training?"

Tyler nodded. "I was deployed to national disasters—hurricanes, wildfires, earthquakes—and worked with FEMA and the Red Cross. Four years ago, I joined the Elite Global Rescue Team, a top-tier, multinational emergency response team handling extreme disaster zones. Things like earthquake zones, tsunamis, and other extreme weather."

Smart, fit, and plows headlong into disaster zones. Rex respected the combination. He decided not to push. If Tyler had a superpower, they would learn it soon enough.

"And Layla? You knew her before she was famous?" Rex wanted to gauge if their past would cause strife among the group. The six of them were here to work together against Kronos in a test of "heart and soul" where the "six align." He didn't want internal clashes to splinter and hurt the team's chance of success in the "fate of all."

"Nah," Tyler said. "She's always been famous. Parents were actors, and she started young. She's another talent in the Sinclair dynasty."

"And her reaction at seeing you?"

"We dated a while back. She never mentioned she could summon the weather—or storms—though, hindsight being twenty-twenty, I think there were signs."

When he didn't elaborate, Rex said, "None of my business," in an ironic tone that suggested he wanted the story.

For sixty seconds, only the sound of their running feet filled the silence.

Tyler sighed. "Look. I get how our interaction that first night came across to everyone. I didn't lie, steal, or cheat. I ended it because our lives were obviously veering in different directions. I was a summer fling for the beauty star before she went back to California and I finished my degree at UNC."

College?

"So that was like ten years ago?" Rex asked, shocked at how raw Layla's emotions seemed to be. When Zoey had mentioned Kitty Hawk Beach, she hadn't mentioned a timeline.

"Yeah."

"And she's still upset about it?"

"Apparently the woman can hold a grudge."

Rex sensed he was missing some important details, but he'd reached the limits of how much he would pry into another man's life.

"It's OK, man," Tyler said. "We'll do whatever we're meant to do—get the tools and seal the breach, like Athena said. Layla'll get over the initial shock of seeing me after all these years, recollect how I'm an insignificant blip in her glamorous life, and it'll be fine." His tone suggested he harbored his own hard feelings about the past.

Toward Layla or toward himself? Rex couldn't tell, but his doubts deepened about their future interactions being "fine."

Regardless of how Tyler remembered events, Layla was a woman scorned. Emotions that jagged might not be so easily smoothed over. The six of them had to function as a team—*pure of soul*, whatever that meant—for their quest to work.

"Thanks for keeping me company," Madison told Layla. "Running has never been something I prioritized." One mile in and she was already breathless. She had her work cut out for her.

The trail wound around the island just wide enough for two shoulder to shoulder. It hugged the coastal cliffs in some places, dipped into shaded ravines in others, and at times disappeared beneath thickets only to reappear around an ancient olive tree or a sun-warmed boulder.

The ground underfoot was uneven but passable—a mixture of compacted dirt, patches of pebbles, and gnarled roots that twisted across the path like nature's warning signs. Wild thyme and oregano burst through the cracks, releasing wisps of scent with every step. Sagebrush, juniper, and mastic trees provided splashes of green amid the rocky outcroppings.

Near the island's center, the trail softened—loamy earth under cypress and pine where sunlight filtered in golden beams through the branches. In more exposed parts, the meltemi wind off the Aegean carried the tang of salt and the distant call of seabirds. Lizards darted across sun-drenched rocks.

Layla chortled. "I'm not back here so that you're not alone. I belong here. My trainers focused on a body with sex appeal. That involves toning arms and legs and honing core strength. Not cardio."

"Whatever you've been doing works. You have a great body."

"Thanks. You're a looker yourself. Tall and long-legged. And that hair. Gorgeous."

"Thanks."

"You and Rex?" Layla asked.

Madison hesitated.

"He looks at you like you're a priceless relic he's afraid to touch—and you stare at him like he's hiding the lost city of Atlantis in his back pocket."

"Yes. I like him. We've only known each other a week, but I'm enjoying the chemistry." After their night under the stars, Rex had granted that goodnight kiss he'd promised. It had been blissfully sweet with an undercurrent of passion that hinted at deeper desires.

"What's not to like? Tall, tan, and fit. Angled jaw and sharp, blue eyes. He looks at you with adoration, too," Layla said.

"Yeah?" Madison felt a warmth unrelated to exercise spread through her.

"Yeah." Layla chuckled. "You might as well seize the moment. Athena sure made our task sound daunting."

"True. And I've never dated anyone who knew my powers."

"I'm betting none of us have."

"I hadn't really thought of that." Madison felt a bolder resolve blossom in her chest.

She also wanted to work the conversation around to Layla and Tyler. But first. "Alexios isn't hiding his interest in Zoey."

Layla shook her head. "He's like a puppy dog."

"You say that only because you've never seen him behead a man."

"You have?" Layla gaped at her without slowing her pace.

"The butler had it coming. Will Alexios's tactic work with Zoey?"

"I don't know." Layla frowned. "She'll admire his fighting skills. Might be flattered by his approach. But there's trauma in her past—her story to tell, or not—not mine. He'll need under-standing and patience. I'm not sure those are virtues men were taught in the BC era."

"You're very perceptive."

"Thanks."

"He has honor, and I think two thousand years in captivity taught him patience," Madison said. As her lungs burned, she wondered why she'd thought talking and jogging would be a good combination.

"I guess we'll see."

"And you and Tyler?" Madison asked.

Layla's expression shuddered closed. "Youthful infatuation. A mistake I won't make again."

Because there was both pain in her words and a finality to them, Madison let the conversation drop.

"Do you know what powers he has?" Madison asked.

"I know he's done extreme rescue his entire adult life. Saved lives. But magic? Not when I knew him."

Madison drew up short on the trail. "There's a path this way. Want to explore?"

"Sure." Layla followed her.

Slowing, they walked the narrow path, flanked by carob trees and kermes oaks, and Madison was grateful for the chance to catch her breath. The trail opened to a short, rocky slope that spread into a white sand beach with aqua blue water.

"Wow." Layla breathed out. "We're so coming back here and swimming."

"The water is beautiful. I could soak up the sun and read a book here for hours."

Layla looked her up and down. "Hours, huh?"

"With five hundred SPF, yes. How are you so tan?"

"My grandmother was Greek. A Papadopoulos. Let's tell Zoey about this place and come back for a dip this afternoon."

Madison nodded, glancing out to sea. The water looked too shallow for any boarsharks—er, Cetus. Would Kronos throw something else at them?

Not on this island, she thought. This had been created as their training sanctuary. Athena had called it a refuge, which surely meant Kronos had no power here.

After five days of training, Rex felt like the team was reaching a rhythm. Everyone had started on the holographic fighting simulator except Madison, but he knew she was working up to it. Each evening, he made sure he found Madison and they shared another goodnight kiss. Each time, walking back to his cabin to sleep alone after losing himself in the taste of her took more effort.

This afternoon, he lounged on one of the beaches beside the other men, resting the body he'd pushed hard in training and watching the sun set while Zoey and Madison helped Layla with her turn to cook dinner.

Tyler sat on one side of him and Alexios on the other in folding chairs they kept stored near the beach.

Tyler had brought a cooler of beer. "You and Madison are a couple? Or something in progress?"

Rex shrugged and grabbed a cold one. "We've only known each other a little over a week."

In front of him, gentle waves lapped onto the sand as the late afternoon sun sank heavy in the sky. If Rex had time with her on the island, just the two of them with no doomsday hovering over them, he could envision bringing her to this spot for a date or romantic interlude.

"Sure. Whatever you say."

"What?"

"I see the way you look at her when she's not looking. I think she's doing some of the same, but it's hard to tell with her glasses."

"She's beautiful." The defensive tone in his own voice annoyed him.

"Just making conversation."

"They like each other," Alexios said.

"I admit to that," Rex said, raising his beer bottle and pointing a finger at the Greek.

"But you're holding back," Tyler said.

Rex considered those nightly kisses and how he'd kept them brief even when he sensed Madison wanted more. "I'm not the settling-down type. I think Madison is."

"A man isn't the settling type until he meets someone worth making the change."

"Oh? So you and Layla—"

"Are ancient history," Tyler said with finality. He glanced at Alexios. "No offense intended."

Alexios grinned. "I do not take offense to your jargon. I was ancient history ... but now I am here, and I will be modern history. Because we are on the subject of women—"

"You like Zoey," Tyler interjected.

"Yes." He beamed.

Rex told Tyler, "He knelt in greeting her when she and Layla arrived in her boat."

"As in, knelt before them when they docked?"

Rex shook his head. "Zoey only, as he accused her of being a goddess."

Tyler raised his eyebrows before telling Alexios, "In this day and age, we don't kneel before a woman unless we're asking her to marry us."

"I would marry Zoey," Alexios said.

"Uh." Rex took a swig of beer. "You don't know anything about her, and you knew even less when you knelt."

"Your assumption is incorrect," Alexios said mildly. "I knew from the way she moved, tossing you the lines of rope, that she has a strong body—a warrior's body. I knew from the way she walked that she has confidence. I knew from her arrival that she was brave enough to seek out an island for answers, suspecting as we did that danger was in store. Now I know she has loyalty— Layla is proof of that—both in friendship and that she saved her life."

"Fair. And remarkably observant of you," Rex said. "I suppose you know some about her character, but there are many women in the world. As in *billions*. Maybe at least try a few of them out before you pick your bride."

"Coming on too forcefully could drive a wedge," Tyler added. "There's no rush. Know each other better first. Women want friendship first. Trust."

Rex nodded. "The marrying kind, yeah. Trust before sex."

"Sex." Alexios stared into the fire.

Rex exchanged a look with Tyler. "I imagine that three-letter word holds a lot of weight for someone who's been celibate for two thousand years."

"But there are a lot of cultural differences now," Tyler rushed to add, tossing an awkward glance at Rex.

"Right." Rex cleared his throat. He could think of a few important ones from his history studies. "Marriage in ancient Macedonia was a social and economic arrangement. Today, women want love."

Tyler added, "Though you still have to prove you can provide financial and emotional support. And if the woman is the breadwinner, you can be supportive in other ways."

"There are no courtesans or slaves," Rex added.

"And you can never force yourself on a woman," Tyler added.

"Understood. I have seen what men have done with the spoils of war. And I have seen officers shame their wives by taking concubines. Over the years, during my golden entombment, I have seen cheating spouses. I would want only one wife as a lifelong companion. She would be my first and last in bed."

Rex choked on his next sip of beer. "Uh, first?"

"A soldier's life does not leave room for women. I needed more status before I made a suitable husband."

"OK." Rex cleared his throat. "We'll use the training here to keep you occupied while Zoey learns more about you, and you both decide if you want to enter a relationship."

"And, I must be occupied with learning to read. I will not make a good husband if I am illiterate."

"We can do that," Rex said, happy to steer the conversation away from long-term relationships.

"I'm sure Layla has books on her shelves inside that yacht," Tyler said. "She always loved to read. She'd let you borrow them if you asked."

Rex studied archaeology because he was inquisitive and curious about puzzles. As such, he so wanted to unpack the history between Layla and Tyler, but that topic had already been deemed off-limits. He would wait and see if it interfered with group dynamics before he dug deeper. For now, they would stick with solving Alexios's challenges.

Rex held up a hand. "We'll teach Alexios to read before the woman he wants to woo ever learns he's illiterate, though I don't think Zoey's the type to judge you for that. The island can provide starter books. Probably also a read-along set with headphones for when you want to study in your room at night."

"Thank you," Alexios said. "It is good to have friends who can help usher me into the modern world."

"Modern, yeah." Tyler chuckled. "And yet somehow here we are, alone on an island, planning to fight a mythological Greek titan using ancient relics."

CHAPTER
FIFTEEN

Madison dressed in flexible cotton leggings that stretched over her thighs down to her calves and a tank top. She'd watched all five other warriors "level up" in the holographic training center. She needed to get her butt into that circle.

The others had all arrived with existing skills: Rex, scrappy fighter, apparently from years of being a scoundrel of an archaeologist, and having to fight his way out of situations he'd likely put himself in; Alexios, who was skipping levels owing to experience in actual wars involving death and dismemberment; Layla, who had clearly trained seriously for her action movie roles; Zoey, whose stunt double work made her a formidable and fierce fighter; and Tyler with quick reflexes from his extreme rescue training.

All the more reason Madison stole out in the wee morning hours to have her first training session. She didn't need to reaffirm what the others probably suspected—that she was the weakest link.

She restored art for a living. Her Q-tips of chemicals to revive vibrant battle scenes were her weapons. She didn't actually enter the scenes. Certainly, had the goddess Athena approached her—oh, say—ten years ago to warn her she would be needed to fulfill a prophecy involving swordplay, she might have chosen a different career path. Maybe. At the very least, she could have taken local aikido classes.

After pulling on her tennis shoes and securing her hair in a ponytail, she slipped quietly down the steps and onto the platform where the training center awaited. Zephyr followed her and sniffed the perimeter. The morning air was cool, and a faint breeze ruffled the surrounding trees.

Walking into the circle, she addressed the magical computer system. "Hello?"

"Welcome, warrior. Identify yourself."

"Madison Katsaros."

"Choose your weapon."

Right. Probably should have picked that out before she stepped into the circle of death—er, training. She chose a Mycenaean short sword, a blade that would be manageable for her. And scrambled back into the center.

"Initiating level."

A creature appeared—a giant snake with half its body raised so it loomed a foot taller than her with glistening oxide green scales, a darting forked tongue, and fangs as long as her forearm. Yellow eyes watched her carefully. With the sword in her right hand, she dipped her glasses down to her nose.

Nothing happened.

"Didn't think so," she said. "Can't blame a girl for trying."

Lightning fast, the snake darted toward her with its wide mouth open and dripping with venom. Shrieking, she jumped back and barely avoided impalement.

"Right. That was probably a missed opportunity to swing my

sword at your head." Bouncing on the balls of her feet, she readied for another attack.

By now, Alexios would've already lunged forward and sliced off its head, but she refused to feel inferior when she'd never had training.

The snake lashed out again. This time she swiped at it but was a good foot short of contacting it.

"OK. We'll chalk that one up to overly cautious."

Circling the creature, she waited for the next lunge. She debated its weakest spot—probably the throat. She didn't think she'd be strong enough to chop its head off, but didn't know if the density of the holographic image was somehow designed to accurately represent that of a snake. Rather than risk it, she would go for the throat if the opportunity presented itself.

They circled each other, and she had a disconcerting thought that in a real battle, there wouldn't be just one snake and she probably couldn't take so much time to kill it.

Well, this wasn't a battle yet. This was training, and levels existed for a reason. She would work her way up to confident and proficient. The same way she'd done for her career, although she suspected she didn't have years before this epic showdown Athena had prophesied.

When the snake came at Madison again, she sliced and dodged, this time cutting through scales. Bile-looking fluid dripped down its neck, but the wound was clearly superficial.

Their standoff became a sort of dance where it would strike and she would slice—sometimes connecting and sometimes not. She was already sweating from the effort.

Finally, she committed, and when it lunged, she plunged her sword upward, through the neck and up into the head. The holographic image fluttered and extinguished.

"Congratulations, warrior, you have unlocked level two. Choose your weapon."

"This one seems fine," she said, feeling a little swell of accomplishment and confidence.

The next monster shimmered into life, a vicious-looking harpy with the face of a bitter, sun-beaten woman, tenacious, yellow-stained claws, gray mottled skin, spiked midnight hair, and waxy bat wings the size of elephant ears.

Unlike the snake, the harpy didn't hesitate to attack with gnashing teeth, swiping claws, and spittle flying from her mouth. She zipped around Madison when she could only duck, dodge, and swat.

"Your damn wings give you the higher ground." Madison breathed heavily now, panting from the exertion.

The creature was quick to avoid her blows, and when Madison got past her defenses, she didn't have enough momentum to cause much damage. She wished she'd taken a break before this next fight.

Won't get that in real life either, said her inner voice.

A grazing claw raked down her arm, and Madison gasped. She hadn't considered that the hologram would cause actual pain. She looked at her arm, but no wound marred it, only shadow pain—the fierce burning of which made her wonder if harpies' claws contained poison.

The distraction of looking at her arm for a wound cost her. The demon bat turned and struck out a wing, slicing the razor-sharp edge across Madison's chest. She screamed from the surprise and pain. Doubling over in agony, her heart threatened to pound out of her chest.

The harpy dove at her, sinking its teeth into Madison's neck. After a brief, sharp pain, the hologram disappeared and the pain with it. Zephyr came to her side, nudging her hand and whining in distress.

"I'm good," she rasped out to reassure him.

The trainer's voice echoed. "You have failed, warrior. You have been defeated. Do you wish to fight another foe?"

Gasping for breath and clutching her chest, Madison seethed. "No. I wish to take a fucking break."

"Madison!" Rex rushed down the stairs and sprinted toward her.

Good. Nothing like polishing off her humiliating entry-level battle debacle by having an audience.

"I'm OK. I'm fine. Just my wounded pride."

He skidded to a halt when he came beside her. "I heard you scream."

"That's because this sadistic training model evidently inflicts pain. Although not the actual wound, thank goodness." Madison gave Zephyr a few more reassuring pats.

"Yeah. Uh. It inflicts virtual pain. You're not hurt?" Rex asked, voice still filled with worry.

"No," she snapped out. Feeling the weight of her failure even more. Having watched a few of the other five sparring, she didn't recall seeing any of them injured in the circle, but maybe she hadn't stuck around long enough.

Alexios appeared beside them. "It is good that you experience pain during training. You need to know you can push through some injuries and continue fighting."

"Well, that's not what happened here." Madison shoved to her feet and wiped the sweat off a brow with the back of her hand.

"You are understandably frustrated," Alexios said. "Every warrior who ever existed started at the ground level. Started with no experience. You will learn, and every day you will grow stronger and more confident." He placed a reassuring hand on her shoulder.

After touching her neck, she drew her hand back to look at it. No blood, even though it had felt like the harpy had hit her jugular. She took a moment to calm herself, because her anger at herself was making her snap at her friends.

When she found composure, she said, "I like that you're a half-full kind of guy. And it's also obvious that I probably need some basic moves. Will you teach me?"

Alexios nodded. "Of course."

Rex said, "I heard you scream, and I thought we were under attack."

Madison shook her head. "I wanted to get on the simulator without an audience." As Zoey and Layla came downstairs, Madison added on a grumble, "Apparently, that's not happening."

Alexios picked up the sword she'd dropped. "Let us cover some basics."

As he led her aside, she heard Rex explaining that what Zoey and Layla had heard was Madison being injured by a holographic harpy and those injuries inflicting "virtual" pain.

A hawk swooped from the sky, spun, and transformed into a man before landing softly on his feet. Everyone stilled and stared at Tyler.

"That's your superpower?" Rex gaped at Tyler.

Alexios grinned. "Magnificent."

Tyler looked around, ignoring everyone's reactions to his display of power. "I heard a scream."

Madison waved her hand. "My bad. Didn't know getting killed by a fake harpy would hurt so much." She glimpsed Layla, who was staring at Tyler through narrow-slitted eyes.

"Any animal or just a hawk?" Rex asked.

"Any animal," Tyler said.

"Like a dolphin?" Layla interjected, voice sharp.

Tyler tucked his hands into his jeans pockets and cast his gaze to the ground. "Those too."

Layla spun on her heel and stormed off. Zoey followed her.

Everyone who remained stared at Tyler. While Madison

appreciated the attention being pulled away from her, she didn't like the discomfort of Layla's unspoken anger toward Tyler. She worried this would only widen the rift between them.

Tyler's mouth drew into a thin line. "I'll talk to her ... when she cools off a little."

"Come," Alexios said to Madison. "Training."

ALL DAY, the sounds of Madison's scream echoed in Rex's mind. He never wanted to hear that sound again, but he wasn't assigned to this quest to shield her. In fact, she might be insulted if she learned the thought had even crossed his mind.

The six of them sat around the evening fire after a hard day of training. They'd eaten dinner in the dining room and moved out to the fire for drinks. They gathered here every few days for the camaraderie, but also the unspoken anticipation that Athena might appear with her next cryptic set of instructions.

"Anyone else feeling a sense of unsettling limbo?" Zoey asked before taking a sip of her beer.

Madison turned her wine glass slowly in her hands. "I'm both nervous and thrilled at this assembly. I've feared this curse for my entire life," Madison said. "Now, maybe it has a purpose. I'd like to hear stories from everyone about how your gift helped you in some way."

Tyler shifted his weight. "Sure. I'll go first. Several of my rescues on the search and rescue team involved shapeshifting, but I have to be careful not to be noticed. One of my most harrowing actually took place just south of here, near Crete. A passenger ferry hit submerged ruins during a storm, capsizing in rough seas. I was in Italy on my way here, but I received an alert on my phone about a flipped ferry. Passengers were trapped as the ship began to sink. I flew a few miles out as a falcon, dove underwater, shifted into a dolphin, and dragged survivors to shore." He glanced at Layla and continued, "More were trapped inside the wreckage, so I squeezed through tight spaces as an octopus, shifted back to man, opened a hatch, and guided them out."

Rex sensed Tyler held details back in his story. "What else happened down there?"

Tyler shifted uncomfortably. "Jackal-headed sea demons."

"Telkhines," Alexios said. "Cast into the sea by Zeus. Amphibious and known for their cursed magic."

"That'd be them," Tyler agreed, voice sounding a little haunted by the experience. "Three of them came at me with tridents and dark water magic. Stirred up the water, making it hard to see while they ambushed me."

"How'd you defeat them?" Madison asked.

"Dodged them as a sailfish and then turned into a great white shark to finish them off."

"Ugh," Zoey blurted. "Why did he go first? No one can top that."

"What's your story?" Madison asked.

"I guess my best one is when Layla and I became BFFs. We were shooting *Wrath of Fates* on a California beach."

"Ooh. That releases soon, right?" Madison interjected.

"Yeah, in a month," Layla confirmed.

"We had just finished filming one of the battle scenes, and Layla's leaning in to kiss the love interest, when a huge lion emerged from the mouth of the cave. Turns out it was a Nemean lion—made of gold."

"And enormous," Layla said. "Big as a car."

"Killed poor Murray." Zoey shook her head.

Madison gasped. "I read about a freak accident on set with a wild animal."

Zoey shrugged. "That was the only rational way people could deal with what they saw. The lion came after Layla next."

Layla interjected, "Zoey dives in, takes me down to the sand, and the lion chomps right into her arm."

Rex thought of the injured arm he'd healed—a lion attack. Had to be terrifying, even though they could speak lightly of it now. Interesting, he thought, considering how all of them faced a trial involving use of their power not long before coming to Milopas.

"I blasted him back with my fire and held him off long enough for Layla to electrocute him."

"Electrocute?" Tyler asked.

Zoey nodded. "Blast of lightning right out of the sky."

Layla arched an eyebrow. "Except she's leaving out the part where it took me half a dozen tries before I finally hit him."

"Zapped him back to Tartarus—or wherever the hell." Zoey stretched her beer bottle toward Layla, who toasted it with her wineglass.

"And we've been inseparable ever since," Layla said. "Mostly because I'm damn well going to keep a flame torch of a friend nearby if Greek monsters are after me."

"Always were smart and beautiful," Tyler said.

Layla shot a look of daggers in his direction. Rex suppressed a grin. Those two would be hell on each other if they didn't resolve their past issues. As long as they weren't hell on the quest for Athena's relics, Rex wouldn't get involved.

Setting down his beer, Rex stood to address the group. "We've all worked hard as we await instructions. And I think we all know whatever those instructions are, they won't be easy and they will be dangerous. With that in mind, I made everyone gifts." He picked up a paper bag off the floor.

"What a thoughtful guy," Zoey teased.

"Yeah, yeah." He reached into the bag and plucked out five tiny vials, each with a thick leather cord tied around it and about twelve inches long. "I, uh, put my tears in these bottles, and I have one for each of you. Best-case scenario is you never need them. But there's a chance, in the heat of battle, I might not be close enough to heal you quickly, so I thought you should wear the necklace into battle so you can heal yourself if the need arises." He handed them out.

"No, shit?" Tyler took the one Rex offered him with a grin.

"It's legit," Zoey said. "A couple of drops and he healed my mangled arm."

Tyler held up his bottle to look at it by the light of the fire. "And this was how you freed Alexios from Midas?"

"He did," Madison said, tying hers around her neck. When she glanced at Rex, her expression was thoughtful and appreciative. "And how he freed my dog and me."

"A wise gift," Alexios said. "We shall all treasure it."

Rex swallowed uncomfortably and rubbed the back of his neck before taking a seat again.

Tyler raised his beer. "A toast. To new friendships, special gifts, and hoping we never have to use Rex's magical tears to heal ourselves." The group collectively raised their glasses to the toast before drinking.

SIXTEEN

Rex had pushed weightlifting hard that day—maybe too hard—based on his aching muscles. He'd also run five miles, swam two, keeping to the shallow waters around the island with Alexios and Tyler, and done an hour on the simulator. Fortunately, tomorrow was one of the days off per week Layla had thankfully requested.

Rex needed to plan a way to finagle some time alone with Madison. Maybe he could take her to that beach spot he'd envisioned. They could picnic, skinny-dip, and kiss more. He wanted to take their relationship to the next level, but he didn't know what that involved emotionally, other than uncharted territory for him. Intimacy would be so much more than physical for both of them and unlike anything he'd experienced before because she truly knew who he was—his past, his powers, his burdens.

He was about to slip into his bed for the night when a knock sounded at his door.

"Come in."

He turned to see Madison standing in sleep shorts and a t-shirt. Long, smooth legs shone in the light in his room. Her blond hair was down in soft, loose waves and different from the ponytail she usually sported for their days of training.

"Madison." Instantly aroused, he wanted to crush her body against his and run his hands over every inch of her but didn't dare move until he knew her intentions.

She looked like a woman ready to tumble under the sheets, but for all he knew she could be here to talk about battle strategy.

"I like kissing you," she said, voice soft and hesitant.

OK, so not here for battle strategy.

"I like kissing you too. I've missed spending time with you. We had so little before the rest of the group arrived. I've been wanting to get you alone," he confessed. He started to explain that he hadn't meant that to sound completely sexual when her smile brightened.

"You have? We've all been a little busy. It's taken me days to work up the courage to come to your room like this."

Like this, he thought, the words swimming in his head. She'd come to share his bed, an offering he wouldn't take for granted.

He moved toward her. "You're the most amazing woman I've ever met. Spend tomorrow at the beach with me. We'll have a picnic, just the two of us."

She gave a soft smile. "I'd like that."

He touched a hand to her cheek, wishing he could see her eyes to see her thoughts. But he didn't need to see her to show her how he felt. Leaning forward, he pressed his lips to hers. She parted them for him and tilted her head back as her body swayed closer. She smelled like warm vanilla.

He took his time devouring her, hoping to show her how much he enjoyed her mouth. He wanted to enjoy more, but without making her feel pressured. They hadn't so much as been on a date, though their living and working situation at the moment eliminated the possibility of usual courtship behavior.

"Let me kiss you everywhere." He kissed his way down to her

neck as his hand roamed along her backside. "I want to taste you. Hear you moan."

Her head rolled back as a soft purr escaped. "So dangerous," she murmured.

"Do you trust me?" He stopped his caresses to wait for an answer.

Her head rose slowly. "I trust you."

Damn, her voice sounded even sexier when it turned husky.

He pulled a strip of black silk out of his dresser drawer, something he'd asked the island for along with condoms, because this moment was a fantasy he'd hoped would come true.

He held up the strip of fabric for her to see. "I'll tell you exactly what I'm doing before I do it. We'll set your glasses on the nightstand, and you can stop me anytime."

"OK."

"Yeah?"

"Yeah." She smiled, more warmly now.

He kissed her again, excitement and a touch of nerves rolling through him. He'd enjoyed the pleasure of women between his excavations, but Madison felt different. This wasn't a tussle in the dark to quickly satisfy hormonal urges. Her trust and surrender added a momentous weight to their activity that had his throat constricting and his chest aching.

With emotions running high and the delectable soft feel of her mouth, he was throbbing to be inside her. He would rush nothing. If she asked for sex, he would willingly oblige, but he wouldn't coerce. He wanted to give, and take only the satisfaction of her pleasure.

"Turn around and close your eyes."

When she did, he slipped her glasses off and set them on the nightstand. Standing behind her, he laid the silk across her eyes and tied the back to secure it in place. He let his fingers trail down her neck, then down her back as he memorized the wondrous shape of her.

She shivered under his touch as he eased her shirt up and over her head, careful not to displace the blindfold. After tossing the shirt aside, his hands came back to her, tracing the curve of her shoulder blades and the lovely line of her spine. She'd come to his cabin braless, which he found all the more arousing.

He trailed fingers over her hips before running his thumbs along the waistband of her cotton shorts. Her stomach quivered beneath his touch as he slid them down her long, shapely legs. She sidestepped out of them.

Standing back up, he danced his touch up her legs and over her red underwear. *Gods of Olympus*, he wanted to bite into that lace and tear it off with his teeth. Instead, he slowly slid the fabric down to the floor.

He eased his hands around to cup her perfect breasts and rub the erect nipples. When she gasped, his hands shook with the effort of his control.

"You feel exquisite," he said, kissing the back of her neck as he kept his hands on her soft flesh. "I'm carrying you to bed now."

She chuckled. "Why? It's like five feet from me."

He scooped her up as she laughed, a sound of sheer delight. He barely registered his aching muscles anymore. Gently, he set her on the bed. Wanting to feel his skin against hers, he took off his shirt but didn't dare take off more and tempt his fragile control.

"I'm going to kiss you more and work my way lower." Now that he could see the front of her naked, he took a moment to admire the round swell of generous breasts and hourglass waist.

Lowering himself over her, he started on the delicate pink flesh. She arched, hissed, and called his name. With his tongue on her breast, he dragged fingers up her inner thigh. She parted. Warm and ready for him, he sank into that eager flesh.

Groaning, she moved her hips in a rhythmic motion as she plunged her fingers into his hair. She would shatter what little control he had left at this rate. He'd never been so turned on by a woman's eagerness for him.

He worked mouth and hand in unison, selecting his speed based on the pace of her hips, until she cried out in shuddering waves of pleasure. When she stilled, he stilled, listening to her panting breaths.

When she moved again, her hands roamed down his chest to the waistband of his shorts.

"Madison," he managed in a croak.

"More. I need you inside me."

His blood thrummed, thick and heavy. "OK. Yes. Uh. Condom."

She smiled as he fumbled in his dresser drawer, discarded the rest of his clothes, and rolled on the condom. He settled over her on the bed and hovered at her hot entrance as he ached and pulsed with need.

"What are you waiting for?" she asked, licking her lips with the blindfold still securely in place.

"Composure. I don't want to hurt you."

In response, she arched up to him, took him deep. She gasped and clutched his biceps. Before he could back out in a panic, she locked her legs around him.

"You won't hurt me."

When she moved her hips, she undid him. First, they started in long pulls and soon moved to heated thrusts. He bent to kiss her, so hungry to consume her, to be consumed by her. He held on, merged physically and emotionally, never wanting to let go of either.

The friction and pleasure intensified, taking him to a glorious peak. When she cried out and quaked around him, she took him right off the edge of that precipice with her.

He buried himself within her until he couldn't tell where he ended and she began. "Madison."

Waves of pleasure washed over Madison. She had no idea two mingling bodies could feel so amazing.

Her eyes were closed against the soft fabric shielding Rex from her power. She wished she could see him when they made love, but his way was safer than risking her glasses falling off and turning him to stone.

Made love?

The passionate coupling had certainly felt like that, but she would keep that part of the experience to herself. Too soon in their relationship for deep emotional confessions.

She rolled to face him where he lay on his back, panting. A fine sheen of sweat covered his chest where she rested her hand. His body was hard muscle and warmth.

"That was nice," she said.

"Nice?" He arched an eyebrow. "Just nice?"

"Well, amazing actually." She stretched up, estimated where her lips would land, and placed a kiss on his cheek.

How soon was too soon to tell him he was the best thing to come into her life ... ever? She didn't want to overwhelm him, especially because she already felt overwhelmed enough for the both of them.

Swallowing her nervousness, she asked, "Can you help me find my glasses so I can see where my clothes are?"

He stroked a finger along the bare skin of torso and down her hip. "What do you need clothes for?"

She gave him a lighthearted tsk. "I'm not making my walk of shame back to my cabin naked."

"Walk of shame?"

She hesitated. Did he sound offended? "No, I don't mean that.

It's just an expression. I've no regrets. In fact, I'm hoping this was the first of many."

"You can stay." His voice held a thickness and vulnerability that had her heart stumbling over the next few beats.

Yes, she very much wanted to stay. Her shoulders drooped. "I don't want to take that chance. I don't want a blindfold to work its way off and accidentally turn you to stone. In fact, I've worn a cover to bed every night since we started living on the island, and sometimes it does slip off."

When she sat up on the edge of the bed, warm hands wrapped around her and cupped her breasts. Rex nuzzled his nose into her neck, sending shivers of delight down her spine.

"Then we'll wait until you're comfortable staying. For now, at least let me take you again," he said. "I want you screaming my name so loud that the word nice is forever erased as a description of anything that takes place in my bed."

SEVENTEEN

Rex flipped burgers on the grill while Tyler stood beside him nursing a beer. The team had trained hard before breaking at two in the afternoon for a cookout. The women practiced archery while the men promised dinner in an hour.

He thought about how far Madison had come in her training. She didn't shy away from the hard work or the training center. She didn't shy away from the relationship they were building either. He'd followed through on the picnic he'd planned as well as the skinny-dipping. Since then, they'd made time to steal a few minutes together each day, even if only during a brief meal looking out over the sea.

The sizzle of beef, smell of charcoal, and Alexios chopping, drew Rex back to the present. The Greek warrior stood in the kitchen preparing burger dressings and making a side dish of revithokeftedes—crispy chickpea fritters—he planned to serve with a garlic-yogurt dip.

As promised, Rex had started the *Star Wars* series with Alexios. They had watched the first three original movies, *Star Wars IV*, *V*, and *VI*, over the course of their time on Milopas, and Alexios was now humming Vader's theme song—"The Imperial March" by John Williams—during his food preparation. He'd been fascinated by the concept of lightsabers, though unimpressed by the sword fighting skills thus far. He admitted, however, that the characters' emotions woven in made the fighting more dramatic. Surely, he would enjoy the Obi-Wan and Anakin battle on Mustafar when they watched *Revenge of the Sith*.

Speaking of sword fights—"My sword arrived in Athens," Rex told Tyler. "I thought we could make a day trip, a break from the island, and all six go fetch it."

He'd had his trophy from his battle against Kharon shipped to Greece, but of course, no delivery system was making a voyage to an island that didn't exist, so he had to pick it up from Athens. If he had to fight in an epic Greek battle, using the sword from around the era seemed appropriate and meaningful. He would just need to polish it up, sharpen it, and give it a new leather handle.

Zephyr's ears twitched as he cocked his head. He'd been lingering near the smell of cooking meat just a few feet from the grill.

"Seven of us," Rex amended.

The dog wagged his tail.

"This is the Kharon sword you mentioned?" Tyler asked.

Rex had told the group the same story he'd told Madison during one of the six's fireside chats when they took turns talking about their lives before Milopas.

"That's the one."

"Think it'll give you an advantage?"

Rex glanced toward the kitchen where Alexios worked. "I hope so. We can't all be battle-bronzed warriors akin to Achilles."

"The man's got moves," Tyler said with appreciation.

"So do you."

"Not like that. Not with a sword."

Rex flipped the patties one by one as he talked. "Who needs a sword when you can turn into a sabertooth tiger?" He'd seen Tyler fight monsters in various forms of ferocious animals in the training simulator.

"Huh. Haven't tried a sabertooth before. I'll have to do that."

Rex took the burgers off the grill and slid them onto a platter. "We should let the ladies know the food is ready."

"Yeah. So … you and Madison …" Tyler let the words hang.

"Yup."

"Those cabins are not soundproof, by the way." Tyler grumbled out the words.

"If you're looking for an apology, you're not getting one."

⁂

MADISON PULLED the string taut and launched an arrow … into the wall behind the target. "Oof." Reaching down, she pulled another out of the wooden box. Archery wasn't her strong suit, but this was one of the many skills Alexios wanted them to learn.

The three women stood in a row, bows in hand, arrows sticking out of nearby straw targets—Layla with more than the rest. The sea breeze tugged at Madison's hair as the sun began to dip toward the horizon.

"You'll get the hang of it," Layla said.

"You certainly do."

"I'm getting better. Alexios says I need to master the bow, so it's been a focus of mine for several weeks."

"Why the bow?" Madison asked.

"He says that because my magical battle skills will incorporate the use of wind and lightning, requiring focus and distance from my enemy, a bow and arrow will help me keep that distance from advancing stragglers when I—and I quote—best the bulk of my enemies with *magic from the sky*."

"He is one of a kind," Madison said. "Optimistic and encouraging." She looked over at Zoey. "And I bet he'd watch all those zombie movies you like with you."

Zoey, ignoring Madison's probe, nocked an arrow. "OK, serious question. Were you guys more NSYNC or Backstreet Boys?"

Layla snorted as she released her arrow. "Please. NSYNC all the way. Justin's ramen noodle hair? Iconic."

Chuckling, Madison missed the target again. "Oh my gosh, the frosted tips! I wanted to dye a pink streak in my hair so bad in eighth grade."

Zoey fired, landing one ring outside of the center target. "I *did* dye a pink streak. My mom made me rinse it out before the school photo. Said I looked like a juvenile delinquent."

Layla hit a bull's-eye and grinned. "You *were* a juvenile delinquent."

"I had butterfly clips." Madison notched another bow. "Like ... *so many* butterfly clips. It's a miracle my scalp survived middle school."

Zoey said, "I once did ten tiny buns all over my head, à la Gwen Stefani. I thought I was killing it."

Layla laughed. "I bet you did! That was the Y2K look. Did you dye it red at the time too?"

Zoey nodded. "Then I hit my angry Alanis Morissette phase. Total grunge hair look for six months."

Layla picked up another arrow. "Anyone else collect gel pens and write *deep* thoughts in glitter ink?"

Madison sighed in mocked wistfulness. "Fantasies about

Leonardo DiCaprio. We were soul mates in my young imagination."

Zoey laughed and unleashed another arrow. "*Titanic* did a number on all of us."

"Meanwhile, I taped MTV's TRL every afternoon and pretended I was best friends with Christina Aguilera." Layla adjusted her stance and took aim.

Zoey tossed her head back. "Oh man, and don't forget 'Total Request Live' drama. You either liked Britney ... or you *were* Britney."

"I was more of a Fiona Apple girl. Angsty but artsy." Madison did a happy jig when she hit the ring around the center circle.

Layla fired. Bull's-eye. "Of course you were."

Zoey scrubbed a hand over her face. "Crazy to think we went from butterfly clips and boy bands to magic powers and monster battles."

"Teen years ...," Madison began wistfully, "a simpler kind of chaos, but I have friendships forming here that I wouldn't trade for anything."

Layla smiled. "And now we get to write our own soundtrack."

"I'll drink to that." Zoey picked up another arrow. "Speaking of ... smells like those burgers might be done soon."

🝈🝈🝈🝈🝈🝈🝈

REX ENJOYED the breeze on deck with Alexios beside him as Layla piloted the yacht toward Athens. They watched for any potential attacks, but the water was calm and the skies were clear. Seabirds wheeled overhead, their cries distant but constant, while dolphins occasionally broke the surface near the bow, trailing the boat in playful arcs. Madison and Zoey took pictures on their smart phones. To the west, hazy outlines of other Cycladic islands emerged—Santorini's cliffs faint in the distance, a plume of white cloud clinging to its volcanic crown.

Two weeks had passed on the island. They ran, swam, lifted weights, fought holograms, and sparred against each other. Alexios created the schedules and incorporated personal one-on-one coaching from him. Now, Rex reflected, he cruised on a multi-million-dollar yacht in the Aegean Sea with an eclectic group he would one day have to trust with his life in battle.

Two weeks of training, and Athena had yet to give them the next phase of their obligations. He had mixed feelings. Though anxious to advance to the part where they sealed the rift and prevented Kronos's rising, any extra time was much-needed additional training.

After long days of intense training, Rex recognized the group needed to take a break. If they were fighting for civilization, then they needed to not isolate themselves entirely from it. They had debated the safety of leaving the island, but it needed to happen. In the interest of both safety and an island reprieve, he asked that everyone come to Athens. In addition, Rex also needed to pick up his sword from the Athens post office.

"How's the reading progressing?" Rex asked Alexios.

On the deck, Zephyr made the rounds to get patted by everyone. Apparently, his last harrowing boat adventure hadn't made him afraid of sea travel, albeit this deluxe mode of transportation was quite different from the *Little Dolphin*—gods rest her soul in peace. And pieces, which they'd dragged aboard *Calypso* to take back to Athens.

"Well. It goes well. I achieved an American grade three level, according to the books."

"You're a fast learner. And Zoey?"

Rex turned his attention to the water, scanning the horizon with the salty breeze on his lips. The coastline of Greece began to form on the horizon—rolling hills of muted green, dotted with whitewashed villages that gleamed in the sunlight like clusters of pearls. Ancient ruins and temple columns peeked out from cliffs and headlands.

Alexios gave a slight shrug. "I ask her questions sometimes to learn more about her, but she gives brisk answers. I think my initial reaction made her cautious. She is politely guarded. Perhaps that is an aspect of the warrior side of her. There is no rush."

"She'll come around," Rex said.

"Do you think so?"

"You're a freaking Greek warrior with a physique that rivals Achilles and hair that rivals Fabio. Yeah. She'll get there."

Alexios smiled. "Who is Fabio?"

"Trust me. It's a compliment." Maybe an outdated one, but Rex recalled his mother's crush on the model while growing up.

In the distance, Athens slowly emerged, modern buildings sprawling toward the ancient heart of the city—the Acropolis rising proudly above it all, golden in the afternoon light.

Closer to the coast or near small islands, he spotted local fishermen in colorful wooden boats, some hauling in nets and others gliding slowly across the waves. Ferries, day-cruise ships, and sleek charter yachts became more common the nearer they sailed to Athens. Music from the deck of a larger yacht trailed behind it. On the horizon, a massive freighter crawled slowly toward Piraeus—Athens's bustling port. The mix of old-world fishing boats and modern vessels reinforced the feeling of sailing between two eras—myth and modernity.

Mercifully, the trip to Athens was uneventful with no new creatures attacking them. Before they deboarded, Rex gathered everybody up on deck. The sun beat down on the stone promenade of the marina, the salty tang of the Aegean clinging to the breeze. Fishing boats bobbed gently beside sleek modern yachts. Beyond the docks, the streets narrowed—paved in smooth gray stone, flanked by whitewashed buildings with iron balconies overflowing with potted plants.

Rex checked his watch. "One hour should be enough time for me to return what's left of the *Little Dolphin* to the rental place and file whatever paperwork I need to for the destroyed boat. Then Tyler, Alexios, and I can go to the postal service and pick up my sword."

"One hour is not enough time." Layla shook her head. "We are making this a girl shopping excursion, also known as stress relief. As a decompression event, we need at least three."

Three hours?

Rex swallowed back a strangled sound and blew out a breath. The curve on Madison's lips suggested she eagerly anticipated some girl time. Far be it from him to interfere with a stress-relief shopping event. "Oookay, three hours. In that case, why don't we meet back at the docks in three hours?"

"Agreed," Layla said with a cheerful smile.

Rex approached Madison who wore a blue cotton sundress and sandals. Dark glasses reflected his face back at him. He picked up a strand of blond hair cascading over her shoulder. "Decompression event, eh?"

"Sounds like fun." She grinned.

"In the interest of letting you have your fun, why don't I take Zephyr? Enjoy your time with your girlfriends."

"Really?"

He reached for the leash. "Yeah. We'll pal around for a while."

She passed the doggy bags in her pocket to him. "Thanks." Leaning forward, she planted a long, savory kiss on his lips.

"I didn't know that would earn me a kiss, but now I'm even happier I offered."

The nights with Madison in his bed weren't nearly often enough, and the time he wanted with her was more than sexual craving. All of this proved to be a strange realization for a man who valued his independence, but he didn't really know what to do with that revelation other than to soak in and savor every moment with her.

Her smile widened. "I'll see you in a few hours."

"Three," he clarified, a little worried the trio would have so much fun that they would lose track of time.

"Three," she reassured him.

CHAPTER

EIGHTEEN

Madison relished the day, walking through the streets with Layla and Zoey by her side. Layla wore capri trousers and a baby blue short-sleeved blouse with puckered sleeves. Her long dark hair was braided to one side. Zoey had her short red hair spiked as usual and wore faded jeans and a fitted tank that showed off her shapely shoulders and arms. They chatted about the sights around them.

Shading her eyes, Zoey glanced back at the dock where colorful fishing boats swayed in the harbor. "I swear those boats look straight out of a postcard."

Madison snapped a quick photo with her phone. "Everything here is color-coordinated by nature. Even the ropes look like curated decor."

They walked through a narrow alley framed by cascading vines, and Layla paused to admire the vivid magentas and purples. "That alley is begging for a dramatic entrance. Someone cue the music."

Zoey snorted. "Only if you promise not to summon a thunderstorm for ambience."

Outside a small shop, Madison slowed her pace listening to the melancholy tune of an elderly man playing a bouzouki. "This is what I imagined Greece would feel like—history in the air, music in the streets."

Was this what hanging out with girlfriends felt like? So blissfully normal. For a little while, she could forget her curse and the destiny of the six.

They ate lunch at Taverna Perivóli in a tucked-away alley in Plaka, the historic old town of Athens. Madison adored the cobblestone street, orange and purple flower-draped balconies, and bougainvillea spilling down whitewashed walls. The taverna was nestled beneath a canopy of grapevines, with mismatched wooden tables and sunflowers in small glass jars. The scent of grilled lamb, lemon, and oregano wafted through the warm air. Locals chatted leisurely in Greek.

Layla ordered xtapodi—grilled octopus with lemon and herbs, Zoey enjoyed eggplant moussaka and fresh bread with Italian seasoning, and Madison dined on grape leaves stuffed with ground lamb. They shared a bottle of Samos, a sweet wine with floral and fruity flavors.

With their stomachs full and the mood light, they traveled to the marketplace and haggled with the vendors over the prices of jewelry and trinkets.

With just one hour left to spare, they meandered along the edge of the Anafiotika district and near a modern-looking spa designed like a sleek sanctuary, where Layla stopped abruptly. The name read "Relaxation Haven" with a flower logo between the words.

"It's a massage clinic." Layla spun to look at them, eyes bright with eager anticipation. "Girls, we have been working out and training relentlessly. We deserve this."

Madison checked the watch on her phone. "We're cutting it close."

"Look!" Layla lifted her arms and pulled the door open. "My muscles are moving of their own volition. I can only follow them!" She walked mechanically, like a puppet on a string, into the massage clinic.

Zoey rolled her eyes, and Madison giggled as they both followed Layla inside the spa.

Madison sent a quick text to Rex: *Stopping at a spa, ten minutes late tops.*

With smooth marble floors, soft blue lighting, and the scent of eucalyptus and honey in the air, the spa felt inviting, harmonious, and almost too perfect. Two closed doors were on opposite sides of a check-in desk. Off in the corner to the right, a fountain gurgled softly as mesmerizing streams of water flowed over rocks.

Confident, Layla sauntered up to the front desk, inquiring about availability.

Madison hung back and whispered to Zoey, "I've never had a massage. What's involved?"

"I've had a few." Zoey shrugged one shoulder and stuffed her hands in her jeans. "We each get our own room. You undress to your level of comfort, lie on the bed, and they do the rest."

Layla turned and grinned at them. "Booked all three of us. Relaxation massages, though I'm sure you can ask for deeper pressure if you want. Madison, what's wrong? You look like you're about to enter the training ring on Milopas."

"First timer," Zoey said.

Layla hooked an arm through Madison's, dispelling any building self-consciousness within her. "Darling, you're in for a treat. They expect you to have your eyes closed and enjoy so don't worry about a thing."

A woman in a gray uniform dress with a white collar entered, holding a tray of three drinks. "Complimentary tea?"

Layla accepted a cup and sipped it slowly. "Mmm. Good."

Madison sniffed hers, and the floral scent sent soothing waves through her.

"It's a blend of herbs for spiritual clarity and rejuvenation," the woman said.

Zoey gulped hers. "I don't know about spiritual clarity, but I could use some rejuvenation."

Madison sipped hers, instantly enjoying the flowery taste with just a hint of honey. Wow. Layla had made the right call diverting them here. As the therapist led her back to the massage room, Madison put her phone on Do Not Disturb to enjoy the relaxation immersion.

Fifteen minutes into the massage, the tension seeped out of her muscles and she felt lulled into dreamy tranquility. Face-down with her head in the cradle, she was in no danger of turning anyone into stone. The heated bed was a warm temperature, and soft music filled the dim room. The massage therapist slathered scented lotion over her bare muscles with expert grace.

Madison could definitely imagine the experience eventually enticing her to sleep. In fact, she wondered if she had dozed for a few minutes.

Rex, Tyler, and Alexios passed through Kallithea, a working-class neighborhood blending modern apartments with weathered tavernas and local grocers. The aroma of baked bread and strong coffee mingled with the sounds of scooters zipping past. Children played in alleys where murals bloomed like urban mythology—gods painted beside pop stars.

As they ascended toward central Athens, the Acropolis peeked above rooftops, a golden crown against the azure sky. They skirted Monastiraki Square, buzzing with life—vendors hawking relics (some real, some fake), buskers playing the lyra, and tourists snapping photos beneath the shadow of ancient ruins.

Yes, Rex decided, they needed this break to unwind and serve as a reminder of the humanity they hoped to save.

From there, they walked up Ermou Street, a bustling pedestrian avenue lined with chic boutiques, bookstores, and jewelry shops. They passed the Church of Panaghia Kapnikarea, one of the oldest Byzantine churches in the city.

They reached Syntagma Square, where the Greek parliament building loomed at the top of broad marble steps. The square pulsed with movement—tourists watching the changing of the Evzone guards, businessmen and women in suits grabbing lunch from vendors, a woman selling pomegranates under a parasol.

The walk had taken them over an hour. Rex passed Zephyr's leash to Alexios and made quick work of retrieving his sword from the postal service. He kept it stored in the long, rectangular shipping box to avoid the awkwardness of carrying a sword through Athens.

On the walk back, the men passed the Taverna Estia just off Ermou Street on their way to Syntagma. The scent of lamb slow-roasting over a spit and the faint strum of a bouzouki from a corner speaker drew them in. The building was tucked into a quiet side alley shaded by olive trees. Stone steps led down into a courtyard where ivy curled around crumbling plaster walls and faded murals of Greek myths peeked from behind creeping vines.

"Estia," Alexios said, looking at one image. "Named for the goddess of hearth and home."

"Sounds like a place of comfort food and soulful conversation," Rex said.

"I could use a dose of both," Tyler said.

A silver-haired woman in a linen apron ushered them to a shaded table beneath a blooming lemon tree and poured glasses of water.

They placed their orders and soon the drinks arrived. Rex had chosen retsina, a traditional Greek white wine infused with pine resin.

"Wine, huh?" Tyler asked. "I think I've only seen you drink beer."

"I like to mix it up. This has an earthy, herbal taste with an old-soul vibe. Feels right for the mood of the afternoon."

"Well, aren't you a connoisseur." Tyler drank his beer, a cold bottle of Mythos. "Alexios, what's that you ordered?"

"Tsipouro. A potent spirit distilled from grape pomace. It is fiery and ancient."

"A drink after your own heart?" Tyler teased.

Alexios grinned, and the men toasted to new friendships.

Rex ordered paidakia—grilled lamb chops seasoned with oregano and lemon, served with golden roasted potatoes. Tyler devoured a souvlaki plate with grilled pork skewers, tzatziki, warm pita, and slices of tomato and cucumber. Alexios opted for something nostalgic in a steaming bowl of fasolada—white bean soup, a dish he said his mother used to make in another life.

Rex and Tyler contributed morsels of meat to Zephyr who seemed content to lie between the two men's chairs.

They ate slowly, relaxing and savoring the moment of peace surrounded by normal people living their normal lives. Rex didn't know Greek, but he'd been in enough foreign countries to enjoy the steady hum of conversation at a restaurant without processing the words spoken.

He glanced at his phone when it buzzed and frowned at the screen.

Stopping at a spa, ten minutes late tops.

Right. He tempered his initial irritation. Madison was being courteous in giving him advance notice. He wasn't used to adjusting his timetable for others, but being part of a team meant being adaptable. Also, kudos to her for embracing this opportunity to relax and bond with the other women. The delay would cost the team nothing and might build on their burgeoning relationships.

As they ate, Tyler and Rex discussed basketball and football, comparing favorite teams.

"So, ancient Greece," Rex said to Alexios to include him in the conversation. "Watch any pankration?" The brutal combination of wrestling and boxing was considered one of the toughest ancient Greek sports. It involved grappling, striking, and choking—basically MMA's ancient granddad. "Or chariot racing?"

"I have watched both. Pankration was a little too violent once you have lived and breathed war and battles every day. Chariot racing entertained spoiled nobles with money to burn as they destroyed perfectly good horses and carts. I am partial to running, discus, and javelin. Tests of strength that harm neither man nor animal."

"Javelin. Cool," Tyler said. "Handy in battle, too."

"I won the javelin contest at the Nemean Panhellenic Games."

"What? Get out. I didn't know we were dining with a celebrity," Tyler drawled, admiration in his tone. "You must have one hell of an arm."

"It has saved my life many times."

Tyler glanced at Rex.

Rex shrugged. "The man knows he's a phenomenal warrior and somehow mixes it with mind-boggling humility. It's a gift."

"Yeah," Tyler agreed. "He probably won some battle single-handedly, saved a few hundred lives, and doesn't want us mere mortals to feel our weakness in his shadow."

Alexios frowned. "No. Nothing like that. Stories like that belong to Hercules and Achilles. I am a man. I did not save so many lives, especially not when it mattered most." His voice trailed off at the end.

"Sorry, man," Rex said, sensing a rare moment of distress in the usually calm warrior. "You want to talk about it?"

He shook his head as if shaking off the memory. "It is, as they say, ancient history."

WITH FULL BELLIES and a low-key afternoon, the mood was relaxed as they made the trek back to Layla's yacht.

Rex texted Madison: *We're here.*

No reply.

Rex paced as another ten minutes ticked by, and the women were now beyond their ten minutes past due arrival time. Angst coiled in the pit of Rex's stomach. Zephyr mimicked him, pacing the road beside him.

"We should go look for them," Alexios said, concern in his voice.

Tyler tucked his hands in his pockets. "Maybe they just lost track of time. Three women together ... stranger things have happened."

"Not Madison," Rex said. "She's meticulously responsible. She would have texted me back by now." He found himself more worried than irritated. But if he was overreacting and this turned out to be the result of poor communication, he'd be sure to give Madison a good tongue-lashing for causing the churning sensation in his gut.

"She didn't say which spa?" Tyler asked.

"No." He wished he'd asked her to text him a photo of where the women had stopped or drop a pin on a digital map.

"We can divide and search," Tyler suggested. "Well, Alexios doesn't have a phone, so he should stick with one of us."

"Let's not split up," Rex said. "If this is some type of danger bad enough that those three women can't handle, then it may require all of us."

. . .

An hour later, frustrated, worried, and tired, they arrived at their fourth massage clinic. At the first three, the staff had denied seeing the three women Rex had described. Zephyr barked and pawed at the ground.

"A promising sign," Tyler noted.

Rex glanced one more time at his phone. He'd sent a text or called every ten minutes and still no response from Madison. When he found her, they were going to make sure everyone connected their phones so that each could find the other's location with an app.

Tyler led the way inside to a cool reception area splashed in relaxing pastel colors.

Alexios drew up short beside him. "The logo out front ... I wonder ... "

His words faded as the scent of sweet flowers filled Rex's nostrils. His muscles relaxed and the tension he'd carried with him these last few hours seeped from his pores. He tried to remember why he'd stepped inside this business.

"Drinks?" A young woman in a plain gray dress raised a tray.

He was thirsty after walking the streets of Athens for the last hour. Maybe a refreshing beverage would refocus his mind on the reason for being here.

CHAPTER
NINETEEN

reamily, Madison shifted her weight.

Did she hear barking in the distance? That couldn't be right. Rex had Zephyr. Unless Rex was here, or man and dog had been separated.

Warmth from the bed oozed a gentle comfort. Why worry about them? They could manage on their own. Besides, her sixty-minute massage would probably end any moment now. The sooner it ended, the sooner she'd be back to training on that island with doom and gloom looming in their future.

Why go back? Why not enjoy an eternal massage?

More barking.

She shifted her weight to move, and her muscles felt heavy. Not relaxed heavy, but immobile heavy, as if the joints hadn't moved in hours. Lifting her head, she rubbed her nose. She thought of the room's fragrance—airily floral and slightly aquatic, like a cross between a lilac and water lily.

Sudden internal alarm had her bolting upright as she pulled the covers around her. Lotus. The smell of lotus flower permeated everything, especially the body lotion.

Oh, Athena. Had they walked right into a trap?

"You're not done yet," her therapist said, voice an easy calm.

Madison turned to look at the woman before she considered the ramifications. The therapist had a waxy smile and expressionless eyes. How had she not noticed that before? Even as the woman reached for her tube of cream, she transformed into stone in mid-action.

Scrambling off the bed, Madison fought back panic as she grappled for her clothing. She could worry about fixing the woman later—unless she was complicit in this scheme, which seemed likely—but right now, she needed to check on Layla and Zoey. And find Zephyr and the man who was supposed to be holding his leash.

Madison glimpsed herself in the mirror as she slipped on her glasses. Her face had a deep, creased, red oval, and her eyelids were puffy. Ugh. How long had she been lying there? She checked her phone. Four o'clock. Wow, so definitely a few hours. When her stomach rumbled, she did a double take on her phone, this time noting the date.

Four o'clock the next day! Bloody hell.

Panic momentarily seized her before she yanked open the door and peered down the hallway. Five closed doors and an eerie quiet spread in one direction. Creepy.

Now what?

Screw it. She would just have to walk in on strangers until she found Layla and Zoey, assuming they were still in massages and not murdered in their sleep.

Oh, Zeus. Please don't let them be dead.

Swallowing back bile as her stomach churned, she opened the first door she came to with a shaking hand and put her left hand to her glasses.

"You can't be—"

Before the therapist could finish her sentence or whip out that scented lotus lotion, Madison stoned her. They could sort out later who to free. For now, she wasn't taking chances.

She pushed her glasses back up. "Layla?" she guessed, based on the dark hair.

"Hmm. What?" The actress lifted her head, looking over at Madison through bleary eyes. "Oh, no, did you not like your massage?"

How congenial was this woman that her concern was about Madison's massage when Madison had barged in on hers?

"I liked it so much that I spent over a day on the table. We all did." She entered the room and picked up Layla's clothes, glancing around as if some other threat might burst from the cupboard or the bowl of hot stones.

"What?" Layla pushed herself up slowly and gaped at the stoned therapist.

"Little hard to get up, isn't it? We need to get moving. We've been trapped here by the power of the lotus."

"The hell?" Layla's tone sharpened.

Madison passed Layla her clothes as the woman struggled to sit up. "Get dressed. I need to find Zoey. Watch your back. I don't know if the plan was just to keep us here indefinitely or keep us until they could ambush us."

"*Ohmygod.*" Layla's face paled.

"You good?" Every minute ticking by added to Madison's sobriety, so she assumed the same would be true for Layla.

"I'm fine. Go. Go make sure Zoey's OK."

Heart thudding, Madison raced to the next door. Barking reverberated at the end of the hall. Madison suspected Zephyr waited on the other side of the door marked EXIT. He would have to wait. She needed to make sure Zoey was safe first.

Without knocking, she barged in, the door banging against one wall. Zoey, who'd been on her back getting a scalp massage, bolted upright as she clutched at the sheet to keep it from falling.

"Move!" Madison barked.

Without hesitation, Zoey rolled to one side and landed on the floor with catlike agility. Madison dropped her glasses and stared at the massage therapist seated at the head of the bed. The woman's mouth stretched wide in surprise as her skin turned rock hard and gray.

Madison slipped her glasses back onto her nose.

Zoey stood, grasping the sheets. "You're going to tell me what the hell is going on, yeah? That was only the best massage of my life."

"And the longest. We've spent a day under the spell of the lotus flower."

Zoey's eyes widened. "The logo? Oh, shit."

Layla burst into the room. "You're OK?" She looked over at Zoey.

"Freaked out, but, yeah, OK."

Madison handed Zoey her clothes. "Look out for each other. I need to check on Zephyr."

"I heard barking. He's here?" Zoey asked. She leaned toward the stoned therapist and poked her with a tentative finger as though not believing the woman had been turned into a statue.

"I don't know how, but that's his bark." Madison raced down the hall, shoving down the bubbling terror at the realization she'd turned three people to stone.

Rex could turn them back, she reassured herself. No authorities needed to know. Glancing up and around, she didn't see any cameras in the hallway.

The door turned and opened easily. Of course, they didn't need to lock doors when everyone lingered in a drug-induced haze.

Wastin' away in Lotusville.

Lookin' for my lost boyfriend and dog.

Ugh. This was a mournful disaster ... not unlike the Jimmy

Buffett song. And Madison only had herself to blame. She'd been so careless not noticing the trap.

Zephyr burst through the doorway and spun in a circle at her feet, tail wagging fiercely.

She bent to pet him. "Good boy. Good boy. How long were you out there?"

The feel of his soft fur had a calming effect on her. She needed to slow down and think. The men must be here somewhere, because Zephyr was. His leash was still attached.

When she turned to look back down the hall, Zoey and Layla were checking the other rooms. Good thinking. They looked like quite the pair with Zoey's hands extended, ready to burn the face off any lotus-bearing masseuses, while Layla wielded a long vase over one shoulder like a baseball bat.

Madison looked at her phone—three calls and three texts. All from Rex. She called him and cursed when the phone went to voicemail. She tried Tyler next. No answer.

"All empty," Layla said when they finished sweeping the rooms. She lowered the vase as Zoey lowered her arms, and they walked to stand by Madison.

"No answer on Rex's or Tyler's phone, but Zephyr's here, so I'm guessing they are too," Madison said.

"Let's search the rest of this place," Zoey said.

Together, the three of them went through the exit door and into the brighter lights of the foyer.

Madison's head whipped right and left. Empty. Another door led to an unknown room. She considered the name of the massage clinic—*Relaxation Haven*. Did the door lead to employee offices or more customer rooms like a hot tub or sauna?

"What's behind door number one?" Layla said with a sneer, clearly still angry about the trance she'd been put into.

She started to march toward the door when Zoey threw out a

hand. "You can't send lightning through the building. Let me go first in case something dangerous is hiding in there."

"Fine," she huffed. "But I'm never leaving my weapons behind again. And for the record, I wouldn't mind using my fists on these freaks."

"Noted." Zoey reached for the door.

"Uh ...," Madison began.

Zoey hesitated. Madison cleared her throat. "I'm not at all one to rush into danger. But use of my power won't set off the sprinkler system or alert the fire department."

"Yeah." Zoey dropped her hand and looked up. "I don't see sprinklers, but I don't want to set the place on fire ... so beauty before brawn."

Madison eased forward, straightening her spine and raising her left hand, ready to drop her glasses if needed.

Beside her, Zephyr whined impatiently.

"Yes, yes." She opened the door.

They walked down a hallway with the sound of music in the distance. When they passed through a glass door, the room opened up into an expansive spa with several pools. Lounge chairs fanned out. One wall contained shelves of rolled towels.

Soothing piano and violin ensembles floated from speakers above. To the left, a rectangular pool with blue and gray tile held rippling water and Alexios floating on his back with his eyes closed. In the middle spanned a half-moon-shaped pool with a waterfall flowing down into the pool in front of a backdrop of staggered slate rocks. To the right gurgled a steaming hot tub where Rex and Tyler conversed with drinks in hand.

Something in Madison's chest eased at seeing the rest of the six safe and whole.

"Hey, Madison." Rex waved at her. "Why don't you join us?"

From a door to the left, a woman emerged—another employee with the same waxy face, pleasant yet flat eyes, and gray uniform. When she saw the trio of women, who were probably not expected to be out of their rooms and certainly not looking quite so furious, no longer under the lotus spell, the woman started to retreat.

Zephyr growled, hair on his neck stiffening upright.

Madison lowered her glasses. She wouldn't risk the employee running back and warning others. *If* there were others. The woman morphed from flesh to stone. The tray in her hand, which contained three glasses of purple liquid and pink ice cubes, faded to gray and the wisps of purple smoke wafting up from the drink vanished.

Rex stood up, swim shorts dripping with water. "Why did you do that?"

She had her glasses back up before she took in his expression. Rather than being frightened or incredulous, he was genuinely worried, as if he instantly accepted she must have a good reason for turning a woman, who by all appearances looked nonthreatening, into stone.

"You're all under a spell," Zoey said.

Alexios righted himself in the water and swam to the edge of the pool toward them, eyes wide in alarm.

"We were just hanging out until you finished your massages," Rex said.

"Don't drink another drop of those." Madison gestured to the drinks beside the hot tub. Because the men hadn't been slathered in lotion, yet had been bewitched, she suspected the magic sedative of the lotus was also in the drinks.

Rex and Tyler exited the water and reached for towels.

"They tried to drug us?" Tyler asked.

"They did drug us," Layla said.

"How long have you been in this room?" Madison asked.

Rex looked around as if searching for a clock on the wall. "At least an hour. We've gone in and out of all the pools while hanging out chatting."

Madison walked to him and held up her phone. "We've been here for over a day. The only reason I snapped out of it was that I heard Zephyr barking."

Alexios climbed a ladder out of the pool and reached for a towel. "Lotus," he said. "We have been under a spell."

"I think the massage lotion they used kept us sedated, and they did the same to you with the drinks," Madison said.

"Then I assume we're getting the hell out of here, right?" Tyler asked, briskly drying off.

"We need a minute to get changed," Rex said. "And I need to find my sword."

Madison nodded toward the woman turned to stone. "She's the fourth one I've turned to stone. I didn't want to take any chances that they could do something else to keep the spell going."

Rex pursed his lips. "Appreciate that. You did the right thing."

His words sent warmth through her. She hadn't realized she needed his blessing for her use of magic, but the approval eased a tightness in her throat.

Rex wrapped the towel around his waist. "I feel like such an idiot. We were so vulnerable."

"Let's just get the hell out of here, and lament later," Zoey said, looking around nervously, though Madison was sure she spared a glance at Alexios's half-naked form.

"What do we do about them?" Madison asked, gesturing at the stone statue.

"Let them be stoned," Layla said on a sneer. "Drugging people and keeping them against their will. I call bullshit. They need to pay the price."

Madison glanced at Layla, wondering what sort of past

trauma might be linked to that statement. They could unpack that later.

"I'm with Layla on this one," Tyler said. "Maybe with a little less vindictive undertone, but if we free them, we don't know what kind of backup they'll call for. I vote they remain in their immobile prisons for now."

"OK. That's settled," Rex said. "We'll get changed and get the hell out of here. Stay in pairs or triplets. No one goes anywhere alone. Back to the boat and the safety of Milopas."

REX STOOD on the deck and watched Athens grow smaller as they sailed away. Careless and downright stupid. All of them. They'd lost a day, and the situation could have been worse if Madison hadn't snapped out of her trance and stoned the employees. They were supposed to be six tough warriors. What did it say about them that they could be rendered immobile by a lotus flower? As self-appointed leader of the group, he keenly felt the weight of his failure.

Inside the captain's deck, shouting erupted.

An unnatural frustration stirred within him. On top of everything, now he had to play dad when adults with godlike powers decided to throw temper tantrums. Couldn't he have a moment's peace?

He stalked up the steps to find the entire crew in the captain's space with Layla at the wheel.

"Whose dumb idea was it to go into the spa in the first place?" Tyler demanded, looking at Layla as if he already knew the answer.

"Mine," she snapped back. "We've been training relentlessly and needed a break. I didn't know the damn place was a trap."

"A massage? Is this really the time for such luxuries?" Tyler asked.

"What the hell would you know about it? You can drop everything to go halfway around the world and rescue perfect strangers. Some of us have jobs. Some of us have agents and fans and other people's livelihoods depending on us. I have connections to maintain so that I have a life to go back to when this is over. I'm basically training to save the world while keeping a day job, so, yeah, I think a little pampering isn't too much to ask." As her anger flared, wind inside the cabin stirred.

Zoey slid closer to Layla as if preparing to defend her.

"You're unbelievable," Tyler snapped. As his cheeks reddened in anger, his face elongated and became covered in short, dark hair. His canines extended as his hands morphed into claws.

"Back off!" Zoey said to him. "You walked right into that spa, unsuspecting, same as us."

"To find the womenfolk," he said on a snarl.

"We didn't ask for your help," Layla said.

"Back off!" Zoey repeated.

"Make me." His voice was deadly low.

Alexios stepped forward as the sound of cold, scraping metal heralded the withdrawing of his sword from its sheath. Eyes hard, he took a stance beside Zoey, making his side known.

Flames danced on her fingertips as she held her hands at her side.

"You planning to burn me, Zoey?" Tyler glared at her, face partly shifted between half-man and half-wolf.

"Zoey!" Madison gasped. She put a hand on Tyler's arm as if to calm him, but he shook her off.

She stumbled back, which had Rex rushing to her side and seeing red.

"You need to calm the hell down," Madison yelled at the group in a tone that suggested she'd lost all semblance of calm.

Layla's eyes flashed as the wind in the room picked up speed, swirling hair and clothing and tossing loose papers.

Zephyr cowered in one corner as if sensing the room was about to detonate.

Everyone had lost their damned minds. Rex felt that swell of raw, unnatural anger again. He balled his fists, ready to join the fight.

Time slowed as he looked at each of his companions—Madison raising a hand to her glasses as if she meant to lower them and inflict her power; Tyler half-transformed beast between canine and man; Zoey ready to burn the next person who looked at her wrong; Layla with a storm brewing on her strained face and inside the room; and Alexios, the most rational of them all, with a sword drawn against his friends.

Rex thought of Athena's words:

The barrier grows weak, his power swells ...
    Six must stand where six once fought,
    With wisdom, strength, and courage wrought.

"Enough!" Rex boomed.

The room went silent and still, even as tension boiled beneath the surface.

"This isn't you. This isn't us. This is Kronos. Can you feel him? He's toying with our emotions, making us want to lash out and fight each other. Madison, you wouldn't stone your friends, but you're thinking of it now, right? Alexios? Drawing a sword against your fellow soldier? Never. Zoey, you wouldn't be so quick to flare your fire without a boost from the king of ill tempers."

As he spoke, Zoey's fire extinguished, Alexios sheathed his sword, Madison lowered her hand, and Tyler transformed back into man. Their faces held some mixture of shock, dismay, and shame.

"You're right," Tyler said. "I'm sorry, everyone."

Zoey sighed and stormed out of the captain's room saying, "This quest sucks."

"I'm sorry too," Layla said, voice a whisper.

Alexios stared down at his hands, looking lost. "He came at us when we were off the island and vulnerable. He used the frustration we all felt against us. Magnified it."

"Now we know he can play mind games," Rex said.

Madison leaned against him. "But not on the island, right? We just need to get back there."

"Working on it," Layla said.

I don't know, Rex didn't say. It seemed Kronos couldn't send any beasts there, but could he try to manipulate their emotions on Milopas?

I don't know.

CHAPTER

TWENTY

Madison sat around the campfire with the sullen group after the Athens expedition. Zephyr curled in a ball beside her chair. The six of them had been somber during the boat ride back to Milopas after their outbursts. They seemed to share their sense of failure in quiet misery.

Layla absently strummed a guitar she'd brought up from her boat as everyone stared into the flames of the fire. When Layla sang, Madison let herself be swept up in the words.

"Oh, city beneath the surf,
Where wise men dare not traverse,
And the demons never sleep,
Where no sun penetrates deep,
And the magic trident glows,
From the depths of fathoms below."

The song flowed beautifully and melancholically, with the ebb and flow like waves making it feel like a pirate's song.

"Beyond the gates of stone,
Where Hercules carved his throne,
The sea runs dark and wide,

With secrets the gods still hide.
No compass can lead you down,
To the lost city and crown.
Oh, city beneath the surf,
Where wise men dare not traverse,
And the demons never sleep,
Where no sun penetrates deep,
And the magic trident glows,
From the depths of fathoms below."

"I feel like such a fool," Zoey said when Layla strummed without singing.

"We all fell for the lotus trap," Tyler countered, his voice bitter with self-disgust.

"Including three of Odysseus's men," Alexios added. "And they lost nine days to the island."

Madison sighed. "That's a little comfort. Still feels like we should have known better."

"I don't know," Rex said. "We were on the lookout for more monsters—boarsharks and golden lions—not sinister massage parlors."

"We learn and we move on," Alexios said, seeming to have shucked off his earlier dismay at his own behavior.

Layla began singing again, and the group fell silent to listen.

"They say the bells still toll,
In halls of coral and gold,
Where kings once ruled the tide,
Before the sea swallowed their hide.
With whispers drifting forever,
The currents guard their treasure.
Oh, city beneath the surf,
Where wise men dare not traverse,
And the demons never sleep,
Where no sun penetrates deep,

And the magic trident glows,
From the depths of fathoms below.”

When she went back to strumming, Zoey told the group, “She wrote this one herself.”

Madison recalled hearing that the actress was also a singer and songwriter, but had never heard her perform. “It’s beautiful. Spiritual. I’ve never been to a concert. Any concert,” she clarified.

“Layla doesn’t do them,” Zoey said. “Her singing is personal. Family and close friends only. I’d never heard her play until we traveled on the yacht, heading to Milopas.”

“I’ve seen it in my dreams,
Lit soft by sapphire beams,
Statues of a thousand sunken years,
Holding anguished weeping tears.
And none return from the gloom,
To tell what waits in that tomb.

“Back to the chorus,” Layla interjected. “Everyone sing it.
“Oh, city beneath the surf,
Where wise men dare not traverse,
And the demons never sleep,
Where no sun penetrates deep,
And the magic trident glows,
From the depths of fathoms below.”

The deep voices added by the men made Madison feel as though she was aboard a wooden ship, rocking through the ocean and revering this city beneath the waves. The melancholy mood soothed into calm. Alexios was right. They learned from their mistakes and moved on.

“You wrote that?” Madison asked. “It’s beautiful in a sad and mysterious way.”

“Just some place I’ve dreamed about but never been. Not sure where it is or if I’d want to go there. I’ve never made sense of it.”

Layla wriggled her fingers and adjusted the guitar. "OK. Let's all sing an oldie but goodie."

She began to strum the melody for "Free Fallin'," and everyone sang along with the Tom Petty song until they were smiling with lighter hearts and eased minds.

❧ ❧ ❧ ❧ ❧ ❧ ❧

MADISON PULLED on her shoes and tied the laces. She worked her messy hair into a ponytail. She'd made love with Rex last night again, something wild and reckless and burning with the desire to feel alive.

They had been training hard this past week since Athens—the humiliation of the lotus encounter and Kronos's subsequent igniting of their tempers feeding their desire to keep the titan buried. Running, swimming, combat training. She was building toned muscles like she'd never had. Though she was still the slowest and lowest level in the holographic dojo, she'd accepted that everyone had different talents and her magical abilities made her a formidable team member. She'd proven that at the lotus spa.

"Hey, you stayed last night." Rex grinned at her, eyes still heavy with sleep, as he propped up in bed on one arm.

She looked at him through her dark glasses. "I couldn't move after we'd ravished each other like that."

"An apt word—ravished."

"Better than nice?"

He gave her a playful scowl. "That word is outlawed in this space."

She laughed and hugged him. "Rex, you're wonderful."

"That's what I like to hear," he said with a lopsided grin.

Pulling back and standing, she rumpled his hair with her fingers. "You're messy and impulsive and a little reckless."

He frowned. "Well, this interaction was headed in a different direction when it first started."

She laughed again, wondering if no other woman had told him his flaws. "You care, and you're an excellent leader. You are wonderful. And I love you."

"That's more ... wait. Come again?" He sat up straighter in bed with a look of panic in his eyes and slackness in his jaw.

She smiled, undeterred by his flustered gaping. Maybe that wasn't the reaction most women wanted, but she'd sprung the declaration on him after sex and after three weeks of knowing each other.

"I love you, Rex Alderman. Take as long as you need to wrap your head around it." She stepped forward, bent, and held his face in her hands. "I love you, and I never thought love like this would be possible." After kissing him, she dashed off to start her morning run.

With her bubbling energy, her feet moved swiftly. She had grown stronger in the weeks since coming to Milopas. She would grow stronger still before the Kronos showdown.

Grinning, she pictured Rex's panicked look. She'd flustered him, and their fearless leader didn't get rattled often.

She didn't need to hear the words back from him. It would be too soon for him anyway.

Today, she would train and give him time and space. Tonight was her turn to cook dinner. He knew where to find her if he wanted to talk, but if he needed more time to process, she'd give him that too.

***

"WHAT ARE YOU WORKING ON?" Madison asked Layla as she entered the kitchen. Having just finished her morning jog, Madison stretched as she talked.

"Had this urge for baklava," Layla said. "I asked Athena—or whoever is providing for us here—for all the ingredients, so I could make the dessert. And here we are." She gestured to the countertop full of said ingredients.

"Bow shooting later?" Madison asked.

"You know it. I like it."

"You're good at it."

"Thanks." Layla tipped her head as she spread out filo dough. "I was thinking of researching bows and coming up with a cool-looking one. Maybe if I ask nicely, Athena could have it made for me. Something sleek and classy."

"Oh, good idea. Perhaps she can scribe some magical runes to help with accuracy or deadliness."

Layla looked up at her from where she was sprinkling chopped pistachios in between layers of filo dough. "I hadn't thought of that. We're fighting a war of the gods using magic. Why not ask for a magical bow?" She smiled as if imagining new possibilities.

Madison leaned on the counter. "Over the years, I've given a lot of thought to what type of glasses I would want if I could design my own and they wouldn't cost me an arm and a leg. I've come up with some sketches and some ideas for materials, but I didn't have access to any of that before this island. Now that I have that, I've been thinking about asking Athena to make them and perhaps incorporating some type of woven magic." Madison still hadn't felt comfortable with the ask, so while she had brainstormed, she'd also dragged her feet on having them made.

"That's a great idea."

"Thanks. I would especially like to see the world for the color it is, not through tinted shades."

"I can see how that would be frustrating."

"On a separate topic, is Alexios making any progress with Zoey?" Madison asked.

"I'm not sure. She's focused on her training and the enormity of our task. As long as I've known her, she doesn't multitask."

"I suppose with his attentiveness and ever-adoring gaze, he's made his intentions known and she can decide if it's something she wants to entertain."

"How are you and Rex doing?" Layla asked. "I mean, if I had to gauge by the noises coming from your cabin at night, I'd say pretty good, but ... " She let the words drift off.

Madison dipped a finger into a drop of honey that had fallen on the countertop. She gave a sheepish smile. "Um. Sorry, not sorry?" She licked her finger before washing her hands in the sink.

Layla laughed. "It's fine. Find enjoyment where you can in the chaos of this thing called life."

"I told him I loved him," Madison blurted.

Layla stilled, holding another piece of filo dough. "You *what*?! You dropped the L-word and didn't even wait for a dramatic lightning strike or near-death moment? Who even *are* you?"

Madison grinned. "It just ... came out. No curses, no crumbling ruins—just him, me, and a quiet bedroom with morning light streaming between us."

Layla placed the dough layer into the dish with dramatic flair. "Ugh, that's disgustingly romantic. I was hoping for at least one monster-in-the-background moment. Maybe a harpy crashing the mood."

Madison chuckled. "Sorry to disappoint the actress. No harpies. Just feelings."

"Well." Layla sprinkled in cinnamon. "Now I have to finish this baklava. True love requires celebratory pastry. Wait. What did he say?"

Madison smirked. "He didn't know what to say, which is fine. I had no expectation of him declaring his love back to me. That's not how it's supposed to work anyway."

"Are you OK? That's a vulnerable place to put yourself."

"I'm OK. Great, in fact. Most of the time with Rex, I feel invincible. He needed to know how I felt, and I needed to say it out loud. So, mission accomplished."

"What if he doesn't say it back?" Layla's eyes widened. "No, that didn't sound right. I didn't mean—"

"It's fine. I understand that's a risk I took. I think he'll come around because I think what we have is tremendously special, but I won't hold it over his head or hold back my emotions just because I got there before he did."

CHAPTER

TWENTY-ONE

The day and evening passed in training, and Madison went to bed alone with Zephyr on his pillow nearby. She fell asleep confident Rex would find her tomorrow and keep the relationship progressing at whatever pace he was most comfortable.

The next morning, Madison woke to the sound of giggling children climbing into her bed. Rising sun cascaded through a window covered by sheer curtains.

"Elena! Ariana!" Madison scolded with humor in her voice.

"Mom! Dad! We want to make pancakes."

Rex groaned even as he rolled over with a smile. "Those must be *your* daughters. *My* daughters wouldn't disturb the sleeping bear."

"Yeah, teddy bear," Elena teased.

Rex let out a playful roar as he captured Elena in his embrace. She squealed and giggled as he tickled her. He had disheveled hair and a thick growth on his jaw, though not quite a beard. When he shot Madison an adoring smile, her heart warmed.

She pulled Ariana into a hug. "Pancakes, eh?"

"Yes!"

"OK. Downstairs. Go get out the ingredients. I'll be down in a minute."

The girls scurried down the stairs as Madison tossed off the covers.

Before she could stand, Rex pulled her back into bed. "Mmm. Love our Saturday mornings together."

She laughed as he buried his face in her neck. She loved the smell of him in the mornings. "I liked our Friday night, too."

"That was fun." He playfully scraped his teeth over her shoulder. "We should do that again. Tonight." He kissed the bare skin. "Or now."

Heat flushed through her. "Now, is pancakes."

He released her. "Tonight, then."

She stood and pulled on her robe, feeling the blissful contentment that was her life.

"Love you," he said.

"Love you too."

As Madison descended the stairs, she realized she didn't have her glasses on—hadn't since the kids came bounding into their room. Disorientation flooded her senses as her heart pounded wildly, making her stop and grip the railing.

Wait, she didn't have children. Then, she recalled the casual "I love you" Rex had tossed her way as if he said it every day. In reality, he'd never said that. She'd only just told him she loved him yesterday, she recalled, as she looked down at the ring on her left hand. She and Rex weren't married.

The surrounding stairway dimmed.

"You can have this future," an impossibly deep voice purred in something that sounded both worlds away and welling up from a deep cavern.

"An illusion." She wasn't living in some fictional house with her dream family. She was on a Greek island, where she'd lived for almost four weeks now, preparing to battle the worst homicidal creature the world had ever known.

"A potential," Kronos cooed.

She couldn't see the titan, but the bone-chilling sensation told her the voice belonged to him. Fear had her heart kicking faster. If only she could get a glimpse of him and see if her Medusa powers would work against him.

"I have the power to remove your curse," he added. "You can have the family you have always desired."

"I love you," Rex's voice echoed softly, followed by the sounds of Elena and Ariana giggling.

Madison's chest ached with the loss of something she had never had. Would never have. "You can't give that to me," she choked out, as her throat constricted. Her body shook, knees trembling, from some combination of fear and anger.

"I can. You need only accept my offer, and you will leave this island with Alderman by your side."

She believed him. Believed Kronos could give her the illusion he showed her. He could trap her in the illusion, trap Rex too, and she would know only blind, ignorant happiness. She only needed to accept the offer. One simple *yes* and this beautiful family would be hers. Guaranteed happiness.

Problem was, she didn't want the fantasy; she wanted the reality. Such a thing required the love and effort of two people, not the fantasy of one.

"You can't give what's not yours to give." Her voice was stronger now as raw fury had her blood pumping hot. "I don't accept, won't accept." Indignation boiled inside her that the titan had tried to exploit her weakness. He had made her feel that family, if only for a moment, but she would suffer the yearning and loss of a lifetime.

Kronos snarled. "I will never let you escape your prison of isolation! You will remain cursed and alone!" he boomed.

The ache in her heart erupted into an excruciating, penetrating cold, as if Kronos had driven an enormous icicle through her sternum. She fell to her knees, clutching her chest.

Bolting upright in bed, she grasped at her breastbone and gasped for air as tears streamed down her face. She clawed away her nightgown, but, in the dim morning sun, nothing protruded from her chest. Moving her hand to her head, she worked to slow her breathing down from the fast, panicked state it had been in.

The pain slowly ebbed, leaving a hollow desolation in its place. She sank back into bed and sobbed.

❧❧❧❧❧❧❧

WHEN MADISON FOUND HER COMPOSURE, she went to the kitchen and started on breakfast—chopping onions and peppers and whisking eggs. For once, she was grateful for the dark glasses. No one could see her red-rimmed eyes.

"What'd the eggs do to you?" Zoey asked, humor in her tone as she approached.

"Huh?" Madison looked down at the frothy, beaten eggs and whisk in her hands.

Layla poured a cup of coffee from the batch Madison had brewed as Zoey walked to the refrigerator.

"You are butchering those eggs," Zoey added.

Madison cleared her throat and set aside the whisk. Pouring the eggs into the frying pan, she stirred them thoughtfully. She considered the titan's threat about her prison of isolation. She wasn't alone any longer. She was surrounded by friends who would and could lend sympathetic ears.

"Kronos visited me in my dreams," she said.

"Oh, shit." Zoey fumbled getting the carafe of orange juice as she pulled it out of the fridge.

Layla dropped into the chair at the kitchen counter, her full attention on Madison, coffee cup in hand. "Tell us what happened."

Madison relayed her nightmare to the women. "I'm seriously pissed," she added after the details were shared. "He fights dirty." She pointed the spatula at them. "Toying with emotions like that. Why are you smirking?"

Zoey, glass of orange juice in hand and joining Layla at the counter, shifted her weight, expression having changed from worry to appreciation. "He underestimated you. I'll bet he thought you would take the bait. Worst case, he probably thought you'd run screaming in fear at his display of power. Instead, you're mad and ready for retaliation."

Madison was grateful for Zoey's admiration of her fighting spirit. A weight lifted knowing she'd had the courage to turn him down. She'd felt so hollowed out by the experience that she hadn't considered how she'd basically flipped Kronos the bird— before, of course, he plunged an imaginary icicle into her chest. Physical pain, as if the emotional suffering hadn't been enough.

"Now we know he can come at us sideways even on the island." Layla snatched a piece of bacon and munched.

"Will you tell Rex?" Zoey asked.

"I don't know what to say. He's spooked enough from hearing I love him. Has barely spoken to me since I said those words—though I fully intend to give him processing time. But what do you imagine he'd feel if I told him I dreamt we had two beautiful girls? And that dream was my version of a perfect life?" She placed a finished omelet in front of Zoey, then placed the butt of her palm against her breastbone where her chest ached. "And they weren't cursed. They were adorable little darlings who didn't turn things to stone."

"How do you suppose Kronos would have delivered on such a promise?" Layla asked.

"I thought he meant to trap me in the fantasy world. He certainly made it real enough."

"Trap Rex in the fantasy with you?"

"I think so." Madison turned, started on another omelet. "Maybe. But I don't want to force him into a relationship."

"Good thing you put the kung fu on Kronos's wazoo," Zoey said around a bite of omelet.

Madison rolled her eyes as her lips quirked. "We're just resorting to rhymes now?" Leave it to her new best friends to make her feel better after tangoing with a titan. "I want to marry Rex someday. He has to want that too."

"In all seriousness, you da bomb," Layla added.

"Thanks."

"Who da bomb?" Rex asked, entering the kitchen and looking fresh from a morning run.

Madison turned back to the eggs, avoiding eye contact so he wouldn't see her recent distress. He couldn't see her eyes, but she was sure the rest of her face would show the strain from last night's encounter. She would tell him when she thought the news would be better received.

He sidled up to her and hugged her back, burying his face in her neck. "Must be whoever is making this amazing breakfast."

"Yeah, you hungry?" She slid Layla's omelet out of the pan, onto a plate, and placed it in front of Layla.

"Hey, you OK?" Rex asked her, spinning her toward him.

Once again, she was glad she could hide her eyes behind her dark glasses. Now if she could just brush off the terrible night. She wanted to avoid questions about it.

"She didn't sleep well," Layla said, covering for her.

When Rex looked at Layla, Madison shot her a grateful look, though she probably couldn't tell.

I have the power to remove your curse.

Damn. She hated Kronos and how he'd baited her.

"I'll feel better when I start exercising," she told Rex.

She would tell him. She just needed to figure out how.

᯽᯽᯽᯽᯽᯽᯽

THAT EVENING, Rex sat staring at the fire, thinking about Madison. She'd declared her love, then distanced herself from him for the next three days. Busy training, she claimed. How was that love? Was she waiting to hear the words back? Shouldn't he say them when he was damn well ready? Maybe he should give her the benefit of the doubt that she was giving him space to figure out how he felt.

He shifted in his chair, body sore from a particularly hard training day. He'd advanced two levels but used several lives trying. Kharon's sword he'd picked up in Athens served him well, though. He felt more powerful with it.

When Tyler and Alexios approached, he nodded in acknowledgment. The three women were in the living room, watching a rom-com.

"Beer," Tyler said.

Rex took the beverage offered. "Thanks."

The other men plopped into empty seats.

"Training goes well," Alexios commented.

"Yeah. That Zoey's a tenacious one," Rex said.

"She's a warrior, like me." His voice was filled with awe and respect.

"And filled with fire."

"Literally and figuratively." Tyler tipped his beer back and drank.

"What about you and Layla?" Rex asked before taking a swig of beer. "Any resolution?"

"She'll come around. Hasn't been interested in talking to me, but we'll hash out the past eventually."

Pain lurked beneath Tyler's nonchalant demeanor. He would have to decide if he wanted to address those feelings while they "hashed out the past."

As for Rex, he could use a little advice. He shifted his weight in his chair. "Madison wants to marry me."

When Rex had walked in on the women talking in the kitchen, he'd first overheard Madison say, "*I want to marry Rex someday. He has to want that too.*"

She had said she loved him, and already she talked about marriage? They'd known each other for just over a month.

"Congratulations!" Alexios said with a beaming smile, making Rex recall when Alexios had told him he had a wife back in Madison's apartment. He'd apparently been on to something.

Tyler stopped the bottle halfway to his lips and turned to stare at Rex. "Uh. What do you want?"

Rex took another swig. "Hell if I know. I thought I just wanted a fling." *Liar,* his conscience told him. He'd known she was more than that the first time he'd touched her. "She's smart and beautiful. Sexy as hell. We both need to burn off the stress of the weight of the world on our shoulders. She's spectacular. One in a million. But marriage? I've never thought about marriage with anyone. Wasn't part of my future plans."

"So you said no?" Alexios asked, face falling and disappointment etched around his mouth.

Rex rubbed his neck. "She didn't actually ask me." He cleared his throat. "She just told me she loves me, and later I overheard her telling Layla and Zoey that she wants to marry me."

"Sounds like you have permission to ask her," Tyler said, tone casual as if they were talking about sports and not commitments. "Also sounds like she isn't pressuring you or placing time limits."

"Yeah, I guess." Rex recalled how happy she'd looked just to tell him her feelings even as he'd sat dumbfounded until she jogged off. Not one of his better moments.

"What will you do?" Alexios asked, leaning forward, the fire-light illuminating his curious expression.

"I don't know, man."

"Question is, what do you want?" Tyler asked again.

"Don't know that either," Rex said miserably. He didn't want to disappoint Madison, but that wasn't a reason to make promises he was unprepared to fulfill.

Tyler crossed one ankle over his knee as he raised his beer and pointed a finger at Rex. "How about this ... picture your life ten years from now. Is she with you?"

Rex let the images flip through his mind—hunting treasure in Peru, plane flights to Dubai, morning coffee in Istanbul, walking along a beach in Monterey. "Huh. I'll be damned."

Madison was by his side in each of those.

Tyler lowered his arm and gave a quick nod of his head. "Guess you have your answer."

CHAPTER
TWENTY-TWO

Rex crouched over the ancient stone tablet, his fingers tracing the grooves of the inscribed symbols, a mix of Greek letters and strange pictographs. He recognized the Linear B script, a rare writing system used by the Mycenaeans.

Instinct took over as he sketched the symbols into his smart phone with a stylus, breaking them into phonetic clusters and matching them to Greek root words. A pattern emerged: Each symbol correlated with a constellation, forming a celestial map. Rex pulled up a star chart app, and mentally aligning the symbols with real astronomical positions. Orion. Lyra. Sagittarius.

Then it clicked—the constellations corresponded to numbers in an ancient Greek alphanumeric cipher. He scrawled the numbers on the ground: 7-1-9-3-4.

Seven steps forward. One step right. Nine back. Three left. Four forward.

Heart pounding with the thrill of the discovery to come, he followed the sequence through the ruined temple, his breath misting in the cold, stale air. As he took the last step, a section of the stone floor sank beneath his weight. His heart kicked up another notch in excitement and anticipation. With a deep rumble, a hidden chamber revealed itself.

Rex stepped into an expansive room and held his lantern high to cast light farther. The smell of dust and metal surrounded him. Walls were lined with treasures of past civilizations—jewel-encrusted goblets, gilded shields, silvered spears, and helmets that still gleamed despite the passage of millennia. But at the heart of the hoard, resting on an ornate marble pedestal, was the true prize.

The golden bow of Apollo.

His mouth went dry. The sleek, impossibly smooth, metallic frame rippled with ribbons of celestial gold. The bowstring seemed to hum with power, as if strung from the threads of the sun itself. The legends claimed Apollo himself had crafted it, a weapon that could strike with the force of divine light, turning arrows into searing bolts of fire.

Rex reached for the bow—

And the chamber shuddered. The light flickered.

A voice, deep as the earth's core, laughed. "You would take it so easily?"

Freezing where he stood, Rex's blood iced with sudden realization. This was a dream. This was no temple, no real discovery.

And Kronos was watching.

This isn't real. I'm on a Greek island with five other Olympian hybrids, Rex thought.

"Riches beyond belief," a deep voice filled the air.

Taking a hard swallow, Rex looked around at the treasure trove—a lifetime of fortune and fame.

The voice continued. "A relationship will tie you down. Chain you to mediocrity. A family will take all of your time and energy. Resources better spent on escapades to find lost treasures."

Rex straightened and glanced around the room again. "This is everything I've ever wanted. The big score."

He felt the truth in the words he spoke. And the hollowness.

"It can all be yours. And more," Kronos said.

Not without a price, Rex knew. "In exchange for?"

"Start your quest for your dream come true now. I know where the treasure is. Leave the island at daybreak and travel to the ruins of Delphi. There, you will receive further instructions."

"You want me to abandon my friends?" Rex ground his teeth together.

"You have bequeathed them your tears. What more should you sacrifice for them? And the woman? She will confine you. Suffocate you. Probably even accidentally turn you to stone."

The image of Madison on the boat when all of them were arguing popped into his head. Mouth hard in anger and determination, she'd reached up to lower her glasses. Rex shook his head and stumbled back, blinking to look around at the golden treasures.

The world twisted. The walls dissolved into mist. The golden statues, chests of precious gems, and priceless works of art faded to gray as they turned to bland stone—the same way living creatures metamorphosed under Madison's stare.

A cold squeezed Rex's heart as unseen chains wrapped around him. The frigid cables tightened until breathing became challenging.

"What say you, adventurer?" Kronos rumbled.

"No." He heaved out the word. "You can keep your offer in hell right along with the rest of you." Rex struggled against the invisible restraints as icy fear coursed through his veins. "This isn't real. You can't do this."

A vicious laugh echoed around him.

Rex's breaths came in short gasps as black dots danced before his eyes. Any tighter and his ribs would start snapping. He thought about crying out for help, but would anyone hear him?

He considered the magic of the island. There was someone who might hear. "In the name of Athena, I banish thee!"

Rex bolted upright in his bed, the room around him spinning as he fought to orient himself. Alone in bed. Gray sky told him it was barely morning on Milopas. A tranquil salty breeze brushed his senses even as the pain from the chains still ghosted his muscles and bones.

Panting and fighting off panic, he threw off the covers and dashed to Madison's quarters. His bare feet thundered swiftly over the cold stone paving.

"Madison?" Jetting through her entryway, he sped past her living room and opened the door to her bedroom. "Madison?" His terrified voice sounded foreign to his own ears.

Bolting up, she reached for her sunglasses. "What? What's wrong?"

"You're OK?" He sat beside her, placing his hands on her shoulders and needing to feel her solid and safe. His thundering heart slowed, no longer threatening to burst out of his chest.

She put her glasses on. "I'm fine. I mean, you've got my heart racing like Apollo's chariot, but aside from that, I'm fine. Whose house is on fire?"

"No one." He dropped his hands, relieved she wasn't hurt. "No one. I had a dream." He scrubbed a hand over his face. "A nightmare from Kronos. I was scared you may have had one too."

She pulled the covers up to her chin. "Not tonight," she said in a small voice.

"Not—?" He leaned back. "What does that mean?"

"You tell me yours first."

"Why? What happened?" he snapped.

"It's personal," she said, her speech sounding fragile as she shrank further back from him.

"You claim to love me. How can you exclude me from something personal?" He stood and paced, worry spiking straight into irritation.

She bristled. "I'm a little new at this love thing. I'm still figuring out how it works. You first."

On a hunch, he asked, "You told Layla and Zoey?"

"Mine was an issue women would understand."

He rubbed his neck, struggling to find calm and balance.

"It hurt. Emotionally," Madison added. "As Kronos intended. I wasn't sure if sharing would drive a wedge between us."

"Seems it already has." Rex glared at her.

Her shoulders dropped slightly. "You're right. I should have shared despite my pride."

Damn. Kronos had hurt her. Something deeply personal, apparently. Rex wanted her to feel comfortable telling him anything, but then she'd told him she loved him and he'd gone momentarily catatonic so maybe he hadn't proven he could handle anything.

Frustrated but thankful she was unharmed, he sighed and sat back down on the edge of her bed. "Kronos entered my dream. He promised me the archaeological find of the century. I only needed to abandon my friends." He closed his eyes and saw the fortune all over again. He'd nearly touched the gleaming bow. "The imagery was so real, as were the suffocating chains he wrapped around me when I didn't leap at the opportunity."

"You said no?"

He stared at her. "Madison, of course I said no."

She shrank back again at his harsh retort.

Baffled and offended that she would think otherwise, his voice hardened. "I'm in this with you. All of us are in this together. Stopping Kronos is nonnegotiable." Softer now, he added, "I would never abandon you."

She nodded, still looking sullen. "He promised me a life with you. A life free of my curse." She fidgeted with the edge of the blanket. "We had two beautiful daughters, Elena and Ariana, and we were spending a Saturday morning together. We planned to make pancakes together. It felt real—this family I've never known. So much love and happiness."

Rex's mouth had gone lax. Madison tried to mask the pain in her voice, but he'd heard it. Odd thing was, that vision appealed to him more than the fortune Kronos had shown him. What if Kronos had promised Rex *happiness for Madison*? That would have been harder for him to turn down. Rex would bet the selfish titan would never have considered tempting someone with a better life for someone else.

"It was just fantasy," she added, voice trembling.

"Madison." Rex pulled her into his arms.

She hugged him back, tight.

"He hurt you," Rex said.

"Um, yeah." She sniffed. "Same as you with the pain."

Rex swore. "I meant the emotional pain. But I hate him for both." He pulled back and wiped tears from her cheeks.

"Chains?" he asked, not wanting to envision her as Kronos's captive.

"Uh, no. Felt like something sharp and invisible straight through the heart."

"You're well now?" He moved his hands to rest on her upper arms.

She nodded. "Were you tempted?" she asked. "Even for a moment by the riches?"

"No. I was pissed he thought I could be bought. I—"

"I was tempted. The dream was so real." Her voice sounded small and fragile once again. "They were beautiful daughters. No scary Medusa eyes. I didn't realize until then that part of me fears passing this curse to them should I ever brave having children."

"Oh, Madison." Leaning in, he kissed her lips softly. "How did you turn down such an offer?"

"Imaginary Rex wasn't *choosing* to be with me." Her tone grew stronger and hardened. "I want the messy reality and free will. I want you worried one minute and mad as hell the next, holding me accountable for not trusting you with my pain, like you just did." She reached up, placed her hands on his cheeks. "I don't want a perfectly fabricated fantasy."

"You're amazing. You know that?" he asked.

"I have my moments." She gave him a light peck on the lips before dropping her hands.

"When did Kronos tempt you?"

"The night after I said I loved you." Her voice splintered with hesitation.

Feeling a bone-deep sadness for her, he took her hand. "But you said no, too."

She wiped under her glasses. "It wasn't real. As much as I wanted it to be real, it wasn't."

Rex pulled her into his arms. "This is why you pulled away from me?"

"I was afraid because I was tempted. He went straight to my weakness. Rex, I would never take away your choice, your free will, to have what I want."

He tucked her head under his chin. "He underestimated you. Underestimated both of us."

After giving her one more squeeze, he pulled back so she could look into his eyes—even if he couldn't see hers. "No more secrets?"

"Yeah. No more secrets." She nodded.

She seemed remorseful enough; maybe he shouldn't push, but he wanted to reinforce another reason her silence was dangerous. "Everyone in the group needs to know what happened. Everyone has a right to know Kronos can reach us through our dreams."

Her mouth fell open. "Oh, bullocks. You're right. I didn't think how I should have warned everyone. That was selfish of me."

Rubbing soothing hands up her arms, he said, "Not selfish. He violated your thoughts and used personal information against you. That's a vulnerable thing to share, especially when you're not used to sharing."

She snorted. "You shared. Ran right over here and shared."

He smirked. "I ran over here because I worried he was doing the same thing to you at that very moment. The weakness he exploited in me isn't a secret—nothing personal. I'm a treasure hunter, plain and simple."

She reached up and placed a hand on his cheek, giving him an adoring smile. "Not so plain, and not so simple." Leaning forward, she planted a soft, sweet kiss on his lips. "Let's tell the others."

⌐⌐⌐⌐⌐⌐⌐

THE GROUP GATHERED around the firepit under the morning sun. The fire burned lower during the day but would spring to life from sundown to sunup. Madison adjusted her glasses, still emotionally raw from her discussion with Rex. He'd called the meeting because the team needed to know about Kronos's ability to infiltrate dreams, tempt, and inflict pain. He was right.

"Rex, you've got the floor," Tyler said.

Rex nodded and leaned forward, the serious expression on his face made more severe by the long shadows of the rising sun. "I had a very vivid, very disturbing dream last night that I believe Kronos instigated. Madison had one also."

Both Layla and Zoey shot looks at Madison, who felt her cheeks redden.

Rex continued, "Kronos gave me a sneak peek into what I could have if I quit the quest."

"Quit? Not join forces?" Tyler asked.

Layla scoffed. "I doubt the titan cares about help from human peons."

"What did he offer you?" Alexios asked, eyes narrowed, as he rested a hand on Zephyr's head, who was making the rounds to meet his daily quota of affectionate pats.

"The archaeological find of a lifetime. And the fortune and fame that comes with such a discovery."

"That's it?" Zoey asked.

"When I turned him down, he wrapped me in chains and squeezed so hard I thought I'd burst. That's when I woke up."

"He hurt you?" Alexios asked.

"Just pain with no obvious injuries."

Madison shuddered.

"But this is good, right?" Zoey began. "Not the pain part, but if Kronos is coming after us—offering gifts for us to quit—then he thinks we're a threat."

Alexios nodded.

"What did he offer you?" Tyler asked Madison.

She stiffened but spoke clearly as she addressed the group. "A family I'll never have. My curse lifted to wake up beside my husband every morning." She tilted her head toward Rex. "And our two beautiful children."

Tyler's eyebrows shot up. "Kronos is a cold bastard."

"I need a moment." Madison stood and hurried away, chest aching. Why couldn't she let it go? Why did it hurt to retell it, relive it?

Before she reached her quarters, muscular arms wrapped around her. Rex spun her into his arms. She hugged him tight, and the aching loneliness ebbed.

"I'm sorry. I need a minute."

"Don't worry about it. Take a minute. Take ten." He didn't let go.

After several moments, he shifted their position so he could kiss her.

When they broke the kiss, she grinned up at him. "Kisses really do make boo-boos better."

He chuckled. "Come back to the group, will you? I want to share how we can kick him out of our dreams."

She nodded. As he stepped back, he slid his hand into hers and led them back to the square. From the trailing conversation, Madison suspected Layla and Zoey were telling Tyler and Alexios about the rest of Madison's dream—the icicle through the heart.

"I wish we could punch him in the chest," Tyler said.

"We will," Rex said. "When we shut down the portal he's trying to tear open, we'll hurt him. But for now, be on guard."

Madison said, "I think he can't physically hurt us while we're on the island, or none of his creatures can, so he's lashing out any way he can."

"Fabulous," Layla said. "One more thing to lose sleep over."

"Maybe not. I may have found a kill switch," Rex said. "I asked Athena for help, and that's when Kronos released me. I don't know if she did something or if he can only hold the illusion for so long, but it's worth remembering in case he comes for any of you."

"Swell. Good chat," Tyler said, standing. "Soldiers gotta train."

"Time for drills," Alexios agreed, giving Zephyr a final rub behind the ears.

"Are we soldiers?" Layla snapped. "Or are we just pawns in the gods' games?"

TWENTY-THREE

Rex knocked on the entrance to Madison's cabin.

"Come in."

When he entered, she was standing near the bed wearing only a midriff t-shirt and panties. She'd pulled the covers back, suggesting she'd planned on going to bed when he'd interrupted.

"Can I join you for the night?" he asked.

"Yes, of course. I'd like that." She crawled onto the bed and under the covers. She traded her dark glasses for her silk eye cover.

He took off his shirt and pants and joined her, sidling up close and trailing a hand over her hip. He pressed his lips to hers for a slow kiss.

When they broke, she said, "I am sorry for not telling you about the dream. I feared your reaction."

"I'm disappointed you didn't feel you could confide in me about this, but I'm not exactly an open book. I can't fault you too much, or that would make me a hypocrite. From now on, no secrets."

"No secrets," she repeated the promise from earlier in the day.

"Are you OK?" If he could see her eyes, he'd know. But with them covered, always covered, he couldn't be sure.

"After talking to Layla and Zoey and then you, yeah, I'm fine. Does my version of a perfect life scare you?"

"I'm scared because I don't like the thought of him invading your dreams and hurting you. I'm not scared knowing marriage and a family are some of your deepest desires."

She cocked her head to one side.

"OK, a little scared," he amended. "I'm relieved you turned him down, but you're strong like that. I'm not sure if he planned to change me or copy me. I don't want to be zombie Rex in your fantasy, and I sure as hell don't want to imagine you procreating with my Kronos-made clone." He rested a hand on her hip and teased her lacy underwear between his fingertips. "I'd probably go into a jealous rage and kill the copy. That would totally mess up your plans."

Madison chuckled. "I don't want a zombie or a copy. Only the real guy. Flaws and all."

"Close your eyes," he said. He took the cover off her eyes and slid it over his. "Only fair," he said. "Wait. Flaws? What flaws? I have no flaws."

He rolled her on top of him as she laughed. Stretching her arms above her head with his hands, he slid her shirt off, guided by the feel of skin and fabric.

"Well, humility sure isn't one of them," she said with what sounded like a grin on her lips.

Naked. Skin to skin. The blindfold seemed to heighten the sensation of her body against his. He imagined her beautiful smile beaming down at him, and he was instantly ready for her. She smelled of warm vanilla. Leaning back, he let himself enjoy her dancing touch and fluttering lips.

When she worked her way lower, he sucked in a sharp breath.

He could feel the devious smile in the kisses she pressed against his lower abdomen before her mouth tipped him into blissful oblivion.

𝍠𝍠𝍠𝍠𝍠𝍠𝍠

Sunlight glinted off steel as the clash of swords rang out. Rex and Tyler circled Alexios, who stood tall and barefoot in the sand, his bronzed arms steady, his eyes sharp and amused.

Rex wiped sweat from his brow, noting the Greek was barely breathing heavy. Six weeks into training and the two of them still couldn't beat Alexios.

Rex dodged a swing. "So, college in the early 2000s. Top five moments—go!"

Tyler parried. "Easy. One—skipping class for Halo tournaments."

"Two—free pizza at literally every campus event," Rex added.

Tyler swung, sneakers scuffing along the stone pavers. "Three—burning mixed music CDs for your crush."

Alexios blocked and frowned in confusion. "You set fire to your songs?"

Tyler laughed. "No, man—'burning' means copying music. We were pirates," he joked.

"You still are," Alexios deadpanned before striking with a feint.

Blocking it with a jarring clash of metal, Rex grinned. "Four—dorm parties. Hardly a care in the world on those nights. Booze and babes."

"And five—realizing your degree didn't prepare you for literal sword fights." Tyler stumbled back to avoid Alexios's next swing.

Cocking his head to one side, Alexios twirled his blade. "Your higher learning sounds deeply inefficient."

Tyler wiped sweat from his brow using the bottom half of his t-shirt. "OK, now you. Top things you'll do when we defeat Kronos and you're free to pursue your own interests."

Without hesitation, Alexios said, "One—ride a horse again. Just for the thrill."

Rex said, "Good start."

Alexios blocked his next swing, glinting metal flashing and colliding. "Two—visit the ruins of Sparta. Bury some ghosts."

Tyler nodded, circling Alexios. "Yeah, I get that."

"Three—see the world. The *new* world. I have fought for emperors and gods. Soon I will live for myself."

They paused and lowered their swords. For a moment, the sound of waves and wind was all that filled the space.

Rex clapped him on the shoulder. "Sounds like a hell of a plan."

Tyler smirked. "Just promise you'll wear a Hawaiian shirt at least once. For the experience."

Raising his blade with a challenge in his eye, Alexios said, "I'll consider it ... if you survive this next round." With a shout, he lunged and training resumed, steel against steel, laughter echoing between strikes.

MADISON LICKED her lips and inhaled the salty breeze as warm sand spread between her toes. She jumped and spiked the volleyball down into Alexios who blocked the incoming projectile but couldn't keep it in play. Rex and Layla gave her high fives as a zing of accomplishment zipped through her. On the other side of the net, Tyler slapped Alexios on the shoulder in a "we'll-win-the-next-point" gesture of encouragement. Zoey picked up the ball to serve.

Zephyr had found a spot in the shade for a nap and away from the shuffling feet and flying sand of the vigorous volleyball match.

In much-needed decompression, the team had taken the day off from training. The toll of the quest hanging over them with no clear timeline, the threat Kronos might invade their dreams, and the relentless training where failure wasn't an option made tempers short.

When they finished the game, they gathered under a large tent to eat gyros and drink lightly sweetened lemonade.

"Next time, we'll have a javelin-throwing contest," Alexios said, a small pout in his tone at having lost the volleyball game.

"You mean a competition you know you're superior at," Rex scoffed. "Not likely."

"Pickleball tournament," Layla said. "There's plenty of room on the training platform for a court. We can have a round-robin of singles and doubles."

"What's the plan tonight?" Zoey asked. "Another *Star Wars*?"

"We finished the first six," Alexios said. "Now we have the ones with Rey to watch."

"As she is the ultimate female badass, I may watch those with you. Unless, oh, is that guy time?" She bit into her gyro and a blob of tzatziki sauce fell out the other end.

"Not at all," Tyler said. "Anyone can join."

"After *Star Wars*, we need a zombie apocalypse movie binge," Zoey said.

"Yes. I will partake in that." Alexios took a sip of his lemonade. "I like the Greek parallels in the *Star Wars* movies."

"Greek parallels?" Madison asked, puzzled.

He nodded. "Many parallels. The hero's quest for certain. Luke Skywalker, unaware of his true parentage, is called to adventure by Obi-Wan, like we are by Athena. He faces trials, gains mentors, and confronts darkness—internal and external."

"Mentors," Madison considered, picking out a fresh cucumber slice from her sandwich and eating it. "Obi-Wan Kenobi and Yoda are like Athena to Odysseus or Chiron to Achilles."

Rex nodded. "The father conflict is another parallel. Luke and Vader parallel Oedipus and Laius—the tension between father and son, the unknowable past, and the struggle to reconcile identity and legacy are deeply mythic." He added tzatziki sauce to his gyro and took a bite.

"Tragic downfalls," Alexios added.

"Plenty of that in the movies and myths," Layla grumbled, eating her gyro with a fork as a salad without the pita bread.

Alexios continued, "Anakin Skywalker to Darth Vader follows a tragic arc similar to Achilles or Ajax. A powerful warrior undone by flaws—pride, fear, anger. His redemption mirrors themes of catharsis and fate versus free will."

"Then, of course, are the mythical creatures and epic battles." Zoey, halfway through her sandwich, licked sauce off her finger. "Strange species, like space worms on asteroids."

Tyler gulped down lemonade after a bite of gyro. "Charybdis from Greek mythology and the Sarlacc from *Star Wars*. They both devour from below. A massive sea monster that swallows ships whole versus a giant, sand-dwelling creature with a gaping maw and rows of teeth, hidden in the Great Pit of Carkoon on Tatooine."

"Seriously?" Layla's face fell as the fork in her hand drooped. "Tell me I'm not losing my yacht to Charybdis."

"Only if you sail through the Strait of Messina," Tyler said. "At least, that's where it is in Greek mythology."

Alexios added, "The Death Star can even be viewed as a modern labyrinth—a place of peril with a central confrontation."

"Pause," Madison interjected. She didn't want to think about monster whirlpools filled with razor-sharp teeth and monster mazes filled with traps. "This is the fun zone. Somehow, movie talk circled us right back around to the quest. New topic. If you could teleport to any place in the world right now, where would it be?"

"Iceland," Tyler said. "Always wanted to see the hot springs."

"Sedona," Layla said. "Amazing spa retreats—none with lotus flowers. Sunrise yoga followed by a three-mile hike followed by an eighty-minute massage. Evening wind down working on my screenplay."

"You're a writer also?" Madison asked.

Layla shrugged. "I have ideas. Where would you go?"

"Tour of all of Greece. The culture, the history, the food." She looked at Rex.

"I'd like Greece, if you're up for company."

"I'd like your company." She smiled, sipping her lemonade and thinking the travel could be romantic with Rex at her side and revealing points of interest the way he had on their brief tour of Athens.

"After, we'll visit Transylvania. See what trouble we can get up to excavating some ruins." He gave her lopsided grin.

Madison chuckled. "I'm intrigued."

"Zoey?" Rex asked.

She wiped her mouth with a napkin. "Honestly—all of you and this place have been the closest to something like home I've ever had. Not to trample on the light topic, but there isn't a place I'd rather be. Doomsday quest and all."

"Well said." Madison raised her glass, grateful for her glasses so the threatening tears couldn't be seen. She'd felt the sense of family bonding between the group and was pleased to know she wasn't the only one. "Alexios?"

"At the risk of being unoriginal, I would echo everyone's desires." He set down his half-eaten sandwich. "I want to see all the places you do, including staying right here because it feels like family." He glanced at Zoey and then Layla. "Including this spa you speak of." He looked at Rex and Madison. "Including modern Greece, though not as a third wheel—as you call it. And including

Iceland. There is no place I do not want to go ... except perhaps upstate New York. I have seen enough of that."

Madison laughed, and Alexios grinned.

"Let's make a pact," Rex said. "When this is over, we set a date and once a year, we all meet back here at Milopas for a few days. We'll drink to memories and see what new places life's journey has taken us."

TWENTY-FOUR

After dinner, they sat around the fire. Rex, Tyler, and Zoey drank beer while Layla, Madison, and Alexios had wine. Rex, Tyler, and Alexios discussed fishing off the shore tomorrow. Zoey asked Layla if she would play the guitar for the crew. When Layla agreed, Zoey bounded up to fetch the instrument.

Another day had passed in over six weeks of training with the usual scrapes, aches, and holographic beheadings—sometimes Madison's and sometimes the virtual monsters she fought. Today, she'd run three miles, swum one, battled a Cerberus, and made the group dinner. Her muscles would be sore and aching again tomorrow. She moved faster and stronger every day and pushed herself a little harder in training. Even though she was still eons behind the others, she took fewer injuries during the simulator, albeit advancement in rank was slow. While the wounds inflicted by the holograms weren't real, the pain sure as hell was. When she fought, she never left the holographic training circle until she had secured victory.

You died in battle, warrior. You failed your quest.

She was damn tired of hearing those words, too.

She would continue to improve because letting her teammates down simply wasn't an option.

Every few nights, she and Rex spent the evening in each other's bed, making love until exhaustion swept them into slumber. Neither of them had further visits from the titan.

When Zoey returned, Layla took the guitar and leaned forward in her seat. Strumming the instrument, she took a moment to make some tuning adjustments. She played Ben King's "Stand by Me." Her voice carried melodically over the crackle of the fire. She had the perfect pitch and silky voice of an angel.

Madison glanced at Tyler, who looked entranced though not surprised, making Madison wonder if he'd heard Layla's beautiful singing from the past they shared.

When the song finished, the group remained silent.

"That was lovely," Madison said.

"A bit old for this crowd, probably," Layla said.

"It's a classic," Tyler said. "Can't go wrong with a classic."

Layla gave him a slight smile before scanning the group. "Here's for fun. This one goes out to Madison for all her perseverance with the hologram training. I need everyone singing." She launched into Chumbawamba's song "Tubthumping."

Instead of drinking different alcoholic beverages, she changed the lyrics to ...

"*Singing the night away,*
Singing the night away.
She fights a centaur hologram,
She fights a harpy hologram,
She fights a snake hologram,
She fights sphinx hologram."

Everyone sang and cheered. Madison joined in and was in

tears from laughing and singing. *Goddess divine*, she'd never felt so much affection and camaraderie from a group of people.

When the flames spiked high, the music came to an abrupt halt. Madison wiped at her eyes as the mood became instantly somber.

Athena appeared in blinding golden beauty above her throne of fire. She had shimmering brown hair framing a face of sculpted high cheekbones, straight nose, and full lips. She wore a Corinthian helmet and a gleaming yellow breastplate with flourishing motifs.

> *"To Crete, you'll sail on a restless tide,*
>> *Where secrets in shadows hide.*
>> *Beneath the isle, so steeped in lore,*
>> *A maze awaits with trials in store.*
>> *Daedalus, the cunning mind,*
>> *Left darkened paths, the lost to bind.*
>> *A labyrinth, both vast and deep,*
>> *Where light is scarce and shadows creep.*
>> *Find the mountain where eagles soar,*
>> *Where gales howl and white waves roar.*
>> *Upon its shoulders, a cavern yawns,*
>> *Where stone is slick and daylight's gone."*

Madison looked around at the group. Was Athena going to breathe anytime soon or sensory overload all of them until some-one's head exploded?

Like mine, she thought.

> *"Step inside, but tread with care,*
>> *For tricks and traps lie waiting there.*
>> *Past blackened walls and endless halls,*
>> *Where echoes play and darkness calls,*

No thread will guide you, no map is true,
For walls will shift and hallways skew.
But heed my words, a path is set,
For those who seek and don't forget.
Achilles's might in armor bright
Awaits the one who proves their right.
Bronze and gold, a warrior's shield,
Forged in fire, on battlefields."

The first relic, Madison thought. They knew this day would come. Aside from training and team building, this was their first real assignment from the goddess. She sat on the edge of her seat, holding her breath as Athena continued.

"But might alone will not prevail—
A soul must pass beyond the veil.
Yet from the ash where hope seems lost,
A phoenix burns through fate's cruel cost.
Its wings shall blaze in crimson hue,
To pierce the dark and guide you through.
So set your course and ride the wave,
Through peril and strife, be strong, be brave.
Now go, my warriors—heed this call,
Or watch as Kronos dooms you all."

After Athena vanished, they remained quiet a long moment. No one spoke or even moved as they continued to stare at the vacant flames. Madison let out her breath in a long, quiet exhale.

"Goddess Athena," Tyler said, "moment killer."

"So ... Crete?" Zoey said, running a hand through her short red hair.

"Anybody record that? That's a lot to remember," Madison said. "We should write that down."

Layla tapped her temple. "I think I've got most of it."

"At least a labyrinth won't be too different from some of my other archaeological expeditions," Rex said.

"*Shifting walls and skewed halls?*" Tyler asked skeptically.

"I said not *too* different," Rex fired back.

Layla set her guitar aside. "I'm not a fan of confined spaces, but I'm learning to trust this team. Good thing I'm learning the bow, 'cause there won't be any way for me to shoot lightning off in a labyrinth."

"We need to go in prepared," Tyler said. "Consider what supplies to take to Crete. And do some recon."

"Flashlights, because I suspect this thing is underground like the mythologic depictions—dank and dark," Zoey said.

Layla nodded. "*Daylight's gone* and *blackened walls.*"

"How about glow sticks too?" Madison asked. "We can drop them along the labyrinth to mark our way back out of the maze. I'm not sure about relying on this phoenix to guide us out." She didn't add that their guide was to appear at the expense of someone dying.

"Brilliant," Alexios said. "We need food and water as well. We do not know whether the armor will take hours or days to retrieve."

Zoey leaned forward. "That's a good thought. Damn sobering too. I suspect Kronos won't let us saunter in there, snatch up something that helps the six of us keep him in his prison, and waltz back out again."

Alexios frowned. "I do not think there will be dancing of any sort."

Zoey just grinned and patted his legs.

"*Tricks and traps lie waiting there,*" Layla repeated, pushing to her feet as if suddenly restless. "Yeah. He won't make it easy for us."

Rex nodded. "We go in armed and ready."

Dreading this part of the discussion, Madison put up a hand and all eyes turned to her. "Are we going to talk about the elephant in the room?" she asked as she lowered her arm.

"Elephant?" Alexios looked around, wearing a perplexed expression.

"The expression means the biggest unspoken part of something," Rex explained. "In this case, Madison is referring to one of us passing through the veil."

"Dying," Alexios said grimly.

Zoey shook her head. "But that makes no sense. Six gods confined Kronos to the other realm. Six superhumans are needed to keep him there and close the rift. We can't do that if someone dies on the first part of relic acquisition."

Layla stood. "Agreed. No one dies."

"And the prophecy?" Madison asked.

"It's wrong," Layla stated simply, slashing a hand through the air. "Or we're misinterpreting it. Some metaphorical veil. We stick together, navigate the labyrinth, and everyone returns here—*alive*. And with the armor of Achilles." With an air of finality, Layla picked up her guitar and strode toward her cabin.

THE NEXT MORNING, Rex had barely finished half of his coffee when Tyler ushered everyone in front of the mounted TV. Madison sat on the floor, leaning against the couch and petting Zephyr. Zoey and Layla took seats beside each other on the couch, coffees in hand. Alexios plopped into the recliner. Rex stood behind the sofa, looking at the screen.

"According to the analysis I ran of Athena's description compared to a topographical lay of Crete, these are the three locations that match." Tyler typed on his laptop, which he'd cast to the living room television.

Rex recalled Tyler talking about equipment he used in his search and rescue work, including topographical maps to know terrain before the team dropped in. Had Tyler brought the equipment here on his laptop or asked the island for it? Either way, Rex appreciated the man's initiative.

"Three hours to sail down there. Then we can spend a day scoping out the location," Rex said.

"I can cover it in less time," Tyler offered.

"That doesn't sound safe," Madison said at the same time Rex said, "We shouldn't do solo trips."

Layla scoffed. "Afraid the rest of us will slow you down?"

Tyler's jaw ticked. "I didn't mean to imply I'm faster or better than anyone else here ... in this form. I'm a shapeshifter. As an eagle, I can cover all of this territory in no time."

Layla gaped at him, but said nothing.

"An eagle-eye view?" Rex asked. "No wonder you chose a career in search and rescue. I bet you were off the charts good."

Tyler gave a half grin.

"World record good," Layla murmured low enough only Rex heard.

"I agree with Rex," Alexios said. "Even with your powers, we should not go solo. A Cetus attacked and destroyed our boat. Layla and Zoey faced a Nemean lion. We allowed ourselves to be trapped in a spa for a day."

Tyler frowned. "What'll attack me in the air?"

"Harpies," Alexios answered without hesitation.

Tyler's eyebrows furrowed and mouth turned down. "Well, I can't fly with anyone."

"No solos," Layla agreed.

He shot an irritated look her way. "Fine. We use tech. We use drones in search and rescue. Aerial views are still our best bet for finding the location of the labyrinth."

"OK. The island will provide the drones, and we'll motorboat down to Crete tomorrow," Rex said. "Today, we pack supplies. Weapons, food, water. Enough for a few days."

Layla arched an eyebrow. "Did you just refer to my yacht as a motorboat?"

"It's a boat and has a motor," Tyler said with a challenging baring of his teeth.

She shook her head, scooped up her coffee, and glided out of the room.

CHAPTER
TWENTY-FIVE

Madison leaned on the rail, the sea spray cool on her skin. After six weeks of relentless training on the island of Milopas, her muscles were coiled for action; her nerves thrummed as the charge of possibility mixed with dread.

The sun broke over the horizon in a spill of molten gold, casting long rays across the glittering Aegean as *Calypso* sliced gently through the waves. A breeze carried the salty scent of the sea, as Layla steered the yacht with practiced ease, Zoey beside her—like twin guardians of fate. Layla was dressed in leggings and a t-shirt with running shoes. Her dark hair was in a tight braid encircling her head. Zoey's flaming hair spiked tall. She wore jeans and a tank top.

Beside Madison, Rex gazed out at the water with a quiet intensity. He wore his usual expedition outfit—khaki trousers and a loose button-down shirt. She hadn't told him she loved him again. He knew it because she'd shown it. Beyond that, she didn't want the repetition of the words to feel like she was impatient to hear them back. In his touch and his eyes, he'd conveyed the power of his feelings. The verbal declaration would come when he was ready.

Alexios stood tall at the bow, scanning the horizon like a warrior reborn in his breastplate and blue jeans, while Tyler pointed out dolphins cresting in the distance, his laughter rising like sunlight. He wore black tactical slacks, a black t-shirt, and a vest with a dozen pockets stuffed with—what—Madison hadn't asked. Zephyr trotted from one crewmate to another, tongue lolling, soaking in the morning excitement.

The island of Milopas receded into mist behind them—a speck now—but its legacy pulsed in Madison's blood. She'd learned more than just how to wield a sword—she'd learned trust. Connection. Purpose.

Still, something gnawed at her gut.

The air felt too calm. The sea too serene. Like the labyrinth beneath Crete, a stillness lay just beneath the beauty—a hush before the storm. She reached up and touched the vial of Rex's tears at her neck.

They headed toward Crete, toward a deeper piece of the prophecy. And though no one had voiced aloud their worry, Madison could feel it in the way their smiles faltered when they thought no one was watching.

Danger—powerful and greedy—waited for them beneath the island.

⌐⌐⌐⌐⌐⌐⌐

As the boat eased into the port at Rethymno, Madison was greeted by a heavier scent of salt mixed with wild thyme and roasted chestnuts drifting in from seaside vendors. Wooden fishing boats bobbed lazily in the turquoise water beside sleek sailing yachts, while gulls wheeled overhead, crying into the sun-drenched sky. The harbor was lined with pastel-colored buildings, weathered but elegant, housing tavernas, cafés, and boutiques.

Just beyond a lighthouse, the labyrinthine Old Town rose in narrow, winding alleyways—a mosaic of Venetian, Ottoman, and Greek influences. Balconies overflowed with purple bougainvillea and laundry lines, and stray cats darted between the legs of passing locals.

The six of them and Zephyr took a van taxi from the docks to the bottom of a hill Tyler had identified as one of three possible locations of the entrance to the labyrinth. There, Tyler unpacked his drone and sent it airborne. Zoey and Alexios gathered around his laptop.

Madison and Layla stood off to one side, packs at their feet. Stuffed with food, water, a hundred miniature glow sticks, a flashlight, and a first aid kit, the thing was heavy. Madison didn't need to carry it any longer than necessary. She bent to pat Zephyr who sat patiently waiting.

Rex opened a long tent bag and began passing out everyone's swords. He and Layla fixed theirs at their waists while the others opted for back harnesses. Madison had tested her sword out yesterday and ensured she could draw it from under her pack over her shoulder. Functional, though not graceful.

Tyler piloted the drone back to their gathering location and stored it away. "Looks promising."

"Ready?" Rex asked the group. When they gave a series of nods, he said, "Let's find the entrance."

Layla recited Athena's words. "*Find the mountain where eagles soar, where winds howl and white waves roar. Upon its shoulders, a cavern yawns, where stone is slick and daylight's gone.*"

What if this isn't the spot? Madison thought, nerves humming with anticipation. She wouldn't be disappointed either way. She wanted the quest and the accompanying dread to be over. But if this wasn't the place, and they had a day of hiking without drama, she wouldn't be upset.

They trudged up the uneven terrain, each with his or her backpack stuffed with supplies. When they reached the top, a plateau stretched to the coast, the size of a football field. The Aegean crashed below, white foam exploding against the sharp, black rocks at the base. Salt clung to the air, and the only sound louder than the wind was the rhythmic boom of the surf.

Madison took in the ocean breeze again and basked in the sun's rays. The temperature had risen to a pleasant seventy degrees.

"Cave's over yonder by the rocks," Tyler said.

Right. They were here with a purpose, which did not include sunbathing in Crete.

They walked near gnarled brush with limestone outcroppings. No signs marked the area. No footpaths wore down the terrain. A cleft in the earth, barely visible from above, led to a narrow stone mouth that opened to reveal a dark, slick cavern veiled in shadow and half hidden behind a curtain of hanging moss.

As she stepped closer, she sensed the pulse of something older stirring beneath their feet—hidden catacombs, crumbling stone sealed for centuries, and the whispers of a maze long lost to time.

"This is the place," she said. By the looks on everyone's faces, they'd also felt ancient power pulsing. They gathered around the opening.

"So, we're doing this?" Zoey adjusted her backpack. "Down into the cave?"

"Six warriors enter. Six warriors exit," Alexios said with the same resolve Layla had used the other night.

"I like that plan." Rex took a swig from his water bottle before sliding it back into his pack.

As they approached, the ground shook with a low rumble. Nervous, Madison took a step back. As everyone watched the cave entrance expecting some creature to emerge, she glimpsed movement at the cliff's edge.

Zephyr dashed toward the precipice, barked, then hastily retreated as six enormous men scaled the wall and climbed onto the plateau. No, not men. Giants. They had palms as big as serving platters and hands large enough to squeeze a human head like a stress ball. Oily, shoulder-length ringlets framed their round faces, which drooped in grim expressions. Matching brown beards dripped from their chins. Two had braids, Viking style. Another's was caked in something dark red Madison suspected was blood.

"*Shitfeathers.*" Tyler scrambled back, ditching his pack.

Rex slung his aside and withdrew his sword with Layla and Zoey following his lead. Alexios was the only person who didn't hesitate. Sword drawn, he'd already charged. He dove between one's legs and hacked at his heel, slicing through the tendon and bringing the twelve-foot-tall angry beast to one knee.

As he fell, Madison noted the enormous spiked club in his hand. All the giants brandished them. His came crashing down, forcing Layla and Zoey to dive in opposite directions to avoid being nailed into the ground.

Rex sprang into action to help Alexios finish the one on his knee while Tyler shifted into the form of an enormous grizzly and tackled the nearest giant to him.

One of the giants with a braided beard stalked toward Madison. Zephyr ran around his feet, nipping at his ankles while narrowly dodging being crushed by those size thirties.

She dipped her glasses and looked over the top of the rim, staring at the giant until he made eye contact. Her heart pounded, and blood pumped hot and fierce as magic pulsed from her like a living thing. She transformed the creature into solid stone, and he froze mid-step, club over one shoulder, and eyes locked in terror.

As she slipped her glasses back up, panting and drained, the world seemed to sway around her. She fought to stay upright, remembering how the large boarshark had left her drained as well while the human-sized masseuses had less effect.

Zoey and Layla charged the red-bearded one. Rex and Alexios had slain the first one who lay in a gruesome pool of his own blood while the body looked to be rapidly decomposing and shrinking in on itself as the skin turned a bilious green color.

A club the size of a battering ram swung toward Madison. She pivoted enough to avoid the spikes and a direct hit. Even the glancing blow from the tip of the lumpy weapon was enough to send her sprawling.

Pain flared in her chest from the blunt force trauma before she hit the ground in a tumble. Light blinded her, and she squeezed her eyes shut. With the impact, her glasses had flown off her face.

The roar of distant crashing waves and steady whoosh of the ocean breeze pierced the battle cries of her friends fighting for their lives. She had to help them and couldn't do that blind.

Risking a look, she kept her gaze cast down at the ground. She spied her glasses three feet away. Something wet dripped from her nose. Wiping at her face, she drew a blood-covered hand back. No time to worry about a battered nose. As she tried to move, the dull throb in her side spiked to sharp pain.

Is this what broken ribs feel like?

She crawled to her glasses, panting. Instead of catching her breath, her gasping worsened. She couldn't get enough air, and a tightness spread beneath her ribs. Stretching her arm, her fingers brushed the glasses.

Thunderous stomping closed in on her. By the feel of the shaking ground, another giant approached. She wouldn't survive a second blow from one of those clubs. She had to look.

When she rolled onto her back, her eyes took a second to adjust to the bright sun. Sure enough, one monster barreled toward her.

An enormous ball of fur pounced on the giant's back. Tyler sank teeth into the creature's shoulder and claws into his arms just as Kronos's minion made eye contact with her.

Power beat forth, and her vision blurred momentarily. The giant's skin blanched as his pupils dilated in surprise and his movement slowed.

The bear looked up in her direction, surprise registering in his large green eyes.

No, Tyler!

Her stomach lurched, and she tried to mentally reach for the magic and pull it back. Unrelenting, it barreled toward Tyler. Mahogany fur turned gray as beast and animal toppled forward, an immobile heap of fused stone.

Madison's fingers closed over her glasses, and she wrenched them on before scanning the battlefield. Zoey shot streams of fire toward a giant she and Layla had maneuvered to the edge of a cliff. Shielding his face with his club to avoid the burning flames, the monster stumbled back and over the edge.

The other giant Tyler had been fighting before he'd come to her rescue lay face down on the ground, bleeding from gashes and bite wounds. His gaze was fixed in a death stare as his face slowly caved in and began to dissolve. The remaining four functional Olympians attacked the last one.

Gasping and unable to get a deep breath as her vision blackened at the edges, Madison reached for the vial around her neck. After popping the cork off with her thumb, she poured the contents onto the exposed skin at the nape of her neck. Warmth spread through her, and the pain eased. She could take a deep breath again, even though darkness continued to overtake her.

She should get up and help her friends, but her body was limp and spent. Oblivion swept her away.

CHAPTER

TWENTY-SIX

The wind tore across the mountain plateau, whipping sand and grit against Rex's face. He squinted into the brightness as the last giant barreled toward them—dented and rusted armor creaking and a spiked war hammer dragging deep gouges through the stone with every step.

"Hold the line!" Alexios barked, already moving into position with his shield raised and sword braced.

Madison was behind that line, lying on the ground, unmoving, with Zephyr pacing around her.

Rex gritted his teeth and adjusted his sword grip. "That's a hell of a line to hold," he muttered.

To his left, Zoey advanced, fire sparking across her outstretched hands. "I've got this side," she growled. "Let's roast this bastard."

Layla hovered beside them, sword out in front with wind curling protectively around her. Dark clouds swirled, moving in from the distance.

The giant struck first. It brought the club down on Alexios, but the warrior dove and avoided the spikes.

Rex moved in, slashing low—his blade scraping across bronze-plated flesh but failing to bite deep.

Zoey darted in at an angle, hurling a spear of flame and causing the giant to spin with a roar as he lashed out a tree-trunk-sized leg.

The impact of his kick landed square on her thigh with a sound like splintering timber. Zoey flew backward and hit the ground hard, her leg twisted all wrong.

"Zoey!" Rex shouted.

Her flames sputtered out as she reached for her mangled leg.

"Keep him busy!" Alexios yelled.

The giant roared and swung again—Rex ducked, only to stumble into a side blow that nearly took his legs out. He rolled away, coughing with ribs burning.

"Layla!" he called.

Already moving, Layla raised both arms and let the pressure drop. A wall of wind slammed into the giant, staggering it, just long enough for Alexios to rush in and drive his sword between its plates of armor—an opening from Rex's earlier cut.

"Now, Rex!" Alexios shouted.

Rex surged forward, sword angled and sliced at the creature's Achilles' heel.

"Layla—push!"

She did. A burst of gale-force wind roared past them. The giant wavered, pinwheeling his arms in an attempt to keep from falling. It plummeted onto the jagged rocks below, roaring all the way down.

Zoey groaned. With a pale face and quivering hand, she was dribbling Rex's tears onto her leg.

Alexios ran to her, dropping to his knees.

Rex rushed to Madison's side where Zephyr was nudging her with his nose and whining.

"Madison," he called to her as he knelt and felt for a pulse.

Out, but still alive.

The pressure in his chest eased. He couldn't have checked on Madison sooner, because leaving the fight before it was finished risked harm to his teammates.

"She's OK, boy," he reassured the dog.

The vial lay open and empty. After losing five years of his life when she'd flown through the air from the impact of the club, he wasn't surprised she'd needed it. He'd feared the blow had killed her until he saw the second giant turn to stone. Madison's handiwork.

And poor Tyler. Rex glanced back at the petrified eyesore of the two figures. Alexios sprinkled his vial over Tyler, freeing him from immobility. Off to the side, Layla was bent over vomiting as Zoey—back on her feet but barely—comforted her. Rex suspected the actress wasn't accustomed to the sight of blood and decomposing bodies—at least real ones and not CGI. Tough one, that Layla. Kept her composure until the fight ended.

Tyler stumbled off the giant's rock-hard back and shook his grisly head. After transforming back into human form, Tyler thanked Alexios.

"Status check?" Tyler asked, voice hoarse as he looked around with a slightly dazed expression.

Alexios said, "All giants are dead. All Olympians are alive."

"They're decomposing," Tyler said, awe and revulsion in his voice.

Rex supposed that was how the supernatural world remained undetected. The evidence simply vanished.

"Layla?" Tyler glanced her direction as he rubbed his temples.

Alexios shrugged. "Normal post-battle stomach ills. She will be fine."

Rex turned his attention back to Madison. "Honey? Madison, can you open your eyes?" He raised her torso, cradling her in his arms. "We need to go back to the ship," Rex told Tyler.

Bending over, Tyler put his hands on his knees and shook his head. "But, we're here. You want to retreat?"

"We're in no shape to explore the labyrinth today. Layla's sick, Madison nearly died, Zoey just healed her broken leg, and even you're unsteady. We go back to the island, lick our wounds, and regroup."

Alexios walked to Layla and Zoey, explaining the plan to return to Milopas. Neither of them objected.

Rex patted Madison's cheek. "Sweetheart, I need you to wake up."

Her color was good and her breathing even. They could carry her down and to a taxi, but her walking would be easier on all of them and with fewer questions from onlookers.

"Madison?"

When her forehead wrinkled, he suspected she was blinking her eyes open.

She gripped his bicep. "Rex! Is everyone OK?" Sitting up, she wrapped her arms around him.

"Everyone's fine." He hugged her back, needing the reassuring contact. "We're all OK."

"Tyler. Oh, Tyler!"

"Present and accounted for," Tyler called.

"The giants?"

"We're safe. They're all dead," Rex said. "And, uh, decomposing. Can you walk? We need to return to the boat."

"What about the cave? The labyrinth?" Madison asked.

"We can't face more monsters in our current shape," Rex said. "Now that we know the location, we'll rest, recuperate, and get more supplies. Let's call this first attempt our scouting expedition."

"But the delay—"

"Will be better than us all dying. Athena waited over six weeks to send us to Crete. She can wait one more day."

"Um, yeah. Right. Let me try standing."

He helped her to her feet and ensured she was steady before he took a step back from her.

Alexios handed Rex his backpack. "I will carry Madison's pack. You see that she safely reaches the bottom."

Rex pulled on his pack straps. "Thanks. Ready?" he asked her.

She nodded. "Let's get out of here."

WEARY AND SULLEN, Rex and his team and Zephyr took a cab back to the yacht, and Layla sailed them home. The ship had enough room to sleep all of them, but they opted for the safety of their island given the danger of boarsharks, Kronos mind tricks, or whatever else he might throw at them.

Back on Milopas, food was spread out on the kitchen table—a meze platter.

"Is this a consolation meal?" Layla asked, walking up and plucking an olive off one of the platters.

Famished, they ate the meats and cheeses. Rex heaped up a pile of feta, graviera, kasseri, and honey-drizzled manouri beside Greek sausage—loukániko—according to Alexios, pastourma, and cured pork. He added a side of stuffed grape leaves. He paired it with ouzo from the carafe on the table.

After everyone ate and showered in varying order, the group gathered around the fire.

"Alexios, Greek warrior," Rex called to him. "We need you to give us a battle summary. What we did right, what we did wrong, what we can do better."

Alexios set his glass of water aside, stood, and addressed the group. "We rushed into battle, myself included. We should have retreated, formed a line, and thrown together a quick plan of attack. Rex and I finished the one on the ground but probably could have immobilized some others while allowing the more inexperienced fighters kill the first one."

Zoey interrupted, "I can tell you right now. I would not have been able to slit the throat of a person—or living thing—on the ground the way you did." She raised her hand in surrender. "It had to be done. I'm not criticizing. I'm merely saying that, my first time in battle against something human-ish, I don't think I could've done it. Next time," she said on a huff. "Next time, I can. I know they meant to kill us all."

"Madison must not lose her glasses," Alexios continued after nodding an acknowledgment to Zoey. "We need something to secure them better."

"I'm sorry, Tyler. I'm sorry, everyone."

Rex reached over to hold her hand.

Alexios shook his head. "That is not a criticism or failing on your part. Please do not misunderstand. You took down two of them yourself. *By* yourself." He turned to scan the others. "Tyler, all of you, if a monster in proximity to you is in the process of turning to stone, thank Madison silently and do not look in her direction."

Tyler rubbed the back of his neck. "Yeah, lesson learned."

"I'm sorry," Madison murmured again.

"We learn, we fix it, and we move on," Alexios said. "No more guilt. No more apologies."

Madison gave a resolute nod. "You're right."

Alexios continued, "If we had formed rank, it is possible Madison could have turned them all to stone before any of us had to draw our swords."

"Six in one blow? My mom used to read me a book called *Seven in One Blow*." Madison shook her head. "As much as I like that thought, those giants were the second largest thing I've ever turned, and it took something out of me. I don't think I could've done all six, but maybe half."

"Half is good, baby," Rex said, squeezing her hand. "I'll gladly take half."

"But good to know your power has limits. We all have our limits. It is wise to know them," Alexios said.

He took a sip of his drink before continuing, "Speaking of limits. Rex's tears worked magically to heal Madison and Zoey as intended, but it seems that when injuries are severe enough, there's no immediate restoration of energy or ability to rejoin the battle. In summary, the tears are a safety net against disability and death. They won't help us win any battles."

Zoey put a hand to the vial around her neck. "I like my safety net."

Layla patted Zoey's shoulder. "You saved our lives."

Zoey exhaled shakily. "Yeah, well. Next time, *you* get drop-kicked by a giant."

Alexios glanced at Rex. "I meant no offense about the tears."

"None taken. And point taken. My magic will save a life but not save the battle."

"Layla." Alexios turned toward her.

"Sorry about the vomiting," she said.

"Not something requiring an apology." He waved a dismissive hand. "You waited until the battle was over, so your stomach endangered no one. You brought your wind, but where was your lightning?"

"We were fighting so close together, I didn't want to hit anyone."

"Then we must practice precision. We will go to the beach and set up targets for you to hit. This will wait, as it is of less importance in a cavern. However, we did not bring your bow thinking it wouldn't be needed in the close quarters of the labyrinth and were surprised by an outdoor ambush."

"Bring the bow." Layla nodded. "Duly noted."

"Thanks, Alexios," Rex said. "That covers everyone. And we'll do this again after every skirmish. It's how we'll get better and develop as a team. Tonight, we rest. Tomorrow, we sail back to Crete and try again."

TWENTY-SEVEN

Madison stared at her dresser and picked up her new glasses. They were a single, sleek horizontal band that ran across the eyes, resembling a streamlined visor rather than traditional glasses. Thin but sturdy, it curved gently to match the contours of her face. The band connected seamlessly to a flexible, reinforced strap that wrapped around her head to keep it secure during intense movement in battle and keep sweat from getting into her eyes.

She studied the glasses with awe and building excitement. The front "stripe"—the visual shield—had a smoky, mirrorlike finish from the outside, giving the impression of a burnished strip of blackened silver or dark chrome. Up close, intricate etchings shimmered across it—ancient symbols of warding and protection, designed to amplify the shielding against her petrification powers.

From the inside, she could see clearly. The transparent material filtered the "petrifying" element of her gaze, allowing her to fight without fear of unintentionally freezing her allies. The inside of the band had a soft, almost velvetlike cushioning where it contacted the skin, to avoid any discomfort during prolonged battle.

Wanting to check them in sunlight, she stepped outside and the lens dimmed slightly like transition lenses.

Rex, who'd been walking toward her cabin, stopped. "Whoa. Those are new."

"I designed them." She raised her chin in a show of pride. "The shield over my eyes is a hybrid of impact-resistant graphene composite and alchemically treated crystal—ultra-light, shatter-proof, and magic-conductive. It allows visible light through, but blocks the mystical wavelengths tied to my curse."

"Very cool. You can see fine? I can't see through them at all—not unlike your dark glasses." He leaned in to inspect them.

"I can see better, actually. I see normal light now instead of through the dark glasses."

He cupped her chin and turned her head from side to side. "And they're strapped on so they won't fall off."

She nodded. "The band is made of flexible titanium-infused nano weave, wrapped in leather for comfort and additional magical insulation. I think Athena enchanted the leather, because it seems to adjust automatically to movement."

"You asked the island for this?"

"Yes. I gave Athena specific details on what I wanted. I've spent a lot of time thinking about what I'd want to wear if money and materials were unlimited."

"Classy and practical. Well done." He planted a kiss on her cheek. "Oh, and I can tell better when a smile reaches your eyes. Or if you're giving me the one eyebrow raised in skepticism look."

"But wait ... there's more." She tapped on the side of the band without pressing the circular button. "There's a discreet tactile switch. When pressed, an ultra-thin layer embedded in the shield retracts and deactivates the mechanism blocking my power."

His lips curved in appreciation. "You can stone monsters without having to remove your glasses."

"Exactly. Less risk of losing them altogether. Push the button again and the internal filtering layer is deployed."

"Brilliant."

"Thanks." She gave his cheek a peck. "I'm off to let the others know so they don't think I just beamed down from the *Starship Enterprise*."

MADISON HAD SHOWERED and changed into pajamas for the night when Rex knocked at her door. She finished brushing her damp hair and slid on her new glasses. Her heart did the same quick, happy skitter every time she saw him.

"Hey," she said.

He took her hand. "I have a surprise for you. Come with me."

Allowing herself to be dragged along, she smiled at his boyish excitement. "Where to?"

"My bedroom."

"You know I like that type of surprise."

He paused, pulled her against him, and kissed her. "There'll be some of that too," he said before continuing them on to his cabin.

She giggled as he tugged her inside and into his bedroom.

"For you." He gestured toward a mirror. "Or, for us," he amended.

The mirror featured an ornate mahogany frame styled with carved acanthus leaves. It was mounted on a sturdy, matching wooden base. Reflecting in its pristine surface were her and Rex, who watched her expression.

"It's beautiful."

"You're beautiful." Standing behind her, he swept her pale hair back.

"Thank you, but we're preparing for a battle to prevent the unleashing of a Greek titan into the world. What's the mirror for?"

He rested his hands on her arms. "Do you trust me?" His breath on her neck sent ripples of anticipation down to her toes.

"We've already established that I do."

He whispered, "I want to see your eyes when I make love to you." When she stiffened slightly, he added, "Through the mirror."

"Rex, that's so dangerous."

"It'll work." He kissed her neck as his hands moved to her hips. "You have my tears if anything happens to me."

She glanced down at the vial around her neck, which Rex had refilled for her. "Yes."

His caresses had her blood thickening and body warming.

Reaching up, he took off her eye band and set it carefully on the nightstand. "Look at me in the mirror, Madison."

She lifted her gaze to see the man she'd fallen in love with and began falling all over again. His gaze fixed intently on her, with an expression both dazzled and smoldering.

"Your eyes are breathtaking," he said. "A mix of blue, green, and even purple. I saw this combination of colors once while cave diving in Central America, where sunlight and darkness met over ocean water."

His hands worked to slip her shirt up and over her head, all while watching her through the mirror.

Scooping up her hair, he brought it around to tumble over one shoulder. "Just lovely."

His hands came around and cupped her breasts. Watching herself be touched, feeling his calloused, tan hands against her soft porcelain skin aroused her to a sudden, aching need. She tipped her head back and sucked a long breath into her lungs.

He kissed a warm trail along her neck. "You're smart and strong and so damn sexy. You take my breath away."

She loved his touch, his words.

When he trailed fingers down her bare skin, he watched her reaction in the mirror with an intense gaze. The caress had her wanting more. She backed up to press against him. Wrapping warm, firm arms around her, he massaged her breasts with his left hand as his right dove lower and inside her.

She moaned her approval.

He kissed behind her ear still keeping his eyes locked on hers.

"Rex, I need you."

"You have me. All of me, sweetheart."

"In me," she insisted.

He took a step back and stripped. When his hands were back on her, he eased her forward and onto the bed on her hands and knees, still facing the mirror.

"This OK?" he asked.

"Yeah." Her body tingled with anticipation.

He eased into her, filling and stretching until they completely joined.

"You feel so good," he said, voice raspy. "Keep your eyes on me."

She did and saw his face fill with passion and pleasure without the dark-tinted filter of her sunglasses. He moved in long, exquisite strokes, drawing out the sensation.

"Your irises are gorgeous. So many colors."

Her fingers curled, fisting the blanket. "More," she demanded.

He gave more, gave faster. Positioning his hand above where they joined as he rocked into her, he took her into a wild climax.

Trembling with delicious aftershocks, she held herself up until Rex crested the peak of pleasure. After his release, he held her tighter and buried his face in her hair.

🏛 🏛 🏛 🏛 🏛 🏛 🏛

Because they now knew the location of the labyrinth, they docked the ship on the side of the island nearest the hill. Rex ignored the churning and tightening in his belly.

Just another excavation, he told himself.

More at stake than just treasure, though. More at risk than just his safety.

He scanned the group and felt the strain. They were focused, but clearly bore the weight of the task at hand in the stiffness of their posture and tension around their mouths.

Glancing at Madison, he was reminded of their passionate lovemaking. Her eyes gleamed a beautiful kaleidoscope of color. He liked knowing he now had a way to see them and watch them fill with desire and love.

Now, with glasses in place and sword on her back, she was ready for battle.

How he loved this woman.

And hadn't told her yet. He'd never said the words to any woman, because he would absolutely mean them when he did. And he didn't waffle. Last night, he'd nearly told Madison, but didn't want her thinking he would spout such feelings the eve before tragedy might strike, just in case he didn't get the chance to later.

Damn. What if he didn't get the chance later? Nope. Six into the cave. Six out of the cave.

That is the plan. No deviation.

He could tell Madison he loved her after completing the mini-quest for Apollo's armor.

With packs on their backs, they started the ascent, ready for giants, should they pose an obstacle. The mid-morning sun and blue sky promised a pleasant day—just not for them because they would be deep within the belly of Daedalus's labyrinth.

Rex felt no rumbling of the ground, but perhaps Kronos would throw different creatures at them this time. Zephyr wandered off to sniff the ground where the giants had died at the cliff's edge.

"It's quiet," Tyler observed when they reached the platform.

Layla shot him a *"why-did-you-just-jinx-us?"* look, and Tyler replied with a smug shrug.

When Rex reached the small opening, he shone his flashlight into the abyss, wondering what Kronos's next trick would be. "Looks like stairs down and opens to a landing. How about we go down two at a time? Then no one is ever alone, and we have protection from front and back until we're all down there."

"Good plan," Alexios said. "Madison with Rex. Tyler with Layla. Zoey with me."

No one argued. The pairings made sense in Rex's mind. Madison and Layla had distance offense with the Medusa powers and the bow, so they should be paired with men who used melee weapons. Zoey and Alexios in the back put their strongest fighters covering the flank.

Taking Madison's hand, Rex led them below. As soon as they stepped off the last step onto stone flooring, sconces lining the walls flared to life with an eerie, unnatural flame—blue at the core, gold at the edges. By the light of the flames, the walls were a textured, glossy obsidian.

Madison pressed a hand to the black barrier. "Stone, but smooth like volcanic glass polished for centuries."

This wasn't the crumbling mud and sandstone maze he'd envisioned for an underground death trap—er—labyrinth. Turning, he went back toward the stairs to let Alexios know to send the next two down.

A blast of air knocked Rex backward. When he landed on his butt, the ground shook and shuddered. His pulse skyrocketed. More giants? They wouldn't fit down here, though.

As he shoved to his feet, he looked up at the ceiling. It was …

damn. Nothing but darkness. The walls extended up beyond the light the flames cast, and he couldn't see an end.

Madison came by his side. "You hurt?"

"All good." He dusted off his pants.

With another shake of the surrounding earth, rock collapsed onto the stairs. When the ground stilled and the dust settled, boulders the size of end tables sealed their exit. Rex's stomach plummeted. Their escape route was sealed.

Madison shone her light up and down the enormous rocks. "A cave-in. It's completely closed off."

"Alexios!" Rex bellowed.

Had fighting above triggered the avalanche of rock? What if the other four were hurt and fighting for their lives? How far had Zephyr followed them down?

"They won't hear through that rock." Madison pulled out her phone and looked at the screen. "Service isn't great. Worth a try." She dialed a number. "Layla? Hi, everyone OK up there?" She put the phone on speaker.

"We're good. You're OK?" Layla asked, voice an octave higher than normal.

"Yes. We're in the labyrinth. We have light, air, and a path to the great unknown."

"Tyler turned into a bear again. He's trying to remove the boulders."

Rex leaned toward the phone. "Tell him, don't bother. That will take too long. Those other caves are probably entrances."

Madison cocked her head to one side.

"What?" Zoey asked.

Apparently Layla's phone was also on speaker.

"Think about it. Three possible, similar-appearing caves that all meet Athena's description. We had a thirty-three percent chance of finding it on the first try and did. I bet they're all entry points."

"Could be," Tyler said. "Then they'd also be exit points."

"We will go to a different cave," Alexios said.

"Zephyr's OK?" Madison asked.

"He's good. A little panicked when the cave-in happened, but good," Layla said.

"We'll make our way through the labyrinth, look for the armor, and find another way out," Madison said. "I've a weak signal down here. It might not last."

"Be careful," Zoey said. "I can't find your phone location with my app. Must be too much rock interfering with the signal, but I'll keep an eye on it to watch where you surface."

"Or magical interference," Rex suggested.

"You be careful, too." Madison disconnected the call and pocketed her phone. "Ready?" she asked Rex.

Rex leaned forward, kissed her. "I love you, Madison. I do want to marry you." So much for waiting until this crisis ended. "When I envision my future—any future—you're with me."

"Are you proposing?" she asked, a smile playing on her lips.

"I'm ... yeah, I guess I am."

She laughed as her smile widened. "Well, it's no candlelit dinner, but considering we met in a madman's home who tried to kill us and we've survived a boarshark and giants, we might as well become engaged in an underground magical labyrinth surrounded by self-lighting sconces."

He stepped closer and placed his hands on her hips. "If you ignore Athena's prophecy of doom and gloom and just admire the shining walls and warm light from the torches, it could almost be called romantic."

"That's a stretch, but I like your glass-half-full attitude." She patted his cheek. "Let's get this over with, shall we?"

He nodded, and together they followed the path into the maze. "I have a ring to buy."

"Damn right."

TWENTY-EIGHT

Madison and Rex wandered the blackened halls for what seemed like hours, silence and alertness tiring into fatigue. Distant groans sometimes accompanied a faint smell of metal. She wanted to be excited about his proposal, but they had a labyrinth to survive first.

Tension mounted with every corner they turned that led to another endless path. She wondered if Kronos was somehow watching them, laughing at them. Would they lose themselves before they ever found what they were searching for?

"So, two girls, huh?" Rex broke the silence.

"Oh yes. Their names were Elena and Ariana. Elena had your blue eyes and Ariana, your mouth and violet eyes."

"Are we stopping at two?" he asked.

Surprised, she stammered, "I don't know. I hadn't thought beyond wanting a family, and I shut out those desires years ago to avoid the pain of wanting something I couldn't have."

"I only ask because I will be wholly outnumbered three to one, so we should at least try for a son."

Her lips curved up in a half smile. "Would be fun, trying," she said.

He must have sensed her growing despair, because he was doing that thing where he raised the mood so effortlessly.

A remote creak and faint tremor in the floor had them falling silent. At the end of one hall, the walls opened to reveal a chamber. They glanced at each other hesitantly before stepping cautiously into the room, their footsteps echoing across a polished marble floor veined with silver. The chamber opened wide, lit by a warm, golden glow that seemed to emanate from nowhere and everywhere at once. A wisp of hope blossomed in her chest. Was the armor in this chamber of riches?

Towering columns, carved in the likeness of ancient gods and nymphs, framed the walls. Between them hung immense paintings—scenes of Olympian feasts, battles of demigods, and the sorrowful faces of heroes long lost to myth. Every inch of canvas seemed to shimmer, alive with the touch of masters long dead.

"Wow. Just wow." Madison gaped at the surrounding treasure.

At the center of the room sprawled a breathtaking collection of priceless artifacts—jeweled amphorae, golden death masks, intricate mosaics set into low tables, and delicate ivory figurines no taller than a foot. Wreaths of laurel crowned busts of finely wrought marble. In a glass case, a set of ancient scrolls, the ink still dark as if freshly preserved, seemed to whisper promises of forgotten knowledge. A tang of oxidized gold, tarnished silver, and ancient bronze filled the air and mixed with scents of papery notes, worn leather, oils, and incense.

Rex leaned in to peer at one relic. "It bears the unmistakable seal of Ptolemaic Alexandria."

After Alexander the Great's death, the Ptolemaic period saw Alexandria flourishing as a major center of Greek culture, commerce, and learning. Madison wondered if the scrolls were straight out of the <u>Library of Alexandria.</u> The art restorer in her had her fingers twitching at the thought of preserving the cracked yet magnificent fresco of Apollo chasing Daphne across an entire wall. Everywhere they looked, history and beauty cried out to them: *Take me, save me, study me.*

"No armor of Achilles," Rex said.

Madison stared at a statue of Atlas holding the world. His monstrous muscles strained under the weight.

"No weapons at all," she noted.

Rex straightened, backed away. His body language had her scurrying to his side. "It's not treasure."

"Could've fooled me."

He drew her closer, scanning the room with an expression of one searching for danger, without a hint of the longing and appreciation that had been there moments ago. *"Achilles's might in armor bright, awaits the one who proves their right."* He recited Athena's words.

"You think walking away is proving our right?" Madison asked.

"Yeah. We'd be weighed down, slowed down. And for what? Fortune?"

He was correct. The true prize—the armor of Achilles—wasn't tucked away among these gilded distractions. And somewhere, perhaps even now, the labyrinth shifted behind them.

A sound like heaving bellows filled the room followed by a whoosh of air originating from the statue of Atlas.

"Get down!" Rex cried, even as he covered her body with his.

When the noise vanished as quickly as it came, Rex stumbled and fell. Madison tried to catch him, but he landed on his hands and knees on the unforgiving floor. From his back protruded five eight-inch-long darts.

By the gods.

She would have been at point-blank range of those things if Rex hadn't had them backing away before they fired.

"Rex!" She tugged at him, panic rising in her.

All around them, the walls began to close, a steady but terrifying pace. The treasure vanished behind the walls as the room diminished.

"Rex! The room is shrinking!" Buried alive. The thought made her instantly claustrophobic, and her breath came in shallow pants as if the air was already limited.

His head hung low, like he barely had the energy to hold himself up.

She bent, ducked her head under one arm to hold it over her shoulder, and heaved with her legs. "Move it, Alderman!" she barked at him as she hooked an arm around his waist and grabbed his belt and trousers to haul him with her.

His feet moved sluggishly. Together, hindered by the packs and Rex's injuries, they shuffled unevenly out through the entranceway before his weight became too much for her. They collapsed onto the floor as the chamber sealed completely.

Shoving up, she knelt beside Rex to inspect his injuries. Blood trickled around the wounds and soaked his shirt. Not enough blood to explain his trouble walking. Internal bleeding?

"Get them out," he rasped. "Poisoned."

"Oh, shit."

That room had been a death trap. They could have been hurt, unable to flee, and buried as they slowly died. Her stomach churned in horror, but she shoved it down. Help Rex first, then curl into a ball and weep.

With a tremulous hand, she grabbed hold of a dart and hesitated, not knowing if the tip was smooth or barbed. Either way … "This is going to hurt."

"Yup," he croaked. "Can't heal myself until they're out, though."

With her stomach lurching, she yanked. He let out an agonized groan as the flesh tore wider, ripping her heart right along with it.

"I'm sorry." Using both hands, she grabbed two at a time, hoping to shorten the duration of pain. She pulled quickly, and while he still screamed, she removed the last two and let them fall to the ground with a soft clink. She'd had to torture the man she loved in order to save his life.

He whimpered now, and she shed tears with him. The wounds closed, and the blood dried.

"Rex?" She kept her tone soft.

"I'm OK." He rolled onto his back, staring up at the black abyss of a ceiling above them. His chest heaved up and down for several seconds. "I'm OK," he repeated. "Let's find the damn armor and get the hell out of here."

◧◧◧◧◧◧◧

HALF AN HOUR LATER, Rex finally felt as though he'd mostly recovered from the poisoned darts. His head no longer swam, though he was fatigued from the pain and healing. That had been a clever trap—just what an archaeologist and art lover would stop and admire. If they'd picked up anything to carry out, they would have died in that chamber.

Rex wondered about the others. Had they found another entrance? Were they lost in the labyrinth now, too? Or maybe they were busy fighting whatever monsters guarded an alternate gateway. Madison checked her phone for the dozenth time before shaking her head and re-pocketing it.

They turned down yet another hallway and came to a jolting halt. A hideous creature writhed before them—seven feet tall with the base of a snakelike body. At her waist, she became human form with a shapely upper half and generous breasts covered with a fitted dark bronze breastplate.

She brandished a harpe—the blade of the titans. The hooked sword had a serrated inner edge, sometimes depicted in myth as the weapon Kronos used to castrate Uranus. A weapon associated with divine vengeance made it fitting for Medusa's wrath against humans and gods. Her face was all sharp angles and pronounced cheekbones, but it was the hissing snakes undulating about her head that had Rex instantly looking away and ducking behind the corner.

"Can you stone her?" Rex drew his sword, worrying the suggestion could get Madison stoned, but if the women could turn each other to stone, he could at least free Madison.

"No. I just tried. We made eye contact, and she smirked. Apparently, we're immune to each other."

"You side with the humans and the gods who have cursed you." Medusa's voice was a smooth slither that crawled along Rex's spine, practically teasing him to open his eyes. "Madness. Join Kronos, and he'll set you free."

Rex resisted the urge to look as his heart thudded in his chest. "Talk to me, Madison. What's happening?"

"Snakes. Lots of snakes. Black mambas. They're coming at you. I need you to kill them, and I'll fight her. Don't look at us, no matter what."

He heard a thump, as if Madison dropped her pack, followed by the metallic unsheathing of her sword.

Rex's heart stuttered as he spared a look at the ground in the women's direction and saw the snakes advancing on him. They were probably each ten feet long and glided toward him with deadly purpose.

Clashing of swords filled the room, but he dared not look in Madison's direction. He had to trust she could do this. She'd come far in her training, even in under two months. He didn't have a way to protect himself from Medusa's stare if Madison was injured.

He focused on slicing at the snakes. Zoey's power of flames would sure be useful right about now. Or Tyler could turn into an osprey to kill the damn devils. Instead, he and Madison were by themselves. Athena's prophecy hadn't specified all six would go into the cave—they had made that assumption. Her words, however, had been clear that one would not survive.

Rex retreated, swiping at the snakes, which hurled themselves at him two or three at a time. Fangs flashed, angry hissing filled the air, and dark scales glinted as they attacked. He turned another corner, dodging one that had sprung from the floor with a trajectory toward his head. As he ducked around the wall, he heard the thump of the snake hitting solid rock.

A piercing scream ripped through the air, and had every nerve ending in his body jolting with alarm. "Madison!"

"Stay back!" she warned.

Relief and rational thought returned with her words. That scream hadn't belonged to Madison. He fought the urge to turn the corner and look in their direction, remembering Perseus's tale of how Medusa could still stone, even in death. Was she dead or was Madison still fighting for her life? Fear urged him to call out for an update from Madison, but didn't want to risk distracting her. Instead, he focused on defeating his reptilian attackers.

He continued slashing until bits and bodies of snakes littered the ground and nothing else slithered toward him. Another rumble and groan emitted from the labyrinth.

As he leaned against the wall, catching his breath, he realized he no longer heard the sounds of swords clashing between Medusa and Madison. Panic filled him, and he strained to hear if they were still fighting. He crept to the edge, still listening, and heard nothing.

"Madison?" He had to risk distracting her.

Silence.

Stealing a quick glimpse around the corner, he saw ... nothing. The maze stretched out before him, a long corridor of flame-lit black halls.

What the hell?

He recalled some legends about the maze shifting and changing and Athena's words:

"No thread will guide you, no map is true,
For walls will shift and hallways skew."

And just like that, Kronos had successfully separated them. Was there one wall between them or a great chasm of winding nothingness?

Rex unleashed a string of curse words. "Madison!" He tried to control the thunderous beating of his heart. He still didn't know if she'd won the battle against Medusa. He had to believe that she would.

But would she stay in place so he could pick back up the trail of green glow sticks to find her? And would the glow sticks be of any use in something magically changing form around them?

Mouth suddenly parched from the battle and stomach churning with anxiety, he took a drink of his water. After the momentary pause let him regain his composure, he slid the container back into his pack before he set his jaw in determination.

TWENTY-NINE

Medusa swiped, and Madison parried. At first, she stayed on defense. Soon, she got into a rhythm and remembered her training.

The snake-haired woman's armor was linothorax-layered linen reinforced with bronze plates, but unnaturally blackened and adorned with a writhing gorgon face. Madison's sword wouldn't penetrate the barrier, so she aimed for other weaknesses—Medusa's snakelike lower half, her neck, and under the arms. Madison knew from her art studies that armpits were left uncovered by armor for mobility.

As they exchanged more blows, Madison noted how the bronze plates of armor were thinner near the bottom of Medusa's sternum. Some warriors preferred flexibility over full protection, and Madison would bet the snake woman needed the ability to writhe her upper half in unison with the lower half and so had thinned the bronze to allow for mobility.

As she worked toward an offensive strike, Medusa hissed and fought back. Her wicked sword glided effortlessly through the air and sliced across Madison's arm. The creature clearly had more than Madison's six weeks of training.

Pain stole her breath, and sweat trickled down her neck. Having learned her lesson from the harpy hologram, she didn't take time to assess the severity of the wound, but she could feel blood flowing down her arm. Retreat was not an option, because this was a fight to the death.

After blocking another blow, she bent at the knees, pivoted, ducked, and thrust her sword up and through the chink in Medusa's armor. When she felt flesh give way, Madison poured all her effort into sinking the blade as deep as she could. The woman roared and collapsed as Madison let go of her xiphos and backed away, watching the cursed creature bleed out.

Emotions swirled through her—relief at her win, shock that she'd taken another's life, and pity at Medusa's fate of living in shadows to await a death by someone on a quest.

"You're a traitor to your kind," Medusa hissed as she lay unmoving on the ground in a pool of her own blood.

"I won't let Kronos destroy my world."

"You can't stop him."

"You're wrong."

Medusa's breaths became shallower as her face drained of color. When she breathed her last breath, Madison felt a deep pity for the other woman. Her body didn't dissolve the way the giants had. Maybe that was only a trick on the earth's surface.

Madison needed to cover the woman's eyes to protect Rex. If legends were true, Medusa could stone others even in death. Cringing, Madison grabbed the body of a beheaded mamba and draped it over Medusa's face. Madison's stomach soured, but at least her pulse was finally returning to normal.

"She's dead," Madison called behind her, sweat trailing down the back of her neck. "I've covered her eyes." She hadn't pressed the button to activate her glasses shield, so she didn't turn toward him yet.

Damn. Now she needed to retrieve her sword because she didn't know what other dangers Kronos had in store down here. Placing her foot on Medusa's chest, Madison grabbed the handle. She fought back the urge to gag as she heaved the weapon out of flesh and a fresh wave of copper-scented blood assaulted her senses. After wiping it off on the scales of Medusa's lower half, she re-sheathed her weapon.

Pressing the button on her glasses, she looked around and noticed the unmoving bodies of scaly snakes, but no Rex. She hoisted her backpack on.

Following the trail of elongated corpses around the corner, she found their end, but Rex was nowhere in sight. Had he been kidnapped? Even swallowed by the maze somehow?

"Rex!"

She checked her mobile phone. No service.

"*A soul must pass beyond the veil.*" Athena's words echoed in her mind.

No. Hell no. This wasn't how it ended. She would find him.

With the sword in her right hand, she used her left to snap, shake, and drop the glow sticks to create a trail in case he was somewhere looking for her.

She wandered for what felt like an hour, the dark maze with its cruel silence as her only company. At every turn, she didn't know if she would find Rex, another monster, the armor of Achilles, or the stretch of another monotonous, never-ending corridor.

She sniffed and went to wipe her nose when she saw the blood trailing down her hand from her upper arm and remembered how Medusa had gotten a good strike on her. Fixing it meant putting down her sword to open the vial, and she wasn't willing to risk an ambush from some new foe.

Sᴡᴏʀᴅ ʀᴇᴀᴅʏ ᴀɴᴅ keeping a brisk pace, Rex wound through the maze.

The further he wandered, the more the labyrinth seemed to close in on him. The obsidian walls, once merely towering and dark, now pressed closer as the flickering flames cast twisting, shifting shadows that mimicked movement at the edge of his vision.

The air grew heavier with each step, thick and cloying, as if he were breathing through wet wool. Every sound—his footsteps, his breath—seemed amplified and then swallowed whole, leaving behind a vast, ringing silence that gnawed at the edges of his sanity.

"Get it together," he muttered, but even his own voice sounded small, crushed under the suffocating desolation that wrapped around him.

He looked up again, the walls soaring beyond the reach of the flames, vanishing into a yawning black void. No beams, no end, no comforting signs of structural support—just a sense of endless space both rising up and pressing down. A void hungry for light and hope.

When his gaze drifted back down, a heavy, bleak feeling pressed into his chest. Had he told Madison he loved her just in time to lose her?

A green glow caught his attention. Turning a corner, he saw her trail of glow sticks.

"Madison." The word rushed out of him above a whisper as renewed energy filled him. His feet moved swiftly over the smooth ground as his gaze fixated on the green, glowing path that would lead to her.

After several more turns, he came to a halt at a dead end. Her back was to him, but he recognized the pale hair and backpack.

Holding her sword limply in one hand, she faced gleaming armor on a stand.

"Madison?"

She turned slowly and raised the sword with a shaking arm.

"Madison, it's me, Rex."

Rushing to her, he sheathed his sword and wrapped his arms around her. Real, whole. Not an illusion.

She shook in his arms as she dropped her weapon. "You found me." She leaned into the hug.

"You left a trail for me." Pulling back, he brushed a thumb over her cheek. Looking her over, he noticed then that blood trickled down one arm and sucked in a breath. "You're hurt."

"No worse than having a harpy bite your neck," she said wryly. Her shaking had stopped, and color was returning to her face.

Rex chuckled, even as he inspected the wound. The wicked hook on Medusa's sword had looked like a snake's fang and acted like one, tearing flesh rather than cutting cleanly. He had no trouble summoning a tear and swiping it across her arm, as his heart was hurting at the thought of anything happening to her and the possibility of losing her.

"You didn't heal yourself," he said.

"I didn't want to waste it on something trivial. Didn't know what state you'd be in when I found you. You might have needed it more than I did."

Leaning in, he placed a kiss on her lips.

Rex recited Athena's words as he gestured to the armor.

"Achilles's might in armor bright

    Awaits the one who proves their right.

    Bronze and gold, a warrior's shield,

    Forged in fire, on battlefields.

    You found it."

She smiled. "We found it."

"THE ARMOR OF ACHILLES." Madison stared at the intricately woven breastplate as she held Rex's hand to keep herself grounded. "I expected metal. This looks like it's been spun from gold thread."

Rex reached out and touched it. Of course he did, she mused. The treasure hunter wouldn't hesitate to explore his bounty.

"Soft like leather," he said. "Lightweight and breathable." He hefted it up.

"Will it fit in your pack?" she asked.

"I could stuff it in there, but I'd rather you wear it."

Wearing it out of the maze sounded practical, but, "Shouldn't the better fighter wear it? You'll be up closer while I'm farther away with my powers to turn enemies to stone."

"Madison, down here, we'll only have close-range fighting. I need you to put this on." His imploring tone and vulnerability in his eyes had her dropping her backpack and reaching for the armor. This was not a man who needed much of anything and certainly never pleaded for it. He helped her pull it over her head and torso.

"A little big," she noted. "You should take the shield. It's too heavy for me anyway."

Nodding, he helped her into the vambraces and shin guards. Next, she secured the sword in the straps on the back of the breastplate and put her pack back on.

"All set?" he asked.

"Yup." She tugged at the collar of the breastplate and swallowed. Was it sacrilege to sweat in Achilles's armor? Ugh. Nothing felt right about this situation.

"Let's find an exit."

When they turned a corner, they froze, face-to-face with an enormous beast. He had the bronzed, ripped body of a World

Wrestling Federation champion. Massive thighs and calves tapered into obsidian cloven hooves. Except for a loincloth, he was naked. His bull head had massive bulbous nostrils and menacingly curved horns that topped him out at ten feet tall. A pair of glowing red eyes stared at them. A necklace made of bones stretched around a meaty neck.

In his left hand, he held a giant axe on a long handle wrapped in leather. The edge, sharpened to razor-like smoothness, glinted in the torchlight. He opened his right hand, turning his palm face down, and two dozen of their green trail markers fell to the floor.

Oh, crap. Madison realized their plans to mark their escape route had actually given this creature an easy way to track them.

She reached up to press the button on her glasses, but the Minotaur shielded his eyes with his axe.

Then, he charged.

Rex pulled her back around the corner. "Let's run. He has us by strength, and he's obviously intelligent. We can't outmaneuver him in these tight halls in a fight." Even as Rex talked, the pair of them were already sprinting.

She felt no shame in running. They had what they came for. They'd disturbed this creature's home, and she was happy to leave him to his gloomy, creepy lair.

Every time the Minotaur's thundering hooves got closer, Rex would turn them down a passageway.

We'll never lose him, Madison thought.

He probably knew this maze inside and out—magically shifting passageways and all.

Because the charging bull's wider body couldn't bank the turns as well, they put a little distance between them and him. Rex slowed and pulled out his water bottle, awkwardly bracing Achilles shield under his arm. While Madison appreciated the opportunity to catch her breath, did they honestly have time to stop and hydrate?

At the corner of yet another turn, Rex sprayed the floor, coating the black stone with a layer of water.

"Let's move!" he said.

They sprinted again down a straight corridor. As he took her right, she glanced back the way they'd come. The bull's hooves slid on the slick surface. Unable to make the sharp turn, he slipped and crashed into the wall. He let out a roar that sounded more like frustration than pain.

Rex tugged her through two more turns before drawing to an abrupt halt. As she gasped for air, her stomach plummeted.

Dead end.

"Back, back, back," he ushered her.

When she turned back the way she had come, the beast blocked the path. Hatred and anger glowed in those fierce red eyes, and he smelled pungently of wild bull mixed with mildew and a trace of decay. Her legs went rubbery, but she stayed standing even as cold tentacles of fear wrapped around her.

> *But might alone will not prevail—*
> *A soul must pass beyond the veil.*

CHAPTER

THIRTY

Reaching up, Madison pressed the button on her glasses.

In a quick motion, the monster scraped the blade of his axe along the glassy wall, shaving off pieces of stone. The movement of his blade hurled shards and sparks directly at her face.

Reflexively, she closed her eyes and turned her head to avoid fragments. She felt Rex rush past her and heard the whoosh of air as he withdrew his sword. After reengaging the shield on her visor to avoid accidentally turning him to stone, she opened her eyes.

Rex dodged a swipe of the Minotaur's axe. Sparks flew when the weapon collided with the opposite wall. Rex swung upward, but the bull leaped backward, missing his blade.

Madison drew her sword to join the fight. Using her Medusa powers was not an option with the men so close. If she turned them both to stone but Rex transformed first and the Minotaur achieved one final blow, would Rex's rock form irreparably shatter?

The three of them danced around the confined space. Her heart raced with adrenaline while her lungs still burned from the mile-long sprint they'd done. She knew from her simulator training that she wouldn't be able to block a powerful blow from the creature ten times her strength. She could only dodge.

Defense, then offense.

In quick motions, the Minotaur swung his ax. While Madison ducked, Rex lifted the shield to block a back handed blow from the creature which knocked the shield out of his grasp.

Madison struck out with her siphons. When her sword sliced into the bull's calf and red blood bloomed, she felt some relief to learn he wasn't invincible. But the wound didn't slow him down. Not even so much as a flinch.

He blocked a blow from Rex with his axe as he backhanded Madison. Pain exploded through the side of her face as she tumbled over the hard surface. The glasses stayed firmly on. Scrambling to her feet, she rushed back to the battle, not wanting to leave Rex to face him alone.

The pair had turned during the fight so that the creature's back was to her. She discovered that, with their lives on the line, she had no moral quandary about stabbing this thing in the back.

With sweat in her eyes, grip slick on her sword, and body fatiguing from the exertion of an intense fight after a harrowing run, she felt her body weakening. Slowed reflexes could be the difference between life and death.

As she neared, the Minotaur lashed out a hand, grabbing Rex by the throat at the same time Rex impaled the side of the beast's abdomen with his sword. Despite the injury, the Minotaur didn't loosen his grip. Was he that tough or impervious to pain?

As Madison swung her sword, the bull slung his axe at her. The weapon struck solidly in her chest. While Achilles's armor prevented the blade from slicing her in half, the kinetic energy from the momentum sent her sprawling backward and her sword flying out of her hand. The breath burst out of her as agony lit her stomach and sternum on fire.

Rex, still being strangled, held on to the bull's wrist with one hand while his feet dangled. With his other hand, he pulled a knife from his boot and thrust it up into the Minotaur's forearm. When he twisted the blade, the creature released him and bellowed in pain.

Madison tried to push herself up, but her arms refused to cooperate.

Red-faced and gasping, Rex fell to his knees, taking his knife with him. He scrambled back until he hit a wall, putting a little distance between himself and the ferocious creature.

The beast charged.

"No!" Madison screamed.

The Minotaur lowered his head, dropping the sharp ends of his horns parallel to the ground. He impaled Rex's chest at the same time as Rex brought down his knife into the bull's head.

Rex's arms drooped and his body went limp. Madison's world imploded as anguish flooded every pore of her body. Her heart squeezed so tight she thought it might stop altogether.

The bull shook his head, seemingly unaffected by the knife protruding from his skull. Perhaps his knife hadn't penetrated the thick bone into his brain. He didn't jar loose the rag doll body of Rex stuck to him.

"Rex," Madison sobbed.

He wasn't breathing. Wasn't moving.

She tried to push to her feet again, but strength eluded her. Bullshit. Just bullshit. They weren't dying in this hellhole. Using the wall for support, she pulled herself up, fighting the pain.

A thunderous roar filled the room, but the sound wasn't coming from the Minotaur. Rex, suddenly reanimated, screamed in blood-curdling agony as he grabbed the bull by its horns still inside his chest. As Rex yelled, his body turned a glowing red-orange, the color of a vibrant sunset, before he burst into flames.

Oh, gods. Had he caught fire on one of the sconces?

She reached for her vial of tears, only to find it wasn't around her neck. Had she lost it in battle? Scanning the ground, she spotted it several feet away.

Unnaturally bright fire spread from Rex to the beast, who cried out in surprise and pain. He tried to scramble back and shake Rex loose, but the magical-looking flame quickly consumed the Minotaur's entire body, taking his screams of suffering with it.

As Madison scooped up the vial and ran toward them, the flames flared, bathing her in suffocating heat and forcing her to stagger back to avoid being burned. After the flash, the fire extinguished entirely. Only a pile of ash remained where man and beast had once been.

Crippling silence enveloped the maze.

She crumpled to her knees. Tears streamed down her face. "Rex. No, Rex."

THE MAZE WAS quiet and still.

Madison felt like an utter failure. And Rex died because of her. Maybe if she'd trained harder, fought better, he'd still be alive. She knew she was the weakest fighter. If any one of the others had been down here with him, he'd still be alive.

A crushing pain of guilt and loss filled her chest as she knelt before the cremated form of the love of her life.

Damn the gods, and damn their impossible quest. She had become the best warrior she could be in the short amount of time she'd been given to prepare. His death was on Athena ... and whoever else had pitted the six of them against Kronos.

Minutes ticked by as a hollow ache consumed her. Her heart rate returned to normal, a slow dull thud echoing hollow in her ears, as her breathing came in shaky sobs. With eyes puffy and swimming in tears, her limbs felt heavy and useless with a low burn from the lactic acid build-up caused by exertion.

What now? She had the armor, and people were still counting on them to keep Kronos imprisoned in his world.

Digging in her pocket, she pulled out her phone. No service. She stowed it back away.

Reluctantly, she stood. She picked her sword off the ground, sheathed it, and pulled on her backpack. Picking up the pack Rex had tossed aside, she clutched it and the vial of his tears to her chest. She stood over his ashes once more.

Her heart felt as if it was turning to stone, and the cold heaviness spread into her veins. Better this leaden emptiness than the horrible pain she'd felt earlier.

"I'm sorry I failed you. I swear to you, I won't fail the others."

The ashes swirled. Or had she imagined it?

A small gray tornado of particulates whirled, and she took a step back. A glowing gold spark lit in the center of the ash tornado as it swirled larger.

Red and orange flared to life as the tornado morphed into the shape of a bird with vibrant red, orange, and gold colors. It coalesced into a beautiful, solid figure with long, shimmering feathers.

A phoenix!

She thought of Rex's ability to heal with his tears, and of Athena's words.

Yet from the ash where hope seems lost,
   A phoenix burns through fate's cruel cost.
   Its wings shall blaze in crimson hue,
   To pierce the dark and guide you through.

"Rex!" Hope burst in her chest.

He flapped his wings and rose into the air above the walls of Daedalus's labyrinth. The bird's call—a sound of mixed cry and song—echoed above her.

"I'll follow you!" she called to him. She thought of his healing tears. Of course, he was the phoenix.

He flew forward and around, always looping back to make sure she could see him. His bright colors were a beacon of hope in this dismal cavern.

With renewed vitality, she dashed, backpack jostling. Between the two packs, the ill-fitted armor, and the shield, she felt clumsy and yet the excitement had her feeling lighter than air. She ran until she saw a wedge of golden light she suspected was her exit. Following the phoenix, she burst through the opening and into blinding daylight.

"Madison!" Layla grabbed her.

Rex flew higher into the air as flame burst into Zoey's hands.

"Don't hurt him!" Madison cried. "It's Rex. Rex is the phoenix."

He circled the five of them on the ground, unleashing another cry before spiraling down and crashing to the ground. He curled his red and golden wings around his body as he slowly transformed from bird to man.

A very naked and unconscious man.

"What the hell happened?" Zoey asked.

Madison let out a sob as she knelt to stroke Rex's hair. Alive. He was alive.

THIRTY-ONE

Rex woke, recognizing the feel of his cabin bed and the fresh sea breeze circulating the room. Blinking his eyes open, he spotted Madison curled up in a ball in a chair against one wall. With her glasses on, he couldn't tell if her eyes were open, but she breathed softly as if in sleep.

When he moved, something tugged at his arm. Looking down, he noted an IV in his arm connected to a bag half-filled with clear liquid.

"Tyler thought you might be dehydrated," Madison said. "It's just saline." Stretching, she straightened.

She wore black leggings and a pink tank top. Her hair was pulled into a messy updo, with rebellious blond strands sprouting haphazardly. She must have showered since the labyrinth because the grime and sweat from their time in the pit had been scrubbed away.

When Rex pushed upright, she rushed to him and adjusted the pillows behind him. "Are you hurting?" she asked.

"No." He took her hand. "I love you."

His beautiful, brave Medusa with resolve as hard as stone and heart as full and soft as a cloud.

She smiled. "I love you, too."

"I thought I should reiterate it now that we're not in the labyrinth's clutches, fearing for our lives."

"I know it's true. What else do you remember?"

"Everything except how I arrived back here." He shuddered. "Everyone else is OK?"

"Yes. You're the only one who … died." She choked out the last word.

"Athena doesn't lie. Don't particularly recollect anything as pleasant as a veil, though."

Madison wrapped her arms around him, soft and warm. "I thought I'd lost you." Her voice cracked.

"You're stuck with me. I don't waffle."

She laughed. "Good. I don't want it any other way."

When she leaned back, he scrubbed a hand over his face. "How long have I been out?"

"A day. Alexios and Tyler carried you to the ship and then up the steps and into bed. The group is waiting to convene by the fire when you're up for it. I told them about what happened in the maze."

"I'm ready." He pushed up, weakness tugging at him, but also the urge to get out of bed. "Can you gather them up while I clean up?"

"Of course." She kissed his cheeks before turning away.

"Hey." He tugged her back. "You were amazing."

"You too." She smiled softly before leaving.

Alone, he swung his legs over the edge of the bed and let a wave of dizziness pass. He debated pulling the IV, but thought he might need those extra fluids after all. Apparently, spontaneous combustion inflicted serious dehydration.

Standing, he waited until he felt steady. Plucking the IV bag off the rope and hanger it dangled from, he ambled to the bathroom. He used the toilet, washed his hands and face, and tugged on a pair of jeans. With the IV tubing, he didn't have an easy way of putting on a shirt, so he didn't bother.

By the time he joined the fire, the IV bag was three-fourths empty. All eyes were on him as he approached. Achilles's armor sat off to one side.

"Good to see everyone," Rex said. "Tyler, can you take out the IV?"

"Yeah." From his backpack by his chair, Tyler pulled out a piece of gauze and roll of tape. After tugging out the plastic catheter, he pressed down with gauze over the hole. "I gathered you were the type of man to grab a bull by the horns. Just hadn't pictured it quite so literally until Madison told us the story." He taped the gauze down.

"Thanks." Rex sat down in his chair beside Madison. "I'm happy it's over and won't make a habit of dying. That's a level of pain I wouldn't wish on anyone ... except maybe Kronos."

"You are a hero of legends," Alexios said with encouragement.

"Thanks, man."

"We arrived at the alternate cave entrance, but it wouldn't let us in," Zoey explained. "Layla and I stayed at that entrance in case it opened, while Tyler and Alexios went to the third entrance. They arrived to no opening as well. We stayed in phone contact as we discussed regrouping back at the cave-in or watching the other two locations. We didn't want to split ourselves any thinner than we already were."

"Then, cave opened and you flew forth as a fiery red phoenix," Layla said. "More magnificent than anything CGI could have created on the movie screens."

"You've never died before?" Tyler asked.

"No."

"So the phoenix thing?"

"Had no idea."

"Do you think you have more than one?" Layla asked.

"Life?" Rex rubbed his neck. "I'm not a cat, and I don't intend to tempt fate and find out."

"Let's assume not," Madison said with finality.

"You got the armor." Tyler gestured to the gleaming gold.

"Who's it for?" Zoey walked over, hefted it up. "I say we each try it on, Cinderella style."

"Cinderella?" Alexios asked.

"Classic fairy tale," she explained. "A commoner goes to the royal ball, and the prince falls for her, except she rushes away without telling him her name. She leaves behind a shoe, and he has all the unwed women in the kingdom try it on until he finds her."

"Ah," Alexios said. "In Greek lore, we have something similar in the story of Rhodopis. An eagle steals an enslaved girl's sandal and drops it in the king's lap. Intrigued by the beauty of the sandal and its divine appearance, he sends his men to find the owner through the same trial and error in your Cinderella story." He tilted his head to one side with a grin. "If the armor fits you, who will you marry?"

"Uh. What? No one." Zoey glanced at the armor as if it was a dead carcass. "I just meant it should belong to whomever it fits. No strings attached."

"It's too big for me," Madison said. "I think it will fit one of the men."

Zoey pouted. "Fine." She handed it off to Alexios, who looked around at the group.

"Don't look at me," Tyler said. "Armor doesn't do me any good shifting between animal forms."

Alexios looked at Rex as if afraid he had offended him. "You found it. You should have the first right of refusal."

Rex waved his hand. "A Greek warrior should wear the armor

of Achilles. It's only fitting—pun intended."

Tyler rolled his eyes. "First important relationship and he's already making dad jokes."

"Seriously," Rex told Alexios as he still held the armor. "If it doesn't fit you, I'll try it on."

When Alexios lifted the armor, it caught the light like woven sunlight, every thread of it shimmering as though it had been spun by the gods themselves—well, technically it had as rumor said Hephaestus, the god of fire and metalworking, created it.

"Astonishingly supple," he said as he ran his fingers over it. "As pliable as worn leather, yet humming with strength."

The breastplate molded perfectly to the warrior's torso, the golden surface etched with ancient, flowing designs: celestial maps, crashing waves, rearing stallions, and blazing suns. The scenes seemed to shift subtly when the armor caught the light. The back piece was fitted with a secure, almost hidden slot, a place clearly intended to sheathe a sword without disturbing the balance of the wearer.

"Might as well complete the look," Rex said, gesturing to the vambraces that were part of the set.

Alexios slid the forearm guards on followed by the shin guards, or greaves, which curved around his calves. "Same blend of protection and freedom of movement."

When Alexios finished securing the pieces, he didn't just look like a warrior—he looked like a legend born anew.

Cheeks looking suddenly flushed, Zoey sat back in her chair and crossed her arms. "Yeah. It belongs to you."

Rex glanced at Madison, who was grinning at Zoey's interest in Alexios.

Madison. The amazing woman who'd proven Rex's heart wasn't made of stone. She was everything he'd ever wanted and thought couldn't possibly exist. She knew about his powers, was willing to fight darkness by his side, trained and fought relentlessly, and had given him her love unconditionally.

Reaching over, he took her hand and brought it to his lips, where he kissed the back of it. He would make sure she knew he cherished her.

But before they could start a life together, they had a titan to beat back. And before that they had two more artifacts to find, as prophesied by Athena.

While they awaited her instructions, they would continue their training.

"Dojo tomorrow?" Tyler asked.

"You know it," Rex said.

~~~***Stay tuned for Book 2 in the Olympian Awakenings Trilogy***~~~
~~~

OTHER BOOKS BY CB SAMET

Looking for more romantic suspense? How about with an urban fantasy twist? Check out The Shadow Guardians trilogy.

Get *Raven's Flight, a prequel novella* for FREE. In my newsletter, you'll learn about me, special discounts, and new releases.

Raven's Flight, prequel novella

Raine Down, Book 1

Rosalyn's Run, novella

Storm Surge, Book 2

Anka's Orb, novella

Sky Fall, Book 3

Meridian File / Masters File / Box Set 1

McMillan File / Maltisse File /Box Set 2

Storm File / Sullivan File / Box Set 3

Sharp File / Sizani File / Box Set 4

Rivera File / Rucker File / Box Set 5

Richmond File / Redwood File / Box Set 6

Atlas File / Angel File / Box Set 7

Rider Novellas:

Cabrera File / Connor File

Cassidy File / Christmas File

Buy all four!

The Dr. Whyte Adventure Novels

Thriller Series

Black Gold

Whyte Knight

Gray Horizon

Sweet Romantic Suspense

"Well-written... tales of love and ghosts."

— KIRKUS REVIEW

IN BOXED SETS

**Love action/adventure and strong female leads in a fantasy world?
Check out my other genre:**

The Avant Champion Fantasy Series

FOLLOW ME

Follow me on other platforms for updates and new releases:

Bookbub: https://www.bookbub.com/authors/cb-samet
Facebook: https://www.facebook.com/authorcbsamet/
Instagram: instagram.com/cbsametauthor
Goodreads: https://www.goodreads.com/author/show/6012528.C_B_Samet
Chirp: https://www.chirpbooks.com/authors/cb-samet-audiobooks
TikTok: https://www.tiktok.com/@cbsametauthor

Checkout my other contents:

Pinterest: https://www.pinterest.com/novelsbycbsamet/pins/
YouTube: https://www.youtube.com/channel/UCggCBJuL3QpElmz77LaY56A
My website: www.cbsamet.com